I

Anders

and the Cr

Virtual Destruction

Virtual reality is the technology of the future. And in a supersecret installation in Northern California, under the most restricted security, one of the top scientists in the field is about to be murdered. . .

"The A & B Team strikes again! A taut SF mystery set inside one of the country's most sensitive installations."
—Allen Steele, author of *The Tranquillity Alternative*

"Blends hard SF and detective fiction to preview the dazzling next step in virtual reality . . . the VR gimmickry is fascinating."
—*Booklist*

"I like hard SF, and I love a good mystery. This one has the best of both worlds. There's a sequence in this book I will never forget!"
—Jack McDevitt, author of *Engines of God*

"A killer of a mystery."
—*Newsline*, Lawrence Livermore National Laboratory

"A fast-paced, fascinating techno-thriller that takes the reader down one potential future path." —*Paperback Forum*

"The lollypops for many hard-SF fans will be the speculative VR system which is the immediate scene of the crime, and the actual Lawrence Livermore National Laboratory which is the community that provides the setting, victim, and most of the suspects." —*Locus*

"Anderson and Beason are true 'insiders' in the world of government research laboratories." —*Livermore Independent*

"The authors have a fine grasp of character and a slick writing style." —*Science Fiction Review*

And don't miss Craig Kreident's next thrilling adventure, coming soon from Ace Books!

Ace Books by Kevin J. Anderson and Doug Beason

VIRTUAL DESTRUCTION
FALLOUT

Other Novels

IGNITION
ILL WIND
ASSEMBLERS OF INFINITY
THE TRINITY PARADOX
LIFELINE

FALLOUT

KEVIN J. ANDERSON
DOUG BEASON

ACE BOOKS, NEW YORK

This book is an Ace original edition,
and has never been previously published.

FALLOUT

An Ace Book / published by arrangement with
the author

PRINTING HISTORY
Ace edition / March 1997

The Putnam Berkley World Wide Web site address is
http://www.berkley.com/berkley

For information about the works of Kevin J. Anderson and
Doug Beason, read http://www.wordfire.com

Make sure to check out PB Plug,
the science fiction/fantasy newsletter, at
http://www.pbplug.com

ISBN: 0-441-00425-3

ACE®
Ace Books are published by The Berkley Publishing Group,
200 Madison Avenue, New York, NY 10016.
ACE and the "A" design are trademarks
belonging to Charter Communications, Inc.

PRINTED IN THE UNITED STATES OF AMERICA

10 9 8 7 6 5 4 3 2 1

To the men and women
of the Nevada Test Site
—who endured long hours
and separation from family
for their nation's defense.

ACKNOWLEDGMENTS

As usual, a great many people helped us in the writing of this book. In particular, we would like to thank: Janet Berliner, Mark A. Johnson, Brooke Buddemeier, Deb Ray, Kathleen Dyer, Leslie Lauderdale, young Chris Westbrook, Gorgiana Alonzo, Ginjer Buchanan, Kristine Kathryn Rusch, Brian Lipson, Richard Curtis, Amy Meo, Lil Mitchell, Rebecca Moesta Anderson, and Cindy Beason.

AUTHORS' NOTE

Although the Nevada Nuclear Test Site, the Device Assembly Facility, Nellis Air Force Range, Groom Lake, and other places in this novel actually exist, the authors have taken liberty in detailing the descriptions, not only to add to this story, but to prevent any unwarranted breaches of national security. No nuclear storage compound exists at Omega Mountain. The authors have never had actual access to the Device Assembly Facility or the supposed Groom Lake installation known as Area 51, and all characters and circumstances depicted herein are purely the product of the authors' imaginations. All details involving security, nuclear weapons, and other devices can readily be found in declassified public sources.

All circumstances and characters in this novel are fictional. The views and opinions, expressed or implied, are solely those of the authors and are not meant to reflect the views of the Department of Defense, the Department of Energy, the Nevada Test Site, the U.S. Air Force, the FBI, or the Lawrence Livermore National Laboratory.

"Nuclear weapons and nuclear weapon systems require special consideration because of their policy implications and military importance, their destructive power, as well as the potential consequences of an accident or unauthorized act. Therefore, safety, security, control, and effectiveness of nuclear weapons are of paramount importance to the security of the United States."

—from "Joint Policy Statement on
Nuclear Weapons Surety"
Dick Cheney, Secretary of Defense
James D. Watkins, Secretary of Energy
June, 1991

"Seven hundred of the eight hundred pages of the START agreement that deal with verification are a waste of money."

—Vadim G. Osinin,
staff expert, Supreme Soviet
Committee on Defense and Security

"The person who survives the first year in [the nuclear test program] is probably going to be here for the rest of his career."

—Robert W. Kuckuck,
Deputy Associate Director for
Nuclear Testing, Lawrence Livermore
National Laboratory

FALLOUT

PROLOGUE

Monday, October 20
8:10 P.M.

Device Assembly Facility
Nevada Nuclear Test Site

Alone in a highly secure facility deep inside the Nevada Nuclear Test Site, inspector Kosimo Nevsky stood over the deadly radioactive material that had fueled the Cold War.

The vast, warehouselike Device Assembly Facility was dark, quiet. This late at night most of the workers had gone to their cozy American homes, while the rest of the Russian disarmament team had been shuttled to their Las Vegas hotel to gamble in the casinos. Some team members viewed the expedition to the United States as a holiday, rather than treaty-mandated work. But they had to wrap everything up, nice and tidy, by Friday for the summit meeting between the American and Russian presidents.

For now, that meant Academician Nevsky had to put in the extra hours to double-check what appeared to be a serious discrepancy. Yes, he would have a surprise for the American president. Besides, he didn't mind the opportunity to be alone.

His own security escort, PK Dirks, had wandered off with typical lack of attention to his job. Appalling, given the sensitivity of the information in the warhead-dismantling section of the facility. The Americans relied too much on their badges and fences and sleepy guards.

With no one around, Nevsky slipped a small flask from his front pants pocket and gulped two long swigs of the smooth bourbon. Kentucky bourbon. Another interesting experience. During his evenings in Las Vegas, he had grown quite fond of it, and he intended to consume as much as possible before he returned home to the traditional, but still effective, bottles of vodka he kept in the freezer compartment of his refrigerator in Moscow.

Feeling the sour-mash bourbon burn down his throat, Nevsky stashed the flask again and used a pudgy hand to caress the metal-walled glovebox containing the radioactive plutonium cores, or pits—components of a disassembled U.S. nuclear weapon, now lying in front of him behind a protective glass plate.

Another warhead dismantled, destroyed, awaiting verification. Part of the upcoming international show, so the two presidents could clasp hands and celebrate a safer world in front of swarms of paparazzi, flashing cameras, rolling videotape. Politicians would claim all the credit, while Nevsky and his seven companions would do all the work. He hoped someone bothered to give them a medal at least, a trinket he could wear.

In the harsh lights, Nevsky's reflection glinted off the glovebox, distorted from the safety glass. He saw unruly white hair like a corona surrounding a bald spot above a fleshy face.

In front of him the nondescript weapon cores were warm, gray metal spheres the size of Ping-Pong balls. But when inserted into a critical weapon assembly, surrounded by high-explosive implosion lenses and precisely machined metal casings, each little sphere became a seed of Armageddon, no longer needed in a post-Cold War world.

The three gloveboxes sat within white-painted fortress walls formed by stacked concrete blocks, creating a secure corner of the Device Assembly Facility, which the Americans—loving their acronyms—called the DAF. Security cameras hung from the metal rafters, but they did not track his movements. Deactivated? Budget cuts, perhaps? This "Pit Assembly Area" had originally been constructed to build nuclear weapons, but with the downsizing of the global stockpile, it now provided a natural place to *dis*assemble warheads. With proper international oversight.

The KGB had once expended enormous effort to gain any detail about these weapons. Yet here he was, Ambassador Kosimo Nevsky, former Director of the prestigious Lebedev Institute and now leader of the disarmament team, given total access—alone!—to the heart of the U.S. nuclear arsenal.

But then, when the Americans spent all day displaying their every secret inside the Nuclear Test Site, what was left for a spy to discover? It would have been superfluous. Or was the very openness a clever distraction?

These plutonium pits had been salvaged from weapons decommissioned from the active nuclear stockpile. That stockpile still threatened Russia and the rest of the "near abroad"—which was why Nevsky had to be absolutely certain that each of the serial numbers and entries corresponded to their appropriate components on the voluminous list.

The other inspectors had snickered at him for doing the work of a mere clerk. But he had been chosen as team leader and had been given ambassadorial rank for this assignment—and he had decided to work late to complete this random check, rather than running off to drink and gamble with the rest of the Russians. Nevsky had been criticized for his frequent drinking, and his deputy, General Ursov, bristled at the mere thought of being subordinate to a civilian leader, but Nevsky did take his work seriously.

Scratching the rounded skin of his neck, which was just starting to develop into jowls, he stepped back from the glovebox and frowned, looking around again for his escort,

PK Dirks. Until now, most of the Americans—especially their beautiful and wonderfully competent protocol escort, Paige Mitchell—had insisted that the Russian delegation follow strict rules to the smallest detail. But fifteen minutes earlier, Mr. Dirks had been most anxious to leave Nevsky, claiming pressing business of his own—probably off taking a pee.

Nevsky turned impatiently; he did not wish to continue the tedious work without the American oversight, in case any questions or accusations were raised later. He liked being alone, but he had to follow protocol. He called, "Mr. Dirks! Hurry up, please? Where are you?"

No reply. No sound came inside the DAF except for the distant growling of forklift trucks and machinery in the cargo-crowded high bay on the other side of the Pit Assembly Area.

Scowling, Nevsky turned back to the glovebox, wanting to take another gulp of the delicious bourbon, but he decided not to. The flask would have to last him for another hour or so. For now he had to complete his work, official escorts be damned. He had not flown all the way from Russia for an unreliable *technician* to delay him.

On a table piled with documents, he pulled out a red notebook, fumbling through pages of handwritten notes until he came to *Decommissioned Serial Numbers*. Placing the notebook on the top of the glovebox so he could read it, Nevsky plunged his hands into the thick rubber gloves in front of the unit. Reaching inside, separated from the radioactive material by only the thickness of a glove, he flexed his fingers. The black gloves felt remarkably more flexible than the unwieldy ones he had used for training back at Lebedev.

Grunting, Nevsky peered at the serial numbers he had recorded in his notebook. He carefully picked up one of the three plutonium pits and brought it close to the glass. The number matched. He moved it to a mass balance inside the glovebox, powered up the electronic scale, and waited as it found a fiducial, the zero point reading.

When he placed the pit on the scale, the red digital numbers flickered, finally matching the mass he had written down. He expected no surprises, but it had to be done. Nevsky wasn't tired. If he wished, he had all night to verify the other pits. Earlier today he had felt too rushed, with the other team members anxious for more tours, more food, more fun. If mistakes were found later, Nevsky's head would be on a platter.

Painstakingly, he verified each serial number and carefully weighed each pit. Finished, he moved to the second of the three gloveboxes in the Pit Assembly Area, carrying his notebook with him. As a reward to himself for his efforts, he took another drink of bourbon from his flask.

Still no sign of PK Dirks. Perhaps the technician had abandoned him intentionally to tempt him, trying to provoke an international incident. Some of the Test Site workers would welcome a return to Cold War days, as would some of his own colleagues.

Inside the second glovebox, the weapon cores were again warm to the touch, even through the rubber gloves. Nevsky wondered where this particular warhead had been targeted. *Had the Americans planned to vaporize my beloved Lebedev with one of these finely machined spheres?* The thought sickened him.

With his musing, he almost missed the mass inconsistency.

Nevsky stopped and returned the pit to the scale. The reading was low, only by a fraction, but too low for the amount of plutonium that should have been present. The gray metal seemed a different color, its temperature cooler than the others.

"Ah! What is this?" He picked up the pit and squinted at the serial number. Yes, two numbers transposed in the middle—and he had nearly misread the code. When he placed the sphere back on the electronic mass balance, the number jumped on the LED, then stabilized—again, at the wrong value.

"Do you think you can squirm out of treaty obligations? This is a mock pit—what have you done with the real thing?"

He decided to call the team in immediately, dragging the other inspectors from the casino floors. He would waken General Ursov in his hotel. As military liaison to the disarmament team, Ursov would immediately send an encoded message to Moscow.

A sound came behind him. Dirks must have returned at last! Nevsky placed the mock pit back inside the yellow safe circle. His hands still thrust inside the glovebox, he half-turned to look behind him, ready to confront the technician escort with what he had found.

He caught only a glimpse of the raised crowbar—

Nevsky tried to jerk his hands free, but the gloves were too tight, holding him like a straightjacket. Jerking, he managed to slip his right hand out, lifting his arm to protect himself.

The first blow from the crowbar broke his wrist. Nevsky cried out, but the second blow caved in his skull, squelching any further shout.

Then silence returned to the Device Assembly Facility.

CHAPTER ONE

Tuesday, October 21
6:38 A.M.

Hoover Dam
Boulder City, Nevada

As dawn spilled through the tan rock canyons, Agent Craig Kreident rode in the front seat of the FBI rental car, buckled in and holding on tight as Jackson took the corners significantly faster than the maximum safe speed.

In back, dark-haired agent Ben Goldfarb had stopped his usual banter, leaving quiet and intense Jackson to concentrate on driving. Craig glanced at his watch, seeing the second hand sweep around.

As Jackson curled around another hairpin curve, Craig slid sunglasses firmly in place through his chestnut hair. Tapping his fingers on the seat, he stared out the passenger window beyond the guard rail, seeing the long drop down. The sun grew brighter, funneled through the narrow canyon cut by the Colorado River on the Nevada-Arizona border.

Ahead, Hoover Dam formed a cliff of concrete, a wonder of engineering that held back the waters of Lake Mead. The dam was a popular tourist spot, and Highway 93 across it was a vital lifeline between Nevada and Arizona.

If the radical militia group, the Eagle's Claw, succeeded in blowing up the dam, repercussions from the resulting disaster would approach biblical proportions.

Craig tapped his fingers again, swallowing in a dry throat. He looked at his watch once more. The second hand still hadn't completed a full circuit of the dial. The worst part was not knowing how much time they had.

Reaching the bottom of the grade where the road and Hoover Dam spanned the canyon, Jackson pulled smoothly into the empty visitor's parking lot next to an old exhibit hall. He jammed the shift lever into park, lurching to such a sudden stop that Craig jerked against his seat belt.

Goldfarb popped open the back door, sliding out. Craig unbuckled, grabbed the small walkie-talkie on the seat, then pushed open the passenger side door. He reached in his jacket for his FBI badge and ID. "Let's go!"

Two law-enforcement vehicles marked with *Hoover Dam Police* and one National Park Service jeep waited there. Three policemen and a park ranger stepped forward, ready for action. They seemed relieved to see the FBI. One policeman wiped a hand across his forehead.

While the spotty early morning traffic continued to drive by, curious onlookers turned their heads. Craig pushed his sunglasses against his face, adjusting the shoulder holster beneath his dark suit jacket. "I'm Special Agent Craig Kreident," he said, "in charge of this operation." Exchanging names like rapid gunfire, Craig introduced Agents Ben Goldfarb and Randall Jackson, while the two policemen and the park ranger gave their own names.

"Is this all the backup we've got?" Jackson asked, shading his dark eyes and scanning the canyon walls as if searching for hidden snipers.

"For now," one of the Hoover Dam policemen said. "More on their way, another dozen park rangers, plus three Boulder City police officers."

"Park rangers?" Goldfarb raised an eyebrow.

The ranger settled his hat firmly on his gray-streaked dark hair. His face was tanned and leathery, as if he had spent his entire life under the desert sun. "We have minimal law enforcement at the dam itself, especially before the Visitor's Center opens and the tours start. The National Park Service representatives at Lake Mead, Grand Canyon, and Death Valley are the closest Federal law-enforcement agents."

"Good enough," Craig said, fidgeting, anxious to get moving. "We'll take all the help we can get, sir."

"We've been here and vigilant since we received your message an hour and a half ago," said the second policeman, flushing beneath his freckled skin, "but we don't know exactly what we're looking for."

The other policeman looked more bothered by Craig himself than the threat of the explosives. "Agent Kreident, the Eagle's Claw and their militia counterparts have been blabbing to the newspapers and radio stations for months. What makes you believe this one's not just another false alarm?"

Craig frowned. "Because this one's real in my opinion, sir."

Goldfarb smiled and stepped into the conversation. He was a head shorter than Craig with deep brown eyes and a sunny smile; he used the smile as a weapon more often than his own handgun.

"I've checked up on the Eagle's Claw," Goldfarb said, "and I've read their collected letters in the evidence file—cheery reading, let me tell you. Typical right-wing militia organization, so patriotic they're bloodthirsty. America for Americans and none of this 'world policemen' crap—that's their own words. They want no more foreign aid, closed borders, protectionist trade policies. They hate the United Nations with a passion, because it 'waters down American ideals and dilutes the sovereignty of our nation.' "

Robbins, the skeptical policeman, took off his wire-rim glasses and swiped them across the front of his shirt. Craig noticed beads of sweat on his forehead. "People around here are a bit more conservative than in San Francisco," he said. "Isn't that where you're stationed, Agent Kreident?"

"I've been assigned to this case, sir," Craig said firmly. "Where I live has nothing to do with this morning's operation. Even militia members are entitled to their own opinions, so long as it doesn't spur them to violence. I think that's what's going to happen this morning—violence, and a lot of it."

"But what evidence do you have?" Robbins said, hooking his eyeglasses over his ears and straightening them. He squinted toward the dam's broad expanse of gray-white cement. The waters of the river far below and the Lake Mead reservoir above looked deep blue, peaceful in the morning.

Craig responded matter-of-factly, forcing himself to stop fidgeting for just a moment. "We . . . received a note."

The FBI had been keeping tabs on various militia groups, especially since the Oklahoma City bombing, the Olympic Park bombing and the Freemen standoff in Montana. During their investigations, they had increased surveillance on certain ones they considered most dangerous. Though the Eagle's Claw spent most of its time on propaganda and misinformation, the FBI had sent an undercover agent, William Maguire, to join the militia and investigate their activities. For two years Maguire had submitted regular reports, which had grown sparser but grimmer in the recent six months.

Unlike their frequent letters full of empty threats, the Eagle's Claw had issued no warning, promised no action against Hoover Dam or the hydroelectric generating station. But yesterday Maguire had been found dead in his house trailer on the outskirts of Boulder City.

It might have appeared to be a simple heart attack—though Maguire submitted himself to regular physical exams, and no prior inkling of a health problem had ever been found. But then a hidden note had been discovered next to the phone on an innocuous-looking pad of message paper, five sheets down. Maguire's house cleaner, also an FBI courier, knew where to look.

According to the scribbled message, the Eagle's Claw intended to strike Hoover Dam this morning, planting explosives in strategic positions. Maguire had been prepared to call in a full-fledged FBI assault—but he had died of his convenient "heart attack" the same evening.

"What's so special about another note?" Robbins said sourly. Craig could see that the man liked wearing his uniform but didn't like to be called upon to do his duty.

"I'm inclined to believe this one, sir," Craig said, then turned smartly, cutting off further conversation. "We don't have many men, but we have to act now. Have we contacted the foreman of the red-eye shift?"

The second policeman nodded. "Yeah, a man named García. He's standing by for further instructions from you."

The park ranger looked up as a heavy truck crossed the dam and rattled past, heading up into the hills toward Las Vegas. "I hope we don't have to blockade this highway. This'll be a monumental mess if we can't wrap it up before the Visitor's Center opens at nine."

"We'll take care of it," Jackson agreed tersely, standing tall and dark under the morning sun, not sweating a bit.

Seeing a gap in traffic, Craig jogged across the narrow highway and looked down to the generating stations, the heavy transformers and turbines far below at the bottom of the dam next to a set of administrative buildings.

"All the hydroelectric machinery's down there, Agent Kreident," the ranger said as he approached. "If somebody wants to cause mischief, there's your best bet. They can't do much to damage the dam itself. It was designed to withstand a 6.9 earthquake and made with enough concrete to construct a highway from San Francisco to New York and still have some left over."

"It would take an atom bomb to wreck that," Goldfarb said.

"Be thankful the Eagle's Claw doesn't have one of those," Craig said. He pointed to the generating station and a single-lane roadway on the Nevada side of the river. "How do we get down there?"

Silver-painted Frankenstein machinery hugged the canyon wall—conversion transformers that took the power from hydroelectric turbines and changed it to alternating current, sending it through high-tension electric wires that ran across the river up to naked trestles on the canyon rim above.

On the opposite side of the river, rock alcoves contained more heavy machinery, needle valves that had once been used to shunt the flow of the river during the construction of Hoover Dam. From beneath the dam and the hydroelectric generators, the swirling cold currents of the tailrace eddied where water sloshed out from the churning turbines.

The shift supervisor came out to meet them, moving furtively, as if he didn't want anyone to see him there with three FBI agents. Craig took the initiative and stepped forward. "You're Mr. García?" He extended a hand.

The compact man had wiry gray hair beneath a yellow hard hat. His face wore a wizened expression, and his brown eyes flickered between fear and indignance at the suggestion that one of his workers might be involved in a conspiracy to destroy the dam.

"I'm not keen on the idea of accusing my crew," he said. "I like to think they're trustworthy enough to hold their responsibilities, or they shouldn't be working here in the first place."

"I'd like nothing more than to be proven wrong, sir," Craig said, brushing his suit jacket, glancing at the dam, adjusting his shoulder holster. "But unfortunately we must take precautions. Can we get everyone into a secure area without arousing their suspicions? That'll give us the freedom to inspect for sabotage quietly. At the moment, they don't know *we* know."

García nodded. "I've called a meeting of Team B. They should be waiting for me in our conference room, and I've telephoned the five maintenance and support workers. They'll be in my office and not at their stations. The other workers are all in the administration structure beneath the main dam, where it'll be easy to keep track of them."

"Excellent, Mr. García," Craig said, trying to be firm yet supportive, thankful that the supervisor hadn't lost his cool. "Keep your people busy, hold your meeting, tell the others to wait. We'll search for evidence of explosives or any other kind of sabotage."

García bolted to do as he had been ordered, holding his yellow hard hat. Craig gestured to the others. "Jackson, Goldfarb, go take the admin offices, make sure somebody's in every room. Keep a tally." He directed the three policemen and the park ranger to take other levels inside the warren of tunnels within the dam and the cliffside, the upper machinery rooms and the hydroelectric stations.

Craig himself took the main generating floor. The echoing chamber was like an enclosed football stadium, an airplane hangar filled with horizontal turbines each the size of a circus tent, thrumming and whirring. The Colorado River poured through spiral intake pipes that spun flywheels. Atop each generator, white lights indicated which turbines operated and which ones sat idle.

Craig moved uneasily, walking across the sealed cement floor. The sound of his footsteps vanished in the throbbing vibration of the turbine generators. The vast room had the atmosphere of a high-tech haunted house. He felt as if someone might be there, watching him, though García claimed to have accounted for all of his employees.

Craig crept slowly around, studying the turbines, looking for any sign of tampering, loose access plates, boxes or packages that could have been explosives. He didn't know what he expected to find, but he had to keep moving. He glanced at his watch once more.

After he had circled the third generator and bent toward the fourth, he saw a man emerge from one of the many tunnels that connected elevator shafts, access halls, and river bypass tubes. The stranger wore the jumpsuit and hard hat of a dam worker, but he moved with a furtiveness and quickness of purpose that did not mesh with someone just going about his daily duties.

Craig stepped out of his hiding place, withdrawing his 9-mm handgun and his badge. "Federal agent," he shouted. "FBI. Remain where you are, sir."

The stranger stepped backward and froze, then he spun into action. Though Craig had been prepared, he didn't react fast enough when the stranger snatched a small revolver from inside his overalls, cocked it, and fired in a single, swift motion.

Craig dove behind the shelter of the turbine. He heard the man running, heavy work boots echoing in a humming background of main generators.

Pulse pounding, Craig snapped up his own Beretta, but the stranger fired quickly three times in succession. Bullets ricocheted off the curved metal hulls of the hydroelectric turbines; one bounced with a high-pitched whine from the solid stone wall.

Craig cautiously peered around the curve of the tall turbine, ready to jerk back, hoping he could react fast enough the moment he saw a muzzle flash. The terrorist knew his location, but Craig had lost track of where the stranger had fled, where he might be hiding. He yanked out his walkie-talkie. "Goldfarb, Jackson, all officers—I need backup down at the main generator room. I've found our customer."

As the others rapidly acknowledged, Craig switched off the speaker; it wouldn't do to have a squelch of static or an unwelcome voice coming at the wrong time.

The tunnel was empty now. Craig couldn't tell if the terrorist had ducked back through the labyrinth of passages, or if he had hidden himself somewhere in the cavernous main generator room.

Craig hustled cautiously, keeping low. By the book, he should have called out and demanded that the man surrender—but those procedures were better left for fairy tales. This man wouldn't surrender unless he had absolutely no other chance. Fanatics were fanatics, whatever the motivation.

He heard a scuffed footstep, saw a steel-toed work boot—then the man sprinted out the open doorway to the outside at the base of the dam, by the spillway and the turbine outflow that became the churning tailrace beyond the generators. Perhaps the terrorist had a getaway vehicle among those parked on the narrow access road.

Craig ran after him, dumping caution now that the suspect had fled outside. He did not dare let the militiaman slip away.

Sunshine dazzled him for a moment, but Craig didn't waste time with sunglasses. He blinked repeatedly, trying to focus as he rushed blindly forward. The militiaman had turned right, racing down the asphalt access way. As Craig rounded the corner, he saw the suspect duck behind a twelve-foot-high transformer.

The terrorist popped out from cover again and fired. Craig shot back, but both bullets missed. He dove behind one of the generators, spooked by DANGER—HIGH VOLTAGE signs mounted on the machinery. The high-tension wires suspended across the canyon contained more electricity than he ever wanted to touch. . . .

Craig glanced between the steel tie-downs that held the transformer machinery in place against the canyon wall. He debated waiting for his backup—but by that time the man might have slipped away. He clicked his walkie-talkie. "This is Kreident. I've got him at the transformers. Hurry."

Craig dashed away from the big transformer and slipped between the next two, advancing on his quarry. He made another jump and scrambled behind the transformer.

The militiaman fired once at him as he peered out, but Craig waited an extra second. He knew he was getting closer. His own handgun remained drawn. He took the time to put his sunglasses on now, so the light would not dazzle him when he leaped back out of the shadows.

"You can't get away, sir!" Craig shouted, his words carrying above the loud buzz of the transformers and the vibration communicated through the rock wall from the spinning turbines.

The militiaman didn't answer. After what Craig hoped was an unexpected interval, he bolted out again, trying to go around two more stations in the row of transformers—but the terrorist had been waiting for him, taking no cover whatsoever, standing out in broad daylight, his revolver pointed directly at Craig's chest.

Craig dove to one side as the man shot once. The bullet came close enough to burn through the sleeve of his jacket. He felt a sting, but didn't think he had been seriously injured. But he was totally vulnerable, dead in the man's sights . . . and the terrorist did not hesitate. The man followed him with his weapon—

Craig shot while rolling on the ground. His bullet spanged off the metal transformer behind the terrorist, causing him to spin about and smack his wrist into the machinery. The weapon clattered to the ground, and the militiaman scrambled for it as Craig fired again at his feet. A white starburst of ricochet blossomed on the concrete by the scuffed work boots.

Craig steadied his own Beretta. "Hands up! Move it!" He

had the man helpless, unable to do anything . . . except surrender.

"Let's just take this from the top, sir," Craig said. His voice was even, professional, uninflected. He had learned to be calm, never to lose his cool even in a standoff such as this. "You are under arrest—and you are going to tell me exactly what you've done to sabotage the dam."

The militiaman looked at him with an astonished expression. Craig was amazed at how . . . *average* the man looked. Medium height, medium build, mousy brown hair, plain features—not handsome, but not ugly. He was the sort of man who worked in every out-of-the-way gas station, in every hardware store, any service industry where the customers forgot their helpers moments after leaving the store. He could move about anywhere without being noticed. No doubt that was just what the Eagle's Claw had intended.

Except now this man had been caught in the main generator room of Hoover Dam, shooting at an FBI agent. The terrorist's eyes took on a glazed look, as if he had somehow been programmed with a different routine. "It's too late. The bomb's already set and ticking. You'll never find it in time."

"Yes, I will," Craig said, striding forward and extending his gun, "because you're going to tell me where it is."

The militiaman took a step backward, blocked by the deep river channel and churning cold water pouring through the bottom of the dam. Across the canyon Craig saw the concave plane of concrete, a barrier holding back Lake Mead. If that dam broke in an explosion, the stampede of water would reach all the way to Mexico in a few hours. Hundreds of thousands of people could die—and Craig had no time for kid gloves.

"You're going to tell me, and you're going to tell me now." Craig's voice carried sufficient threat and absolute certainty—but the man took another step backward. His face turned grayish, resigned.

"You're *already* in dreamland, man, if you think I'm going to tell you squat." He glanced over his shoulder and saw the churning water below, the rushing Colorado River that swept through the canyon.

"You've got no place to go," Craig said.

"I can go to Heaven," he answered.

Craig lunged for the terrorist, but the man leaped backward over the edge, falling down. He struck the rocky wall once, leaving a reddish stain, and then plunged into the rushing tailrace, which sucked him under before sweeping him downstream.

Finally, moments too late, Jackson, Goldfarb and the others charged out onto the service road next to the conversion transformers.

Craig stared over the edge at the roiling water, gaping in disbelief at what the terrorist had just done. But the shock paralyzed him for only a few seconds before a greater horror struck. He turned and ran toward the others.

Now he knew the bomb was ticking. And with the militiaman dead, they had very little chance of finding it in time.

CHAPTER TWO

Tuesday, October 21
6:45 A.M.

Rio Hotel and Casino
Las Vegas

Swiping groggily with her left hand, Paige Mitchell missed turning off the alarm on her first two attempts. The room was dark, and she knocked over the glass she kept on the nightstand, spilling lukewarm water on the bedspread, the floor. That, if nothing else, woke her up.

Pushing aside the tropical bedspread, she leaned over and fumbled with the clock radio, finally clicking off the music. Red numbers blinked 6:45 as she turned on the light in the unfamiliar bedroom. Another hotel, another bed far from her home in Livermore, California. This was Las Vegas, at the Rio. Her bed sat on an oval pedestal; jungle-patterned curtains hung in front of a window that covered one entire wall.

Paige ran a hand through her mussed blond hair and made her way to the bathroom. Frequent travel was the price of her job working for the Department of Energy's Protocol Office, a job that often didn't seem like work at all, even if she had to walk on eggshells every day to keep the team of sometimes volatile Russian disarmament inspectors on track, to soothe their indignant threats of pulling out.

Only a few more days, though. By the end of this week, the team would have gone through their paces, filled out the forms, and completed the treaty-mandated disarmament inspections, just in time for the international nuclear downscaling summit. The eight inspectors were scheduled to meet with the U.S. President late on Friday, when he made a quick stopover in Las Vegas, then depart on Saturday morning, when everybody could go home. Mission accomplished, the world saved once again. . . .

Last night, DAF manager Mike Waterloo, whom she'd known as "Uncle Mike" since she was a little girl, offered to help Ambassador Nevsky at the facility after hours, leaving her to baby-sit the remaining Russians. Once they got away from the bleak Test Site, the seven stuffy men had consumed their comrade's share of alcohol, feeling no guilt about leaving their team leader behind to keep working. Paige had left the men to their own celebrations, returning to her room for a long hot bath and a good night's sleep.

Still trying to wake up, she rummaged through the drawer and pulled out a sleek black one-piece swimming suit. Even with her frenzied schedule, Paige insisted on maintaining her own routines. She'd have time for a brief swim down in the pool, then she could pick up coffee and a bagel to take back to her room while she changed for another day at the Nevada Test Site, or NTS.

She eased to the floor and started her stretching exercises, taking long, deep breaths. Paige held a hand over her head and slowly extended it until she could grasp her foot. She'd put up with the hectic schedule for four more days, then she would be glad to see the Russians off.

The phone rang just as she switched to stretching her left leg. The clock blinked 6:53. Had she ordered a wake-up call? But when she answered the phone, the voice on the line sounded worried. "Paige?"

"Yes," she said, initially startled. "Uncle Mike? What's wrong?"

"Please come out to the DAF as soon as possible." He sounded grim. "There's been an . . . accident. Last night."

"An accident? What is it? Is everyone okay?"

"Ambassador Nevsky—he's dead. As the DOE representative, please get over here as soon as you can. I need . . . I need your help, Paige."

Shocked, she gripped the phone tightly. "I'll be there within the hour."

Before she hung up, he spoke in a voice that seemed stronger, as if he took heart just from knowing she was on her way. "We've got an international incident on our hands, and we need to move quickly—otherwise the whole disarmament process might blow up in our face."

CHAPTER THREE

Tuesday, October 21
7:15 A.M.

Hoover Dam

Take charge. Think fast.

Craig Kreident couldn't spend days pondering the ramifications of his decisions. Too many lives depended on his reaction time for him to hesitate. And he had to get it right the first time.

He pointed to Goldfarb, Jackson, and the other law-enforcement agents. "Fan out now. We've definitely got a bomb, but we don't have a bad guy to help us track it down. The clock is ticking, people—move it!"

García, the shift foreman, looked grayish and sick. He had seen the militiaman throw himself backward into the churning water, and now he stared with disbelief at Craig's pronouncement. "A bomb? For real?"

"Yes, sir," Craig said. "Did you recognize that man?"

García swallowed, then shook his head. "Didn't look like anyone I know on shift."

"Could have been an infiltrator," Jackson suggested.

"Mr. García, sir," Craig said, trying to keep his voice calm; even a hint of uncertainty would rattle them all. "It's time to evacuate your people from the dam. Get them away from here and up to safety. We don't know how big the bomb is, or when it's set to explode, or who could be hurt. Then I need you to help us out."

With wide eyes, García turned and ran for a facility telephone mounted in a utility shack.

Craig turned to the three Hoover Dam policemen. "One of you stop traffic on the highway. Get somebody up there to put up roadblocks. I don't want anyone driving across this thing if there's going to be an explosion."

Robbins brightened as if he suddenly realized he would rather be stopping traffic than searching for a bomb. "I'll do it." He ran back to his police cruiser and leaped in.

"Jackson, where's our backup? When is Explosive Ordnance Disposal going to get here?" Craig said, turning in a circle, trying to determine where best to begin their search.

Jackson glanced at his watch, pushing back the sleeve of his suit jacket. "The EOD team was on their way from Boulder City. Should be another fifteen or twenty minutes. We've got thirteen more agents coming in from Las Vegas, but we're on our own for the time being."

"Best we can do, I guess," Craig said. "We have to be fast and efficient."

García trotted back up, cradling his yellow hard hat, his face flushed. "I sounded the evacuation," he said, breathless.

Craig called out, "Mr. García, help us think of where someone might place a bomb around here. Where would it cause the most damage?"

The supervisor looked up at the transformers, down into the channel of water where the terrorist had vanished, then up at the concrete expanse of the dam as though he couldn't fathom anyone trying to destroy his precious machinery. "Do you want to cause structural damage, or knock out the power-generating capability, or flood water through the diversion channels?"

Goldfarb cleared his throat impatiently. "Hey, guys, if I could make a suggestion *while we're looking inside*—the Eagle's Claw wants attention, right? They want to do something spectacular. They need to make a statement that'll affect lots of people."

"Like cracking the dam and flooding the southwestern United States?" Jackson said.

García stuttered. "No way! You'd need to crash an airplane full of dynamite into the dam wall in order to cause that kind of damage."

"Then it must be somewhere inside," Craig said grimly. "Let's move it."

They spread out through the main generating floor. Craig raised his voice, shouting to be heard over the hum of the machinery. "Mr. García, I spotted our suspect leaving that tunnel. Would you accompany me, please? Jackson, Goldfarb, you keep checking out the generator room. I looked at the first couple of turbines, but our guy could have rigged something else."

"You bet," Goldfarb said. The two agents set off at a rapid pace, while Craig and the shift supervisor rushed into the tunnel.

The tunnels ran through the canyon walls and the immense concrete dam like a network of blood vessels. Lit by garish round spotlights, the rock walls were rough and rugged, dusted with salty secretions. Haphazard sheets of corrugated plastic hung from the ceiling and walls to deflect dripping water that seeped from the rocks. Concrete gutters ran alongside the walkway.

"This tunnel goes to one of our main penstock pipes used for shunting the water in an emergency," García said. Perspiration covered his face.

"And if one of those pipes were to be breached?" Craig asked. "Would it flood out the entire dam?"

"Not really," García said. "The pipes are dry now. We've only used the shunt once, ten years ago, when there was a flood condition in Lake Mead."

Craig scowled. "Any other ideas where he might plant his explosives?"

García screwed up his face. "Agent Kreident, this place was built to last two thousand years. I don't believe there *are* any single points of failure."

"Even if somebody blows up the generators?" Craig said, glancing at his watch again.

"We've got eight generators on this side alone," García answered, nervously rubbing his hands together. "Arizona has nine on the other side. You could blow up one or two of the turbines, I suppose, but it still wouldn't cause immediate and irreparable damage."

"Unless whoever planted the bomb didn't know that," said Craig, looking around at the enormous machinery.

The two men jogged through the passage, looking at the power conduits and side storage chambers, but García dismissed all those as being unlikely targets. Craig began to wonder if the terrorist had managed to set up his explosive after all, or if he had merely been lying to cause a panic. The bomber could have a last laugh at the FBI's expense, knowing the agents would frantically close down the dam and search fruitlessly for hours.

But Craig couldn't believe the militiaman would be willing to die for a practical joke.

The worst part was not knowing how much time remained. The bomb could explode in the next ten seconds . . . or the terrorist could have set the bomb to detonate hours later when hundreds of tourists were streaming through Hoover Dam.

Every sound made Craig tense. What if more than one saboteur had crept into the passages that morning? Craig grabbed the small walkie-talkie, which he had switched off during the shootout, and turned on the speaker.

Goldfarb squawked at him in a highly agitated voice.

"Craig, dammit, why don't you answer? We've found it! The bomb's down here."

"Acknowledged, Ben," he said quickly, covering his surprise. "Tell me the details—we're on our way."

"Here in the generator room. It's hooked up to the first two main turbines. It looks homemade, but complex. You know how touchy those things can be."

"EOD should be here any minute," he said. "Is there a timer? Can you see how much we've got left?"

"Six minutes, Craig. Piece of cake."

"Six minutes!" Craig felt his heart leap. He started running, then stopped. "Mr. García, maybe you'd better just get out of here."

The supervisor didn't need to be told twice as he raced for the high-speed service elevator. "Just don't let my dam get ruined, Agent Kreident," he called over his shoulder.

Without answering, Craig raced down the tunnel back to the main generator room. Goldfarb crouched beside one of the enormous turbines while Jackson stood tall and stern like a traffic-crossing guard, motioning Craig to where the bomb had been planted.

Goldfarb looked up, his swarthy face flushed, his skin speckled with perspiration around his normally infectious grin. "Five minutes flat, Craig," he said quietly, whipping his palm across his brow.

Craig bent to inspect the device tucked under the generator cowling, connected to a similar homemade bomb linked to the second generator.

"If those Explosive Ordnance guys don't get here soon, I'm going to start yanking out wires," Goldfarb said. "Or would you prefer to have the honor, Craig—you're the senior agent."

"I don't have a clue how to disarm a bomb," Craig said, squatting beside the other agent. For anything other than simple plastic explosives, Bureau policy was 'Leave it to the professionals.' "I always meant to learn one of these days."

"Well, here's our chance for on-the-job training," Goldfarb said bleakly. Craig saw that his partner's hands were shaking.

"Yo!" Jackson said as the elevator doors opened. Two men wearing helmets, visors, and heavily padded olive-green body armor sprinted out.

Craig stood up, feeling a wash of relief. "Step lively—you've got five minutes left on the timer."

"Uh, four minutes," Goldfarb said.

The first EOD expert whipped out a pack of tools from his side and dove to the bomb as if he were sliding into home plate. With his clear visor down, he pushed himself to within inches of the device, studying the wires. The second man moved to block Jackson, Goldfarb, and Craig from the explosive device. "Please get out of here, gentlemen. We need to work alone."

"I'm staying here," Craig said firmly.

"No, sir—that wouldn't be smart. If something goes wrong, everyone is at risk. There's nothing you can do except get in the way. Don't waste time arguing with me."

Craig blinked, abashed, and realized the EOD man was right. "Sorry."

"We've got two bombs," the first EOD man called out. "Actually more than two—this pair of explosives is hard-wired to the timer, but there's also a transmitter, maybe to broadcast when the timer goes off. I've got to work on disconnecting both of them, and we're running down to the wire."

"Please leave," the second EOD man said again. "We've got to concentrate." Then he turned, ignoring the FBI agents.

"You heard the man," Craig said. He and Goldfarb and Jackson strode outside to the narrow access road below the dam, next to the rushing water where the militiaman had plunged to his death. The park ranger and the first Hoover Dam policeman had already climbed into one vehicle and started their engine.

Jackson raced for the front seat of the car, with Goldfarb following close behind. "Come on, Craig!" Craig paused, though, as he stood beside the transformer towers and high-tension lines extending across the canyon.

García's words echoed in his head about blowing up the turbines, how generators on the Arizona side or other turbines on the Nevada side could easily pick up the slack. However, if all the towers were destroyed and the power cables severed, electricity would certainly be cut off. Enough to black out major portions of several states.

Adjusting his sunglasses, he scanned the base of the metal towers; a rugged handhold and foothold path led to where the steel support beams had been anchored to the rock.

Then he spotted the block of grayish-blue substance affixed to the base of a power transmission tower.

Another bomb. Crude and simple—but still destructive.

A naked wire strung to the next tower and the next one down the cliffside. Craig drew in a breath. There were three of them. *That* must be where the detonation signal inside the dam would be transmitted to. "Oh, great!" he whispered.

Climbing over the concrete barrier, Craig began to scramble wildly up the rocks, painfully aware of how little time remained. His tie and jacket flapped as he bent over, clambering up the incline.

"Hey!" Goldfarb shouted, hanging onto the car door. "We've got to get out of here." Then he too noticed the claylike blocks of plastic explosive.

Craig reached the base of the first support tower, and then his foot slipped from the granite outcropping. He reached out with his left hand and grabbed the metal support of the high-powered transmission tower—hoping too late that the metal itself wasn't electrified. He held on, swinging himself up, scrambling with his feet for purchase.

He saw the plastic explosive. Words had been scrawled on its side with a black magic marker. FOR VICTORY AND FREEDOM ON OCTOBER 24!

Craig had less than a minute remaining, perhaps only a few seconds. If the EOD people didn't prevent the detonator signal, this explosive and the others linked to it would blow up.

He didn't have time to call the other EOD man. He didn't have time even to get out of the way. Craig gritted his teeth, swallowed hard. Simple plastic explosives didn't have complex machinery. He just needed to remove the initiator. If he disconnected the detonator, it would not trigger the bomb. Probably not.

Sure, it would be simple.

He reached out to grab the wires. The first lead came out with a pop, severing the electrical connections thrust into the soft explosive. He tugged on the other wire, pulling the connections from the next block at the second power-transmission tower. The others were just part of a series circuit.

Craig stood looking at the detonator in his fist, his heart pounding. Then he tossed it away from him as if it had turned into a snake—even the detonator cap would take off his hand if he was holding it when it went off.

Finally, slumping, he saw Jackson and Goldfarb hurrying up to the cliff wall, calling to see if he was all right.

The EOD men emerged from the generator room removing their helmets, beaming. "A minute to spare," the first one called. "We could have done it twice."

"These are the other explosives," Craig said, slumping down, suddenly weak. Now he finally had a chance to reconsider the words written on the soft substance.

FOR VICTORY AND FREEDOM ON OCTOBER 24!

It had been standard practice for military men to paint

names or messages on their bombs before dropping them on an enemy, whether it be Saddam Hussein or Adolph Hitler. In *Dr. Strangelove* the two atomic bombs had been named "Hi There!" and "Dear John."

But for all the planning the violent members of the Eagle's Claw had intended, Craig couldn't believe they had made such a stupid mistake as to get the date wrong. He glanced at the calendar function on his watch, checking just to be sure, then he shook his head.

October 24th was still three days away.

CHAPTER FOUR

Tuesday, October 21
8:51 A.M.

Device Assembly Facility
Nevada Test Site

Paige spotted Mike Waterloo waiting for her outside the barbed-wire gates of the Device Assembly Facility. Dirt berms rose on either side of the thick concrete walls. Two security observation towers, like turrets on a castle, stood out at prime vantage points.

Uncle Mike looked grim-faced as she pulled up in her white Ford pickup, identical to most other government vehicles at the DAF, except for the pine-tree air freshener dangling from her rear-view mirror. Three green NTS security cars had parked beside the barricaded entrance; a Clark County ambulance from the base hospital in nearby Indian Springs AFB had backed up to the glass front door, leaving its red emergency flashers shut off.

Mike Waterloo unfolded his arms and left the shade of the cargo doors. Wearing a threadbare short-sleeved yellow shirt and worn blue pants, the lanky man looked tired . . . and *old*. His thin arms stuck out from his body like two sticks. "Thanks for coming so fast, Paige."

She gave him a quick hug. During the glory days of the Cold War, Uncle Mike had regularly flown out to Nevada with Paige's own father, where they worked together on nuclear test explosions. Mike's wife Genny had died four years ago, not long before Gordon Mitchell had succumbed to cancer. Since then, Mike had drifted away, but Paige felt delighted to work with him and the Russian inspectors, getting in touch with him again. It had seemed a wonderful assignment. Until now.

As she reached across the seat to grab her day planner, Uncle Mike set his jaw. "I don't know what we're going to do when the news media gets hold of this. There's so much riding on this international inspection."

"Has the word gotten out?" Paige remembered when she had been blindsided back at Livermore after a controversial scientist had been found dead in his laboratory—and half the free world had found out before anyone could exercise media damage control.

He shook his head, then led her toward the guard gate. "I thought it should come from you. I've got our security folks watching the scene to keep it secure and untouched."

"Good work." She tucked the day planner under her arm, took a deep breath to calm herself, then set about getting the facts. "I last saw Ambassador Nevsky just before the rest of us left to go back to Las Vegas, but you and he went to the cafeteria instead. Explain to me again why he needed to come back to the DAF after working hours."

Uncle Mike held open the glass door to the security portal. Paige unclipped her laminated NTS badge and temporary DAF Access badge, handing both to the guard through an opening in the thick window. She walked through the metal detector, then waited for him on the other side.

Mike's shoulders were drawn forward in a stoop. "Nevsky had taken extensive notes earlier in the day, and he said something didn't seem quite right to him. But I think it may have been a ploy to snoop around in the DAF, judging from where he was found."

"Snooping around?" She arched her eyebrows. "*Spying*, you mean?"

Uncle Mike shrugged. "You tell me."

A mirror set in the wall revealed a security camera; radiation and particulate detectors hung from the ceiling. Paige and Uncle Mike walked past the guards and headed through the vast high-bay facility. The cavernous interior of the DAF gaped three stories high. Stacked concrete blocks formed a maze of temporary barricades.

"Nevsky and I got back here around eight o'clock," Uncle Mike said. "PK Dirks was working the late shift, and he agreed to watch the ambassador in the Pit Assembly Area—but I guess he wasn't watching very closely." He clamped his jaws together in annoyance.

Paige nodded, remembering Dirks, a good-natured, laid-back technician manager who coasted along in his position, not terribly devoted to his job.

"Nevsky was verifying serial numbers on pits from decommissioned devices. That's when our friendly Russian apparently stepped out to go to the bathroom—but instead of going to the head, Nevsky decided to go exploring in the DAF. PK didn't even see him, wasn't watching."

"Dirks left the ambassador alone in the area?" Paige frowned. "That's totally out of line."

"Technically yes, but the DAF has guards, and that hallway is completely sealed. You said yourself, why worry about the Russians seeing anything? We're showing it all to them in the first place. We got careless."

"The media's going to have a field day," Paige said with a groan, running a hand through her long hair, adjusting her barrette.

Uncle Mike looked sickened. "What can I say? PK screwed up. It was late at night, the Pit Assembly Area was empty in the off-shift, and Nevsky must have taken a wrong turn. It can be a maze in here sometimes."

"But how was he killed?" Paige asked.

"One of our forklift drivers, Carl Jorgenson, was stacking crates on the second tier when one fell. This is a warehouse, and that type of thing happens—not often, but cutbacks affect everything. Jorgenson was rushed, trying to do two jobs—he's a contract worker and wanted to make sure he didn't get laid off in the next reduction in force." Mike shrugged. "Nevsky was just unlucky to be standing in the wrong place when it happened."

He stopped by a door set into a concrete wall, ran his badge through the card reader, and punched in a series of numbers. The door swung open, showing a shadowy alley sectioned off by wooden crates. Paige could smell a musty odor from stored material that had sat around for years.

A team of medical workers huddled together where a large crate lay splintered on its side. Paige drew in a breath, searching for calm as the medical techs looked up. One squatted by a pool of dark liquid spilled on the floor. Blood.

Paige's heart raced as she stepped back from the mangled corpse. The Russian's arm was crumpled over his head as if he had tried to ward off the falling object at the last moment. His skin looked battered, his face grotesquely rearranged like a sagging rubber mask with the facial bones pulverized underneath. Pools of dark blood had soaked into the wooden sideboards of the crate.

"I guess he won't be going home with the rest of the team on Saturday," she said.

Uncle Mike slid an arm around her shoulder and nudged her from the grisly sight. He seemed even more sickened than she did, self-conscious about offering Paige his comfort. His face had a sad, hangdog look. She could smell his Brut aftershave, a scent that reminded her of her childhood.

As DAF Manager, Uncle Mike would consider himself ultimately responsible for the death, and the accident investigation just might cost him his job. He now wore the same expression she had seen when Aunt Genny had died—a vacant, stricken look that had lost all hope.

Mike and Genny Waterloo had been frequent visitors to the Mitchell home back in Livermore, alternating visits at Christmas, coming out for the Napa Valley balloon festival. Their families had lived next to each other in small suburban homes in the early days of the Livermore Radiation Lab, when most of the town had been employed in nuclear weapons work. Since Genny's death, Uncle Mike had buried himself in his job, first as a member of a U.S. inspection team traveling in Russia, then appointed to manage the DAF, with all the responsibilities—and headaches—that entailed.

Including the death of a high-profile Russian disarmament inspector.

Hearing the security door open behind her, Paige turned to see a red-faced man in a brown Russian military uniform charging ahead of an NTS security escort. The guard huffed to keep up with the big-shouldered man.

Paige braced herself as General Gregori Ursov pushed his way into the crowded warehouse area. Silver-haired Ursov was slightly shorter than Paige, but held himself erect. His weathered face looked as if it had been chiseled out of hard stone with a blunt instrument.

"Explain this to me! I have been able to get no information from DAF personnel. Is Ambassador Nevsky truly dead? I intend to file a protest because of this brick-walling!"

Paige moved to meet him, already selecting the best path as peacemaker. "No one is attempting to, uh, stonewall you, General. We are still trying to determine—"

His glance seizing on the fallen crate, Ursov brushed past her and strode to the body. Ursov stood stoically, staring down at the pool of blood, then knelt in front of his comrade. He reached out to touch Nevsky's arm. "*Idiot,*" he muttered, as if the ambassador could hear him. The Russian word was the same as English.

Uncle Mike looked helplessly at Paige, and she stepped forward. "Sorry, General, but you'll have to step back. Please don't touch anything."

Ursov remained squatting, studying, but did not touch the body. He spoke without turning. "I demand full reports, full investigations."

Paige spoke quietly. "These people are trying their best to determine exactly what happened, General. It appears to be a tragic accident."

Ursov turned to glare at Paige. "How could this happen? This place is supposed to be the most secure facility in all of the Test Site. You insist we have escorts every time we take a piss or blow our noses, and yet Ambassador Nevsky is allowed to wander until a *crate* falls on his head? Unbelievable!"

"The ambassador's escort left him alone for only a moment, General," said Uncle Mike. To Paige, he sounded more forceful than he had in years. "We don't know what Ambassador Nevsky was doing over here or what he was looking for. This is a restricted area, clearly marked, and he should not have trespassed."

Ursov raised his eyebrows in disbelief. "It is after nine o'clock in the morning, Mr. Waterloo. If this so-called accident happened last night, why wasn't I notified until now?"

"We are just beginning our investigation, General. We've been working diligently all night."

"It took you *all night* to identify Nevsky? Preposterous!" Ursov pressed up against Uncle Mike as if to intimidate him, though the DAF Manager towered over the Russian by a good half foot. "You will grant me immediate access to a telephone so I may contact my embassy."

"Certainly, General," Paige said, stepping up to them.

"We will keep you informed of the investigation as it progresses."

Ursov remained toe to toe with Uncle Mike. "Without Ambassador Nevsky, I am now officially in charge of the disarmament team—as I should have been in the first place. You will ensure that our activities remain precisely on schedule. We have only three more days to complete our assigned activities, and I have no wish to stay in this desert wasteland an hour more than necessary. If the summit meeting does not take place as planned, it will prove quite an embarrassment to both of our governments."

"Ambassador Nevsky's death was an accident, nothing more," said Uncle Mike coolly. "You must make that very clear to your embassy."

"I demand an autopsy of the body, and a review of your safety procedures," said Ursov. "We must have this all documented and submitted before I can transmit my final report to our president when he meets with your president."

Paige stepped up and tried to defuse the situation. "Certainly, we'll order the autopsy." She wasn't sure why Ursov would insist—Nevsky had plainly been squashed like a bug, and there wasn't any question as to the cause of death. "But it might take a few days for a detailed analysis."

Ursov snapped his head around. "Very well, Miss Mitchell. Let us call the *surviving* members of my team, so we may begin our tours for today."

CHAPTER FIVE

Tuesday, October 21
11:08 A.M.

Hoover Dam

Though Craig and his partners had prevented disaster at Hoover Dam, he could not congratulate himself on wrapping up the case. The Eagle's Claw investigation remained wide open.

He had found no leads that pointed to the ringleader responsible for planning the terrorist strike, or the probable murder of undercover agent Bill Maguire. The body of the bomber had vanished into the churning Colorado River—and Craig had no further evidence, no place to turn, despite the support teams of additional agents from the Las Vegas Satellite Office.

After Highway 93 had been reopened to traffic, the flood of cars came through. Drivers honked or glared because of the inconvenience; rubberneckers tried to determine the cause of the shutdown. When the news helicopters and vans arrived, Craig remained down at the base of the dam, where there would be less chance he'd be pegged for an interview.

Now, alone, he stared into the deep cold water of the tailrace, feeling his legs shaking in the backwash of adrenaline and suspense from his brush with death. He tapped his foot, burning off nervous energy. García had told him the water was fifty feet deep with heavy currents, and cold, fifty degrees.

The walkie-talkie squawked at his waist, breaking his concentration. Jackson's voice came over the speaker. "Agent Kreident, come in please. Over."

Craig listened as Jackson spoke in his quiet, professional voice. "The search helicopters have spotted the body. It's washed up against some rocks in a jog in the canyon a mile downriver. We can get you there in a few minutes if you want to be present for the recovery."

Shading his eyes, Craig took one last look around the dam, the power-generating apparatus, the administration building at the base of the structure. "Yeah, I don't want to miss the excitement."

At the water's edge Craig worked his way down the rocky ledges to the river. Sand and rocks the size of marbles dribbled down the incline; the sky burned a bright blue.

Two rescue workers went about the grim task of fishing the battered corpse out of the cold current. Craig's black wing-tip shoes had not been made for rugged climbing, but he managed. The day had grown so warm that he even stopped to loosen his tie.

The bomber's body was bruised and broken, livid red welts on pale white skin, as if a gang of thugs had beaten him to death. His dam coverall was ripped and stained, his face hideously bashed in. Craig doubted the man carried any sort of identification—and if so, he didn't trust it to be legitimate.

Agent Jackson appeared grim, as usual, watching the proceedings from a low outcropping. His suit and his shoes were already covered with mud, but he didn't mind getting himself dirty. Sweat glistened on his dark skin.

Goldfarb stared at the smashed body as the rescue workers hauled it dripping out of the river; he walked quietly away, his skin pale and pasty. Craig wondered if the dark-haired agent wanted to be sick privately, but instead he saw

Goldfarb pull out his cellular phone. The other agent took a few deep breaths, then punched in a number from memory.

Craig looked down at the dead bomber, remembering how this man had been shooting at him not long ago. He had stared the terrorist in the eyes, his gun drawn, holding the suspect backed up against the drop-off. He had known the man was a fanatic. He should have considered the possibility of self-sacrifice . . . but it was too late now. The body lay crumpled and broken. He hoped the militia group wouldn't turn the man into a martyr.

"We'll get dental records," Jackson said, then knelt to hold up the man's mangled hands, inspecting the fingertips. "And prints . . . most of them anyway."

Craig nodded. "If this guy has any criminal record at all, we'll ID him."

Goldfarb came up, his mood dramatically changed. "I found something else that ties together," he said excitedly. "I called my wife back home. She's got one of those 'This Day In History' books. Guess what significance October 24 holds?"

Craig gave the other agent his full attention. "So, what happened then?"

"Well," Goldfarb said, "in 1604 James I was proclaimed king of Great Britain, Ireland, and France . . . in 1964 the country Zambia was created out of Northern Rhodesia and Barotseland . . . in 1931 the George Washington Bridge opened in New York City and Al Capone was sentenced to prison for tax evasion." He raised his eyebrows as Craig waited patiently. "And also, ready for the drum roll? *It's the date the United Nations was founded.*"

Jackson nodded. "The Eagle's Claw hates the United Nations and anything that smacks of a world government, of interfering in national problems."

Craig tapped his fingers together, still pondering. "But if

they were blowing up the bomb today, why are they touting their victory on October 24th? That's not until Friday."

Craig stopped as a cold shiver went down his spine. "Unless they plan to escalate their reign of terror, climaxing on the anniversary. And if this"—he thought of the gigantic dam, the power lines and the generators, imagining how much destruction would have been caused had they not caught the bomb in time—"if this is just the first step, what are they planning for the main event?"

CHAPTER SIX

Tuesday, October 21
11:30 A.M.

Nevada Test Site

With a drawn-out sigh, Paige hung up the phone in Uncle Mike's DAF administrative office. She stood in front of his gray government-issue desk. "That'll make the bureaucratic pack rats back at DOE Headquarters scurry during their afternoon coffee breaks."

"I take it DOE didn't handle the call too well." Mike swiveled forlornly in his chair.

"At least I got through to the Assistant Secretary's office. The case officer said they'd handle the fallout and disperse the news to the On-Site Inspection Agency, the Defense Special Weapons Agency, and the State Department, who will pass it on to the Russian embassy to confirm Ursov's own report." She pulled in a long, slow breath. "They're mostly concerned with how this is going to look on Friday. You know the President had planned a short stopover in Las Vegas on his way to the summit in L.A.—now, they're wondering if the President should even show."

In the front room, Mike's hard-as-nails "moat dragon" Sally Montry rattled the keys on her word processor like machine-gun fire, filling out all the official forms for everyday business as required by regulations and established NTS procedures.

On the wall behind his desk hung a diploma from Cornell, an NTS Excellence in Service award, a photo of the OSIA inspection team in which he had participated two years earlier in Russia; no family photos. He and Aunt Genny had had no children, but Paige was his goddaughter.

Paige cleared her throat and turned from the memories. "We're supposed to continue the inspection process as if nothing had happened, get the Russians on today's scheduled tour of the explosive bunkers and Frenchman Flat—just as Ursov requested. They're not going to let this stop the President from showing up at the airport to thank the disarmament team, and they certainly won't cancel the summit plans."

Uncle Mike shook his head in disbelief. "I was supposed to take the Russians to see David Copperfield at Caesar's Palace tonight."

"My guess is they'll want to go. Might keep them in a cooperative mood for the last few days." She took a deep breath. "We've got to hold on by our fingernails until Friday's over."

Uncle Mike nodded soberly. "We'd open ourselves to accusations of noncompliance if we didn't show them everything on the schedule." He snapped his glance up, as if he had just realized something. "Uh, PK Dirks was supposed to lead the tour today—should we change that, in light of his misconduct last night?"

Paige shook her head, tossing her blond hair. She fixed the barrette, clipping her hair back. "No, any change might look like we're admitting to some wrongdoing. Send Dirks along with me, same as on the printed schedule. We can't do anything here until we get a preliminary report from the medical examiner and the safety team looking at the accident site."

Uncle Mike stood up, all business. "I've already placed the forklift driver, Carl Jorgenson, on administrative leave.

In an accident such as this, we're required to keep him out of the workplace pending a full OSHA investigation. He feels terrible about the whole mess—but Nevsky shouldn't have been wandering around in a restricted area. He's as much at fault."

A knock came at the door, and Sally Montry poked her ash-blond head into the room. "PK's here, Mr. Waterloo." Sally wasn't beautiful, but the statuesque attractiveness made people think of her as a "handsome" fortyish woman. Uncle Mike had often commented on her impeccable competence.

"Thanks. Send him in."

PK Dirks stood uneasily outside the door. He looked at Sally with a strange expression, but the secretary walked coolly past him. Dirks flicked his eyes, then stepped into the administrative office. "The rest of the inspection team is here," he said with forced good humor, scratching his reddish beard, "whenever Ms. Mitchell is ready to head out."

Uncle Mike looked at Paige wearily. "Want me to go along?"

"I can handle it," said Paige. "I've given my cell phone number to the ME, but I need you here to field general calls. Half the State Department will want to fly into town within the next few days, so anything you can do to satisfy them will help me."

"Sally can let them know it's all under control—she's good at that."

Paige nodded to PK Dirks, following the chubby, bearded technician out of the offices. "Let's round up the Russians and go sightseeing."

The white government van hummed along on the two-lane road, heading south and then west. While Paige drove, PK Dirks sat in the front passenger seat, turning his head to speak to the seven Russians in back.

"NTS is a big place, roughly the size of our state of Rhode Island," Dirks said. "I don't know how that compares to the size of old Soviet installations."

The area was dry and desolate, some parts as flat as glass. In the midday sun occasional streaks of paler tan splashed the broad plain like a watercolor wash. Scarecrowish Joshua trees mottled the landscape along with mesquite, brush sage, and gray-green thistles. Jagged mountains lay in angled strips on every horizon. Nothing looked remotely *soft*, as far as Paige could see. The sky was as clear as a blue magnifying glass, but she knew that sudden and violent thunderstorms could roll in at any time.

The Russians spoke little, still in shock at the death of their team leader. Paige knew the thoughts going through their minds: Had it been lax security at the DAF, or was it a sophisticated cover-up for something more sinister? What had Nevsky been doing alone in a restricted area, far from the glovebox?

Paige had seen other accident investigations and the inevitable result. Fingers had to be pointed, and for a tragedy of this magnitude the DAF would have to cough up at least one scapegoat—probably someone like Jorgenson or PK Dirks. She dreaded the repercussions might ripple as high as the DAF Manager, Uncle Mike. . . .

Paige caught a glimpse of figures moving overland across the desert up ahead. People . . . walking along like a group of hikers crossing the road. She squinted. "Who's that?"

Dirks leaned forward. "Shouldn't be anyone out here, ma'am. Slow down," he said. "This is a security zone, not a Boy Scout jamboree."

The three hikers cut across the road as they headed north toward the distant range of mesas. They turned to face the oncoming van as if hoping to hitch a ride. How had they managed to get past NTS security? Several sequential gates phased people into various sections of the site; mobile ground and airborne guard forces monitored the area for intruders.

But apparently not well enough.

"Ma'am," said Dirks, speaking more urgently now, "maybe we should use the CB to call security?" The Russians spoke excitedly among themselves, catching a glimpse of what was going on.

Paige handed Dirks the CB microphone as she pulled up next to the two men and a woman. One of the men was extremely thin and tall, with stringy hair hanging from his floppy brown cowboy hat; he blinked behind round John Lennon glasses. The woman was short and pudgy, wearing her black hair in two braids; the other man looked like a weight lifter dressed in a loose, tie-dyed T-shirt.

The tall man waved and gave a goofy grin. "Hey, what's happening?" he called as Paige opened the van door. He shrugged off his backpack and peered up at the van through his dusty, round glasses.

Paige gestured for PK Dirks to remain seated. Her shoes crunched in the sand as the desert heat hit her full force. "May I ask what you're doing out here? This is a restricted area."

"Told you we should have stayed away from the roads," the pudgy woman said.

"I'm Doog, and this is Tina and Geoff," the tall man said with a grin. "We didn't expect to see anybody this far out past the gates."

"Neither did we," said Paige dryly. "Are you aware that unauthorized access here is a Federal offense?"

Tina and Geoff exchanged nervous glances; Doog just shrugged and gave his goofy grin. "We weren't going to steal anything. The Cold War is over, and you guys aren't setting off any nukes anymore—so what do you have to hide?" He waited with childlike anticipation for her answer.

Paige shook her head, trying not to get irritated. "That's

not the point, Mr., uh, Doog. *No trespassing* means *no trespassing.*"

Doog looked at his two companions, who both shrugged in surrender. "We're just taking a shortcut up to Groom Lake. We figured it might be easier to get through the fence this way. No chance of getting through on the Route 375 side. Extraterrestrial Highway."

"Yeah," said Tina, her eyes dark and intense. "You know, *Dreamland.*"

Doog said, "Groom Lake, Area 51—that supersecret Air Force base inside Nellis where the government is hiding a bunch of aliens in one of their hangars. They won't let the public know about it because they're holding negotiations so Earth can be accepted into the galactic union."

Paige lifted an eyebrow. "Aliens? Right—I saw *Independence Day.*"

Geoff nodded, finally speaking, His voice was surprisingly high-pitched for his burly body. "We're sneaking in to get a look for ourselves, find enlightenment, and channel our energy to the stars."

Dirks leaned out the window. "Site security is on the way, ma'am."

"Who are these people?" General Ursov glared out the open window of the van. "Why the delay? Is this another breach in security?"

Paige sighed. *This is going to be one long day.*

CHAPTER SEVEN

Tuesday, October 21
1:45 P.M.

Cane Springs Test Range
Nevada Test Site

After NTS security troops had taken the UFO-hunting trespassers, Paige drove the government van to a line of rocky, brush-covered hills where explosives storage bunkers dotted the gullies and ridge tops.

They passed through a checkpoint where a security officer in sand camouflage fatigues inspected underneath the vehicle using mirrors and a flashlight. Paige couldn't tell if the guard was suspicious of the Russians *per se*, or if his job was just to be skeptical of everyone driving past his station.

Warmed up to his role as tour guide, PK Dirks chatted breezily, trying to make the Russians relax. Ursov looked dourly out the van windows, as if filing away details of the emplacements, the bunkers, everything he saw.

Dirks pointed up the road. "Take the gravel road just before the curve, ma'am," he said. "Go to bunker 87-3—I know the door lock combination."

She pulled up in front of a thick-walled, windowless concrete bunker set into a steep hillside. The bunker had water-stained walls and a heavy metal door. The coded lock consisted of a round ring of numbered buttons. Paige hung back as Dirks punched four buttons in sequence, then tugged on the handle. One of the Russians helped him haul the heavy steel hatch open.

"This is where we store our chemical explosives," Dirks said, reaching inside to flick on the lights. He puffed his chubby cheeks, making his beard bristle out. He gestured for the Russians to enter the claustrophobic building.

Ursov said, "A bunker looks like a bunker, looks like a bunker."

"Maybe they keep more flying saucers out here," Anatoli Voronin muttered, spreading his thick lips in a grin.

Paige had just closed the van door when her cellular phone rang. As she plucked the unit from her belt, Dirks waved to her. "I'll take them in, ma'am." He ushered the Russians inside the bunker as Paige pressed the phone against her ear.

"This is Chief Medical Examiner Adams," said a voice, reedy but firm. Her heart beat more rapidly as she prepared to receive the report about Nevsky's death. "Are you someplace you can talk, Ms. Mitchell? The report is worse than you might have imagined."

Paige braced herself. "Worse than him being dead?"

"Trouble is," the coroner said, "the ambassador was dead long before that crate fell on his head—by at least half an hour. We can tell by the splash pattern and by chemical analysis of the blood. His heart wasn't beating at the time of the massive trauma to his skull and vertebrae. It would seem that the falling crate was a cover-up to hide a major blow to the cranium."

Paige stiffened as the words sunk in. "You're suggesting this was a murder and cover-up, not just an industrial accident."

"No question in my mind. You've got a problem on your hands, and I don't envy you the political hot potato. Not at all." Adams cleared his throat, then continued as if reading from a dry report. "We'll do a full autopsy and chemical workup, but facts are facts."

Paige stared across the wide-open desert, aghast. "Mr. Adams, I'd like to get guidance from the State Department and the DOE." At the back fringes of her shock, she began to feel the impending political implications to Nevsky's death. *Murder* . . . In a flash of panic she hoped no one was listening on this cellular band. "You know about the President's upcoming disarmament summit, the whole reason for the visit of this Russian inspection team. How long can we keep this information from the press?"

"I've got to complete a lot of tests and document the formal autopsy," Adams answered. "Besides, in a sensitive case like this, I'm going to double- and triple-check every result. In the meantime, if people want to assume it was an industrial accident, there's no reason we have to change their minds."

"I understand," Paige said. "I'll get the FBI on it right away."

Paige continued with the formal briefing. "The Nevada Test Site was chosen as a nuclear proving ground in December 1950, to reduce the expense and logistics of conducting U.S. nuclear tests out on Pacific Islands." Speaking the familiar words helped her to wash away the settling numbness. She tried to focus on the task at hand, to keep the Russians from suspecting anything. She took a deep breath. "Our first nuclear detonation occurred a month later, dropped from an Air Force plane onto Frenchman Flat."

"Here?" Vitali Yakolev said excitedly, scratching his flame-red hair and looking around the barren lake bed. The team members seemed fascinated by the wreckage around them, like a Hollywood set depicting a city in the aftermath of a nuclear holocaust.

PK Dirks answered, hands on hips. "You're standing on ground zero."

Paige said, "President Eisenhower declared a moratorium in 1958, but testing started again three years later, after the Soviet Union resumed testing."

Smiling broadly, Dirks tossed a pebble into the distance. "All told, we conducted about eight hundred tests out here, most of them underground." He trudged across the dried mud toward the town ruins just off the road. "Don't worry," Dirks said jokingly, "it's not too radioactive anymore. You hardly notice the glow at night."

Paige knew the background levels were barely higher than anywhere else on the site. She had checked for clearance before putting the mock towns on their schedule; the ruined buildings and bomb shelters were some of the most impressive sights at NTS.

Her mind still whirling about what she had learned from the ME, Paige continued the charade of the tour, waiting for a return call from DOE Headquarters, playing the attentive hostess and tour guide . . . a good protocol officer even in jeans and a denim shirt. She followed the group onto Frenchman Flat, into an uninhabited city that never was.

To study the blast effects of an atomic strike, samples of different architecture and construction materials, arranged in varying orientations, were erected at incremental distances from ground zero. Paige had seen films of the test explosions, how the flame front swept through the artificial town, scattering buildings like matchsticks, igniting rubble as if it were gunpowder.

Cameras planted inside the buildings showed mannequins seated on the furniture, play-doll families engaged in typical household activities, eating TV dinners in front of their black-and-white television sets. The blast wave swept them aside like chaff.

"So this was a town," Nikolai Bisovka said, lighting up another Marlboro. He had grown immensely fond of American cigarettes. "But where is the saloon? Academician

Nevsky would have felt right at home." General Ursov glared as Bisovka blew a puff of smoke. The other Russians exchanged nervous glances.

The tour group crunched through the shattered rubble, the stumps of buildings, thick walls knocked down or caved in . . . twisted ends where steel doors had been *torn* free. Broken bricks littered the ground, but low, gray-green vegetation thrived. They walked under a steel railroad bridge whose immense girders had been twisted and bent like a pretzel.

"You can see where we tested different designs for bomb shelters," PK Dirks said. "For a while it was a status symbol in this country to have your very own bomb shelter. My parents built one when I was a kid."

"In former Soviet Union, *everyone* had bomb shelter," Bisovka said, blowing away a cloud of smoke. "But our shelters were also called subway tunnels." The other Russian team members chuckled.

Ranks and ranks of low structures protruded from the sands—reinforced-concrete domes and rectangular bunkers covered with dirt. Many had collapsed like eggshells, while others remained unscathed decades later.

Ursov nodded, his interest finally piqued. "I am curious to see if your successful designs look similar to ours."

Dirks laughed. "Come on—we can look inside the intact ones."

Paige's cellular phone rang again, and she stepped back toward the van, trying to conceal her expression as the rest of the group continued into the abandoned ghost town. A pair of fighter jets roared overhead, streaking low, then pulling up in a high-G climb, performing aerial maneuvers that caught the Russians' attention. They stood outside the rows of crumbling bomb shelter domes, pointing at the crisscrossed contrails of the jets.

On her phone, Paige listened to the filtered voice of

Madeleine Jenkins, an Undersecretary at the Department of Energy who did not mince words. "It was already an international incident when Nevsky was found dead, but now the State Department is reeling. We've got a summit in a couple of days to celebrate the successful completion of this work, to show off our bilateral cooperation. The President is scheduled to meet the team on Friday—what's he going to say?" She sighed. "If this was a premeditated assassination, is it your belief that the other members of the team may be in danger as well?"

"I'm not sure that's the case, Madam Undersecretary," Paige said. "Nevsky was alone in the DAF, and someone may have seen an opportunity. If we keep the other Russians together, there should be no cause for alarm."

"Nevertheless," Jenkins said, her rich voice clipped, her words spoken quickly. She carried out her conversation at a Beltway speed, rather than a casual Nevada drawl. "We have spoken directly with the Federal Bureau of Investigation. Their agent will be working separately from the Secret Service advance team—they'll keep to the airport, since the President won't be on the ground more than an hour."

"The FBI?" Paige said. "I suppose that's standard procedure."

"It turns out one of their best investigators is in your area right now. He's a specialist in high-tech investigations, and I believe you worked with him before on a murder case out at Lawrence Livermore."

"Craig?" she said, surprised. "I mean, Special Agent Craig Kreident?"

"Let me stress, Ms. Mitchell, that the DOE and the State Department have an extraordinary interest in solving this incident quickly. It would be a matter of great embarrassment both to our own President and to the Russian president if this ruins our scheduled disarmament talks. Do I make myself clear?"

"I understand, Madam Undersecretary, but I'm not a murder investigator—"

Jenkins interrupted, "You are an *expediter*—a people person, a protocol officer. Smooth the way for Agent Kreident. Get him anything he needs and do what you can to keep the Russians happy. And don't tell anyone we suspect foul play—not yet."

Paige swallowed, watching as Ursov ducked inside the old bomb shelters.

"I'll call you again when we have arranged all the details," Jenkins said. "Go brief the investigator yourself, so we can keep the number of people involved to a minimum."

Overhead the fighter jets streaked northward toward Nellis Air Force Base. *Probably to see the UFOs Doog and his friends believed in,* she thought sourly. She drew another deep, deep breath of the dry desert air.

The sleek aircraft vanished into the haze at the horizon.

CHAPTER EIGHT

Tuesday, October 21
4:07 P.M.

Hoover Dam

In the bright afternoon, Craig Kreident stood at the observation towers atop Hoover Dam, peering down the vast expanse of concrete like the world's most terrifying ski slope. Traffic rolled steadily behind him; tourists walked from the Visitor's Center to the observation towers to the gift shop.

The area had returned to normal, despite the bustling wrap-up conducted by teams of FBI experts in one of the dam's administrative meeting rooms, which had been converted into a temporary operations center.

Craig leaned against the railing, still exhausted from his adrenaline hangover. He tapped his fingers on the rail, shuffling from one spot to another, though the spectacular view did not change. He watched investigators moving about far below, combing the buildings for other evidence of sabotage.

It felt good to relax, but a sour feeling lingered in his stomach. In his mind Craig could still see the wild eyes of the bomber as he stepped backward, saying, "I can go to Heaven." It was never good to have someone killed during a bust. It demonstrated the volatility of his work, the uncertainty that accompanied every law-enforcement situation. Given a simple twist of fate, he himself could be dead instead.

What could he have done differently, what precautions should he have taken? He'd seen that guilt ruin competent investigators, blunt their edges as they worried too much about consequences to make rapid decisions in the line of fire. He had to work on developing internal calluses.

The law classes he'd taken at Stanford had dealt with such issues in esoteric ways—there, the world was black and white, right or wrong, making purely academic sense. Those self-confident professors didn't have to deal with the gritty world Craig saw; he had realized the difference even when he had worked for a private investigator while putting himself through school.

The last time Craig had let down his guard, during a bust for white-collar crime, the CEO of a small computer-chip manufacturing firm had committed suicide. Had he been at fault then as well? The tragedy had resulted in a temporary administrative leave, but ultimately Craig had been cleared. And what about this morning?

You're already in dreamland, man. . . .

As he stood gathering his thoughts, Mr. García came up to him, removing his yellow hard hat. He ran his fingers through short gray hair. "Agent Kreident, I want to report that one of my workers is missing." Craig immediately snapped to attention. "He was here this morning when I called the meeting, but I can't find him now. With all the mess today, I didn't notice until now. His name is Bryce Connors."

"You got a glimpse of the guy who took a swan dive into the water," Craig said. "Could that have been Connors?"

The supervisor shook his head. "No, that guy was tall and skinny. Connors is short, broad-shouldered, square-jawed, and with very dark hair, the kind that gave him a five o'clock shadow by lunchtime."

Craig remained skeptical. "You don't think he just got spooked and ran when he heard about the bomb?"

"Spooked?" García laughed weakly. "No—Bryce Connors is the type to spit at an oncoming truck. Not real bright, mind you, but cowardly is not a word I think of when describing him."

Craig let the words spin through his mind. His foot tapped faster. Even though all the shift employees were accounted for at the time, one of the legitimate workers could have granted the terrorist access, helped him perform the sabotage. "I want Connors's address," he said, "and his employee record." Flustered, the shift supervisor hurried off.

"Hey, Craig!" Another voice drifted from the far end of the sidewalk. Craig turned and spotted Goldfarb. The curly-haired agent held a cup of coffee from the gift shop snack bar, sloshing a few drops as he waved. "Phone call for you down in the temp CC! It's June Atwood. Says it's urgent."

Craig took a last glance at the water rushing past the rocks below, not anxious to talk to his supervisor back in Oakland. A warm breeze ruffled his hair. Goldfarb strode to the unmarked access door leading to the temporary command center. Craig followed, walking stiffly after such a long day.

The inside of the dam smelled of lubricants, oil, and grease for the massive generators. They trotted down three flights of stairs to a room crammed with agents, some at laptop computers, others going over pictures of the bomb the EOD team had dismantled under the turbines. A low throb of equipment and conversation hummed in the background.

"Which line?" Craig asked as he headed for the phone. Feeling a pang of hunger, he realized he hadn't eaten anything since this morning.

"Over there. We've set up a STU-3." Goldfarb pointed with his coffee cup across the room to where Jackson sat next to a portable set.

Jackson held up the receiver, muffling the phone with his hand. "The Boss herself is getting antsy. And we all know what that means."

Craig dodged a metal table holding computer printouts of MOs and intelligence data on regional terrorist groups. "Why is she calling on a secure phone? Is she worried about the Eagle's Claw tapping into our line?"

Jackson handed the phone to Craig. "Beats me, boss. I only do what I'm told around here."

Craig glanced around for a seat and pulled up an old gray swivel chair that looked as if it had been left there by the original dam construction crew in the 1940s. He grabbed the receiver. "Hello, June."

"Ready to go secure, Craig." His supervisor back in Oakland sounded no-nonsense, and not interested in conversation. The Motorola STU-3, a version of the military's secure phone, could transmit classified information as scrambled electronic signals. The Bureau used it only for particularly sensitive cases. "Do you have a STU-3 key?"

Jackson rummaged in his pocket and pulled out a black plastic key with serrated ridges, metal edges, and a magnetic strip. Craig inserted the card into the base of the phone. "Okay, June, I'm ready."

"Going secure." The line went dead.

Craig turned the key and waited until a tiny message appeared on the LED display. SECRET: FBI OAKLAND CA FIELD OFFICE. Craig heard a scratchy noise over the receiver. "Craig? Are you there?"

"Ready on this end, June." He waited, listening to the barely perceptible pause in the words as the signals were encrypted and decrypted.

"Something bigger has come up, Craig," June said without preamble. "I'm pulling you from the Eagle's Claw case."

Craig nearly fell off his chair. "Bigger? What can be bigger than a bunch of terrorists wanting to blow up Hoover Dam?" The half-second STU delay seemed interminable to him.

"There's been a murder at the Nevada Nuclear Test Site, fifty miles outside of Las Vegas. An ambassador, the senior member of a Russian disarmament team, has been killed, staged to look like an accident. If we don't handle this quietly, we'll have an international incident on our hands. The president has scheduled a summit meeting with the Russian president for this coming Saturday, to celebrate the successful completion of this open-doors inspection. Worse, he's scheduled a short stopover in Las Vegas to personally greet the disarmament team before flying on to the summit. We cannot have an unsolved murder mucking this up."

Craig leaned back in the creaking chair, his mind whirling. "Are you sure it's a murder?" He listened to a faint hiss of static.

"The ME's office says it's pretty plain. The Russian was dead half an hour before the so-called accident occurred."

Goldfarb shoved a cup of sour-smelling coffee into Craig's free hand. "Pretend it's Jack Daniels," he whispered, "and imagine how pissed she'd be."

"So you've got the murder of a Russian national on Federal property. I appreciate the political ramifications." Craig sipped the coffee, trying to maintain his calm. It tasted bitter. "But you don't appreciate how serious things are here. We were lucky to find that bomb before it went off, and there's strong evidence the Eagle's Claw intends to do more acts of terrorism before Friday. *Friday*, June. Hoover Dam was just a warmup act."

June's voice remained firm. "I don't intend to slack off on the Eagle's Claw for a minute—we'll keep the entire team cooking at high heat. I'm just pulling *you* from it, Craig. Your abilities are better utilized elsewhere. Some more agents are coming in, and the Secret Service advance team is there if you need help."

He had a difficult time keeping his temper in check. He set down the coffee, afraid he might accidentally clench his fist and smash the foam cup. "What about Bill Maguire? The Eagle's Claw killed him, June—I know it. There's too much at stake to take me off this case for a simple murder."

"Nothing simple about Ambassador Nevsky's murder," she said, unwavering. "And that was a low blow about Maguire. I felt his death as much as any of you field agents did. But I set the priorities here—do I have to call you back to Oakland so I can explain this face to face? According to airline schedules I can get you here and back there by eleven o'clock tonight. The result will be the same, but you'll waste a lot of hours on the plane."

Craig opened his mouth to retort, but saw Jackson, Goldfarb, and three other agents watching him. Heaving a deep breath, he tried to block the thrum of machinery in the background by putting a hand over his free ear.

"June," said Craig, "I still think it's a mistake—"

"You're the best agent I've got, Craig. " She sounded calm now, persuasive. "That previous case you solved at Lawrence Livermore proved it. You have experience working in government facilities, and I know I can count on you." She fell quiet for a moment.

"This is coming straight from the top, the Attorney General herself. We've only known for a few hours that the ambassador's death was not an accident. The U.S. has not yet released that information because there's so much riding on completing the disarmament process. We've got to hold this coalition together and not give the Russians any reason to back out. We cannot afford to have this fail. By Friday, the disarmament team will have completed their mission, the President will have personally expressed his congratulations, and *you*, Craig, will have solved the case."

"How am I going to conduct this investigation without letting on that we know there's been a murder?"

"Because of the political nature of this death, the FBI

must be called in. You're here, a proven expert in cases involving scientific facilities."

Craig rolled his gray eyes. "Are they going to buy that?"

"Besides, Paige Mitchell is also involved in this case. The two of you worked well together in Livermore. Do it again."

"*Paige* is out here? What is she doing in Nevada?"

"Protocol liaison for the disarmament inspectors. It's a temporary assignment for DOE."

Craig fell silent—that put a whole new spin on things. But still he chewed on his lower lip, unconvinced. "This militia problem could turn out to be the tip of a much bigger iceberg."

"Goldfarb and Jackson can handle it for the next three days, Craig. They'll have help."

"Three days is all we've got until the Claw's deadline. October 24."

"Get over to Las Vegas tonight. Find a room somewhere. Miss Mitchell will be your NTS security escort, and she will brief you on the details. Until then, unless you can talk over a secure phone, the true nature of your investigation remains classified. Understand? Or do you have to fly out here so I can explain it to you face to face?"

Craig tried to keep his voice steady. He answered crisply. "No, ma'am. That won't be necessary."

CHAPTER NINE

Tuesday, October 21
6:30 P.M.

Caesar's Palace
Las Vegas

Trying to maintain his patience and keeping an open "American hospitality" mood, Mike Waterloo drove with his station wagon crammed full of Russians. Six members of the disarmament team rode with him as he fought through the evening traffic clogging the Las Vegas Strip.

After their days in the DAF, he had come to know all the inspectors by name, though now they treated him like a mere chauffeur, talking among themselves in guttural Russian, excluding him from the conversation. He clenched his jaws so that a ripple of muscles stood out on his gaunt cheeks, making no comment as the Russians guffawed, sharing a joke—possibly at his expense. He would never know. Their humor struck him as forced, with a slightly hysterical edge, still shocked at the messy death of their comrade.

General Ursov had remained behind in protest, going to his room at the Rio where he was no doubt contacting superiors back in Russia . . . or possibly just documenting the information he had collected from NTS. Waterloo wouldn't be surprised to discover that Ursov worked as a spy for the KGB, or whatever the state intelligence organization called itself these days.

Despite Ursov's protests, the others had overwhelmingly voted to see Copperfield's show. They would hear nothing about changing those plans—dead comrade or no dead comrade.

As Waterloo drove, the Russians marveled at the dazzle of Las Vegas—the epitome of American commercialism. The foreigners acted more excited about seeing a stage magician than about global nuclear disarmament. Maybe if Copperfield could just make the entire stockpile disappear. . . .

Waterloo pulled into the first roundabout parking lot of Caesar's Palace. The palatial building's smooth arches, splattering fountains, and alabaster statue reproductions recalled the golden age of Greece, complete with lovely Corinthian columns, gilt edgings, and shapely curves. He let a valet take his vehicle to the free parking while the Russians boiled out of the front and back seats, gawking at the architecture, the opulence.

This place was very different from what Waterloo had experienced in Russia three years ago. . . .

Following the breakup of the USSR, the Russians and the U.S. had agreed to a bilateral monitoring of nuclear dismantlement. Hence Waterloo's long stay in Russia, and the return visit of this team to the Nevada Test Site.

Waterloo had been one of twelve inspectors arriving in Moscow, a year after the death of his wife, only a few months after Gordon Mitchell had succumbed to cancer. It had felt good to get away.

He and the others had worn badges that sported a bright U.S. flag, which elicited many stares in the airport. Protocol prevented the Russians from physically touching the inspectors, but Waterloo and his teammates were scanned for metal objects. He removed every electronic item from his suitcase, while the customs official studied it to make sure he had not attempted to smuggle any recording devices. His electric razor received particularly rigorous scrutiny.

During the creaking bus ride into Moscow city center, Waterloo had seen few cars on the road. The air was filled with smog, making the gray clouds seem even drearier. He saw no individual houses, only massive state-built apartment complexes. Whole sections of building fronts had fallen away, slumping into disrepair as if no one cared.

Vastly different from the glamour of Las Vegas. . . .

Inside Caesar's Palace, the Russian team wandered through the dizzying maze of lights, blinking slot machines, and video poker games. "We play slot machines here, friend Mike," said Nikolai Bisovka, sucking on another Marlboro. He seemed determined to get lung cancer before he returned to his own country. "You will pick up our tickets, please?"

Waterloo dreaded they would scatter like wild chickens the moment they were out of his sight, but when he returned with the tickets, he was surprised to find the Russians glued to a bank of nickel slots.

Alexander Novikov bubbled with excitement. "I won jackpot, friend Mike! Jackpot!" He rattled a plastic cup of coins, and Waterloo saw that he had collected about four dollars in nickels—the handful of coins must have seemed like a fortune. Novikov took great pride in jingling as he walked.

Waterloo ushered them up the lighted stairs toward the Circus Maximus auditorium. He handed them their tickets as if they were schoolchildren, afraid they would lose their stubs or forget to go to the bathroom before the show started. Filing dutifully to their booth, the group sat back and waved for cocktail waitresses so they could order several rounds of drinks at once.

Waterloo tried to convince himself to enjoy the experience. He had never seen Copperfield's show, though the magician had been playing in Vegas for much of his long career. He and Genny hadn't been to shows in years. As the foreigners spoke in Russian around him, the lights dimmed—and his thoughts drifted back to when the lights had gone out in his Moscow hotel room. . . .

The Hotel Ukraina looked impressive, but old. The walls of the cavernous dining room had been painted with idyllic peasant scenes, huge dancers, farmers, happy musicians. Waterloo went with his companions to a feast of beef pot pies served steaming hot in individual crockpots.

A broad-hipped waitress bustled up and removed the cloth that covered a serving table to reveal an array of trinkets she had smuggled there—nesting "matrushka" dolls, painted eggs, tins of caviar, lacquered boxes. She insisted her under-the-table prices were much better than the Americans could expect to find in the hotel store.

Waterloo had gone to his room exhausted, anxious to be alone. Though meant to be ostentatious, the decor unsettled him—pink walls, green curtains, a pair of chipped end tables sporting small lamps. An empty desk, a tiny black-and-white television in a plastic case, a single hard-backed chair.

While assuring them that there was no crime in Moscow, the senior Moscow escort had insisted they keep their room doors locked, and warned them never to wander around the hotel alone.

Waterloo had been sitting on his bed considering this, when the power went out, cold darkness sweeping down like a Valkyrie—merely one of the frequent power outages that plagued Moscow. On his first day in Russia, he began to count down the hours until he could return home to his own beloved country. . . .

Dry-ice fog poured along the Circus Maximus stage as spotlights stabbed across the vacant space. Electronic rock music blared, a pulsing rhythm in time to the light show. Near-naked dancers swept out from behind the curtains as an empty cage descended from the rafters, dangling on a chain.

The dancers came forward, hinting at more skin than they actually showed, to place translucent white screens around the empty cage. As the music reached its crescendo, fire exploded in the background. The cloth screens fell away, and the lean dark-haired magician appeared out of nowhere. To thunderous applause, David Copperfield took a bow.

Through the stage lights, Waterloo looked to see the Russians delighted at the lights, the spectacle, the *sex*. Gauzy wisps of costumes and flesh-toned leotards made the beautiful assistants look nearly nude as they swirled around Copperfield's dusky handsomeness.

This was why the Russians had come to America in the first place—not to work, not to go through the tedious requirements of the disarmament routine, not to prepare for a summit meeting. But to experience the American flash and dazzle.

Waterloo recalled how the Russians had been displeased with Nevsky staying behind to work in the DAF. If he had only gone with them back to the Rio for the international buffet, rather than putting in extra hours, Kosimo Nevsky would be alive today. It seemed ironic that the only inspector actually interested in the *job* had suffered for that fact, paid with his life.

Not that the job was anything glamorous, but at least Nevsky had been dedicated to it. . . .

When Waterloo and the other On-Site Inspection Agency workers had finally reached their destination—a military base and weapons stockpile in the city of Sarny—he at last began to feel that he was ready to accomplish the task for which he had left his beautiful and spacious Southwest.

The OSIA team began a routine that continued for the next three weeks. Breakfast at 0800, departure for the work site promptly at 0850, work itself at 0900 sharp. The first day it poured down rain. Waterloo stood with the others wearing identical parkas and OSIA baseball caps, watching the step-by-step procedures. Russian escorts followed them suspiciously at every turn.

The SS-20 missiles slated for destruction were huge, fifty feet long and twelve feet high. The Russians used only hand tools for the job—wrenches, hammers, hand saws. Conscripts did all the work while officers supervised.

Waterloo watched one conscript having difficulty removing a hydraulic line because he was turning the wrench the wrong direction. Forbidden to interfere with the work, Waterloo could say nothing, only watch, as the conscript tried one hand, then two hands, then a hammer to break the nut free. When all else failed he cut the line off with a hacksaw, though never once did he attempt to turn the wrench the other direction.

Papers were signed by Russians and Americans, verifying completion of the treaty-mandated work, and then the team returned to watch the process all over again.

The OSIA inspectors lived in a rectangular compound surrounded by a twelve-foot-high concrete fence topped with electric wire. The paper-thin walls readily passed every annoying noise from the outside, at all hours of the night. Water dripped in pipes that ran through the wall next to his bed. The wallpaper had begun to peel in large sections.

It took them a week to discover the hidden microphones, one in each bedroom, several in the day room, another in the hall.

Wonderful Russian hospitality, Waterloo thought now. *Not quite like what we're showing them. . . .*

On the Circus Maximus stage, a blond woman went through a seductive dance with Copperfield, using cloth strips to tie his wrists to the headboard of a simulated bed, which was then surrounded by screens and raised up out of reach. The blond picked up another loose bedsheet, swirled it around herself, draped it over her body—and suddenly Copperfield himself tossed the sheet away, having miraculously switched places with her. When the bed came back down to stage level, the woman lay tied in the same position.

Copperfield released her, then launched into further performances.

The Russians sat astounded.

After the grand finale, Waterloo stood patiently with the Russians as they chattered among themselves. He could tell from the sparkle in their eyes, the smiles on their faces how much they had enjoyed the show. He continued to play nice, nodding, unable to understand a word they said.

It galled him to be so pandering. The Russians, every last one of them, took undue advantage of the U.S. hospitality. At least Ursov had the decency to be enraged at the death of his team leader—but these men seemed to be having the time of their lives . . . and from what he knew of the squalor in Russia, that could well be true.

He urged them through the casino away from the long galleria, because he knew he would never get out of there if they began to look into the stores. For himself, he would rather be home, even if it meant an empty house without Genny . . . at least he could find peace in the surrounding quiet.

CHAPTER TEN

Tuesday, October 21
6:45 P.M.

Excalibur Hotel and Casino
Las Vegas

With the evening, Las Vegas lit up like the Fourth of July. Up and down the Strip, casinos and hotels pulsated with enough light to dazzle the sensors of a weather satellite: bright green illuminating the MGM Grand, Caesar's, and Harrah's; cool blue on the Imperial Palace and Bally's; golden yellow on Treasure Island and the Mirage; crimson on the Rio and the Flamingo Hilton.

Craig took his rental car down Tropicana Avenue past the MGM Grand's monumental crouching lion. To his left, the enormous black pyramid of the Luxor blazed its white beacon into space. When he found the Excalibur, he had to stop himself from laughing at the pearlescent turrets topped with scarlet and blue conical roofs. It was what Craig had expected, but not quite so . . . *exactly* what he had expected.

Knowing Craig needed a place to stay, Goldfarb had enthusiastically recommended the Excalibur. He and his family had vacationed there a year before, and the kids had adored the faux castle, the waving colorful pennants, and the clean fantasy adornments.

"Every hour on the hour an animatronic dragon rises out of the moat, and a knight fights it," the other agent said, grinning as if the casino paid him to be a public relations specialist. "Just make sure your room isn't directly above it, or it'll keep you awake all night."

"I'll remember that," Craig said.

"If you want to see a show at night, they have a medieval spectacle, a jousting tournament, knights riding horses right in the arena," Goldfarb continued. "You sit in the stands and eat a Cornish game hen with your bare hands, just like in the Middle Ages."

Craig had laughed. "I'm not sure how many Cornish game hens were consumed in the Middle Ages."

Now, as he drove under a plywood portcullis, attendants in colorful uniforms trotted up to help him. A young man in pantaloons and a Henry VIII outfit offered to park the car. Craig took his overnight bag and went to stand at the crenelated reception desk where women in medieval costumes stood assisting customers.

Clutching his room key as he went in search of the elevators, Craig glanced at his watch—barely enough time to shower and change clothes before meeting Paige Mitchell. Despite his exhaustion, he was looking forward to seeing Paige again. It would be a pleasant end to a wild day. . . .

After showering, Craig considered wearing the one set of casual clothes he had packed, jeans and a polo shirt . . . but he came to his senses and dressed nicely again. Paige probably wouldn't recognize him otherwise.

He fondly recalled working with her to solve the murder of a prominent scientist at the Lawrence Livermore National Laboratory. There, he had uncovered a web of intrigues and complicated schemes, security breaches and classification infractions . . . but the real killer had not turned out to be at all what Craig expected.

Refreshed but still starving, he returned to the main casino level where he listened to the jangling electronic tones, coins clinking into winnings cups, Keno games, baccarat tables, roulette wheels. The flashing lights and the noise reminded Craig of a giant video game. Couples with small children wandered through, looking at the castle decor, the suits of armor on display, the coats of arms high on the stone block walls. Clouds of cigarette smoke wafted along in weather patterns.

He lingered around the reception desk, pacing near a small sunken bar called the Jester's Court, glancing at his watch repeatedly. Finally he saw heads turn as a young woman entered the casino alone. He spotted the trim, blond form and smiled as he waved to catch Paige Mitchell's attention.

"We meet again, Agent Kreident," she said, looking at him with her bright blue eyes as she extended her hand. He took it, squeezing warmly; she let the grip linger a second longer than was necessary.

"Unfortunately, yet again, it isn't under the best of circumstances," he said. "Does someone always have to die before we get together?"

"We'll see after this is over," she said. Her smile was wide on her delicate chin, her expression bright and wide-awake. She wore a teal silk blouse and tight-fitting black jeans, significantly less formal than when he'd seen her at the Livermore Lab—but the Nevada Test Site was filled with cowboys instead of businessmen. She carried a soft-sider briefcase under one arm, and she reached to unzip it, ready to get down to business immediately.

Craig held up one hand. "Wait. I haven't eaten all day, and if you're going to talk about a case, I have to get some food first."

Craig carried his cafeteria tray, its plates laden with mashed potatoes, chicken, sliced baron of beef, honey-glazed ham, baked fish, steamed vegetables, baked zucchini, rolls and butter, and a salad—he would make a second trip for the dessert bar at the King Arthur's Buffet.

Craig made fast work of his plateful of food while Paige watched with wry amusement, eating more slowly herself. "I'd think the FBI could provide an eating allowance, some kind of per diem so you don't have to starve yourself."

"It's not the money," Craig said wiping his mouth with a napkin, "it's the time." He summarized the day's events at Hoover Dam and the continuing investigation into the Eagle's Claw—an investigation which he had passed on to Jackson and Goldfarb because of the Nevsky murder case.

Taking the hint, Paige took out her soft-sider briefcase, moving salt and pepper shakers to make room for it. "I know you don't want to shift gears," she said, "but if the Russians pull out of the disarmament work, all our reciprocal treaties will be put on hold. The summit gets canceled, the President is embarrassed, and it'll be years before we can build up the same momentum. Friday is their last day—if we can just keep the Russians calm enough, we'll squeak through this."

"Friday is also the day the Eagle's Claw has threatened their big disaster. Not much time for either of us," Craig said, then smiled wearily at her. "But I won't argue with you over which case has the greater importance."

Paige wiped her mouth with a napkin. "I think there could be a lot more to the ambassador's death. Everybody else thinks it was just an industrial accident. The Russians are taking it pretty well, except for the new team leader, General Ursov, who's outraged—but we don't think they suspect foul play yet. We have to put this to rest as soon as possible."

"Three whole days. Lucky me," Craig said, then smiled to take the edge off his comment. "I guess I am lucky in a way. I'd been looking forward to working with you again." He reached over to take the papers she offered.

"I was hoping to see you again, too," she answered, "but preferably under circumstances other than a murder investigation. This is a real political land mine, Craig. Because the DAF was a secure facility with very few people around, we have a limited pool of suspects to interview. We'll get started first thing in the morning—it's too late tonight. An hour drive out to the DAF, and with everyone gone you couldn't see anything but the murder scene."

"Sounds fine." Craig finished his plateful of food and stood up to get dessert. "Now that I've got a full stomach, I can tackle any case."

CHAPTER ELEVEN

Tuesday, October 21
9:55 P.M.

Excalibur Hotel and Casino
Las Vegas

Craig lingered in the swirl of people in the Excalibur lobby as Paige swayed gently out of the casino. The jumbled sounds of slot machines and laughter faded in the background as he concentrated on watching the set of her shoulders, the flow of her hair.

He still remembered the Livermore murder investigation, swimming at the Lab pool and watching the water glisten off her black one-piece suit, sipping a pint of Red Nectar Ale at the Lyons Brewery, watching the wind whip her hair as she drove him in her red MG convertible.

The new case had placed them once again on a professional basis, and daydreaming about a relationship with Paige didn't seem professional. Before, he'd always gone out with someone outside his realm of work, outside his circle of interests, someone with whom he had little in common—

Someone like his former girlfriend Trish.

Craig walked past the huge roulette wheel, the green-felt blackjack tables, people leaning over padded craps tables. He had not played those games, barely even knew the rules—but he enjoyed watching. A Federal agent had to be a good observer. Gray-haired women with pearl necklaces and artificial-looking perms walked by, followed by older men holding plastic buckets of change.

Despite his exhausting day, he felt too wound up, too frazzled, to retire to his room. Craig's feet ached, but at least he was no longer hungry. Trish would never have agreed to eat in King Arthur's Buffet. As a medical professional, she would have lectured him about cholesterol and saturated fat. Trish liked trying to improve him, "keeping him fit for his stressful life."

Two years ago she had packed up and left him and the Bay Area, accepting a six-figure salary at Baltimore's Johns Hopkins to study radiation effects on humans. As a medical student she had been fascinated with the victims of Chernobyl and had begun to specialize in treating exposures . . . though the demand for such specialists was relatively nil. So far.

His old flame was a continent away and had her own life. But a letter he'd received from her three days ago weighed heavily on his mind. *We can still be friends.*

Yeah, right.

But did she miss him . . . did she have second thoughts? And why now?

Petite, with dark hair, deep brown eyes, and delicate glasses, Trish looked quite different from Paige. She kept herself healthy through a carefully watched diet rather than physical activity. Pretty and bookish, Trish preferred quiet days at home, listening to music, doing crossword puzzles, when she wasn't obsessively studying.

Paige Mitchell seemed just as dedicated to her job, just as intelligent—but she still found time to drink in life to the fullest. Bright-eyed, with a dry sense of humor, Paige was a joy to be around. Standing between a row of slot machines that extended out on either side, Craig smiled wistfully.

"Let me guess. You've got a woman on your mind . . . a brunette—no, a blond!"

Craig spun about, startled, and bumped a woman's elbow. A scrawny lady in her mid-fifties wavered in front of him, dressed in fishnet stockings, a deep-cut scarlet corset, dyed red hair under a three-pointed Court Jester's cap. She wore as much makeup as Paige would put on in a year. She carried an empty glass in one hand and a smoldering cigarette in another.

She looked him up and down, then batted her eyes. "I can sense these things, you know." Her voice was rough from too many drinks and too many cigarettes. "I'm psychic, Sweetie."

Craig noticed that her drink had spilled on the floor. "I'm sorry if I bumped you, ma'am. I apologize." He reached out to steady her, and the woman slipped her arm through his.

"The name's Maggie, not ma'am." She grinned hugely at him. "Maggie the Mind Reader. Not one of those telephone psychic clowns—I'm a real performer. So was I right, a woman on your mind—blond or brunette?"

Craig laughed as he steered her to a corner table. "Both, I guess."

"Oooh, dangerous. And her name is?"

"Trish," he blurted before he could stop himself. "Hey, you were supposed to read that from my mind—"

"*Trish,* that's what I was going to say." Maggie batted her eyes again. She brought her glass up to take a drink, but found it empty. Without pause, she snagged a passing cocktail waitress in a scanty medieval-style costume. "This young man's buying me a drink. Make it a double scotch, single malt, neat."

Embarrassed, Craig smiled politely to the waitress. "All right. Let me pay for it now—I've got to be going." He removed five dollars from his wallet, suddenly wanting to go back to his room after all.

Maggie patted the empty seat next to her at one of the slots. "Not so fast, Sweetie. Part of the deal is you have to join me."

Craig started to protest, but gave up. He needed something after today's turn of events. He looked to the waitress. "I'll have a beer, please." Then he thought of Paige. "Uh, what are your premium brands? Any microbrews?"

"Heineken or Corona, if you want premium."

"Heineken, then."

Maggie took a draw on her cigarette and blew smoke away from the slot machine. "You haven't caught my show, have you? It's one of the little floor acts, but they pay me extra to wander the casino and amaze the customers with my mind-reading abilities." She stopped as if Craig should automatically know who she was, but he just shook his head. "I pegged you right, didn't I? Thinking about a girl?"

Craig raised his eyebrows. "That would be a good guess for any single man, alone in Las Vegas, surrounded by these cocktail waitresses."

"Yes, but you're not just any single man in Vegas. You're here on business. You're not here to have fun."

"Another score." The cocktail waitress reappeared at his side and set the drinks on a small shelf between the two slot machines. Craig tipped his beer and turned back to Maggie. "No, I'm not here to have fun. You could tell that by my jacket and tie."

"But you're not an east coast executive—suit's not a designer. I'd guess you're from California, probably work for the government. Serious type. Wear a suit like a uniform, not a fashion statement."

Craig smiled, impressed at her detective abilities, just like a Quantico-trained investigator. "Sounds like you've managed to become a pretty good psychic."

Maggie took another drink. "Damn straight, Sweetie!" She lowered her voice. "You hear plenty of things, dropped conversations, people assuming no one else is listening in the bustle of the crowd. I file it away for future reference, and then if I see them again I amaze them with my talent!"

Craig took a long swallow and pushed his unfinished beer away from him. It was late, and Paige would be picking him up at dawn to escort him out to the Test Site. He couldn't waste any time—June Atwood, Paige, the State Department, even the President were all counting on him to solve the Russian's murder in three days, and he hadn't even been to the scene of the crime yet. "Okay, I'll try to catch your act before I leave, Maggie."

"Friday night's the big finale. Be sure to bring your girlfriend." Maggie finished her drink with a huge swallow. "The blond one. She's got you walking around in a daze."

Craig nodded. Prescient or not, Maggie had hit that nail on the head. Until now, though, he'd thought it was *Trish* who had him walking around in a daze.

CHAPTER TWELVE

Wednesday, October 22
6:50 A.M.

Mercury, Nevada

The straight desert roads made speed limits meaningless, but Craig kept his eyes nervously on the needle hovering at ninety miles per hour. Paige drove with one hand on the steering wheel, as if her government pickup were a sporty MG convertible.

She filled him in on what she'd been doing since they had last worked together. She described her previous week with the Russian disarmament team and tried to establish a foundation for him to begin his investigation.

Highway 95 stretched north to the horizon, and the desert opened up like a bottomless pit with huge skies above, huge horizons around them, and rugged mountains like distant guardians on all sides.

After nearly an hour of crossing barren wasteland, Paige gestured through the windshield. "Here we are, Craig—paradise on Earth." He saw only a single green road sign marking a highway exit. It declared forlornly, *Mercury—No Services.* Paige drove toward a cluster of low buildings several miles away. Large white signs with stenciled black letters warned:

ENTERING THE NEVADA NUCLEAR TEST SITE
PROPERTY OF THE U.S. DEPARTMENT OF ENERGY
NO TRESPASSING

Electrical wires crisscrossed the road overhead, strung from creosote-covered utility poles. Orange balls hung suspended in the middle of the wires, and prominent signs indicated the vertical clearance. Other signs admonished *Caution—Desert Tortoises.*

Paige pulled next to a Badge Office blockhouse and hustled Craig inside. Another sign warned that loaded weapons were not allowed on the site; a large sealed trashbin provided a receptacle for those carrying guns to unload their ammunition before entering the site.

At the counter Paige led him through the steps required to sign in. "Not quite as daunting as Livermore," she said.

"But just as much paperwork." He filled out a form, stating his Social Security number, his employer, and the reason for his visit. Finally, the guard handed Craig a Visitor's badge and a heavy plastic-encased dosimeter that felt like a license plate dangling from the collar of his gray suit jacket.

Back in the truck again, Paige stopped at a line of guard kiosks across the road like toll booths spanning a bridge. Most of the kiosks remained empty, hinting at busier times during active nuclear testing. Now, only weathered signs announced "All Traffic Stop For Special Convoys Displaying Flashing Blue Lights." Craig wondered when the last convoy had gone through.

Paige drove toward Mercury, the central village that housed the NTS administrative and employee offices. Mercury looked like a dehydrated settlement, an industrial ghost town: government trailers, huts, and supply sheds, not to mention a bowling alley, cafeteria, and library. He saw no other signs of civilization. "People actually live out here?"

Paige shook her head. "They used to, but most of the workers moved to Las Vegas, even though it's an hour away. Out in the desert, distances don't mean much."

Flat clearings had become heavy-equipment parking lots, transportainer storage areas, and waste dumps. One lot on the northern edge of town was a graveyard of cable spools, round wooden holders for electrical wire, telephone cables, diagnostic fiber optics, coaxial cables.

Rows of white government cars and trucks were parked together outside the buildings. "See why I keep this air freshener hanging here?" Paige said, touching the pine tree dangling from her rear-view mirror. "It's the only way I can tell my own truck from all those others."

After passing through Mercury, Paige headed uphill over a ridge that opened into a valley so vast it seemed capable of swallowing up an entire Eastern state. Ahead, the road went downhill for a dozen miles. Barren mountains encircling the wide valley looked like mounds of gravel and sand, reminding him of folds on an iguana's back.

As she drove down the long slope, Paige stared wistfully into the distance. Fidgeting, Craig looked at her through his sunglasses, watching the expression on her face, seeing how the sunlight gave a golden cast to her skin.

"My dad used to come out here all the time," she said. "Flying back and forth from Livermore right to Mercury, the Desert Rock Airstrip. The Livermore Lab had a dedicated airplane called AMI, a tan two-propeller F-27 that seated forty people. AMI took off from the Livermore Municipal Airport every morning at six-thirty and came back every day at five. When I was a little girl I could go outside late after school and watch it flying home over the Livermore Valley, carrying my dad."

Craig looked across the flat, imagining the activity during the Cold War. Random lines of roads had been scraped across the dry lakebed, for transport of equipment, trailers, and technicians out to individual test shots. After each underground nuclear test was completed, the obsolete roads were left to slowly grow over again. But the desert was not quick to reclaim its territory.

"We've got another fifteen miles until we reach the Device Assembly Facility," Paige said, "where the murder happened."

She continued to watch the side of the road, studying the mesquite shrubs and the occasional ferocious-looking Joshua tree. Then she pulled abruptly off to the shoulder, the wide tires of the Ford pickup crunching gravel. She flashed him a glance. "I want to show you something."

"We don't have a lot of time to kill," he said, anxious to get started on the case, feeling the deadline pressure before his first day had even begun. He hoped Goldfarb and Jackson would make progress on the Eagle's Claw case today as well. They planned to head out early to the home of the missing Hoover Dam worker to see if they could pick up any clues.

"This spot will do more to give you a perspective of what NTS is about than any other place I can think of." Paige picked her way over the rocks, climbing a small rise ten yards from the road. She looked comfortable in her jeans and short-sleeved cotton shirt. "Before you start questioning people, you need to understand the test program. It's a whole different mindset."

Craig followed her, totally out of place in his formal business suit, too warm, feeling a tingle of sweat, but not yet so uncomfortable that he might need to loosen his maroon tie. He glanced at his watch.

The cleared area gave an unobstructed view of what seemed to be the entire state of Nevada. Two startlingly out-of-place rows of splintered wooden bleachers sat abandoned and alone. The wood had turned gray from decades of exposure to the desert.

Craig blinked in disbelief. "What are these doing out here?"

"These were the press bleachers, official observation stands." Paige gestured toward the dry brown lake bed. "Back in the late fifties, aboveground tests took place out there on Frenchman Flat. The press corps and other VIP guests would sit here and watch the mushroom cloud, clicking pictures, looking through darkened glasses. Also, somewhere out there, soldier volunteers crouched in foxholes, unwittingly exposed to massive amounts of radiation."

"You're kidding," he said. "How could they be so—" He searched for the right word.

"Naive?" she suggested. "They honestly didn't know what they were doing, didn't understand the real nature of the dragon they were tempting. Reporters would sit here with their big cameras, notepads on their knees, applauding the fireball, the mushroom cloud. It was exciting."

"And they did it willingly?" Craig asked.

"They fought each other for the chance." She crossed her arms, tossing her blond hair away from her face. "Remember, back then technology was supposed to solve all the world's problems. Scientists were revered celebrities." She brushed her hands on her jeans. "The aboveground tests took place before 1963. After that, nuclear shots were conducted underground to prevent environmental contamination—if we did a ground burst of one of our modern multi-megaton bombs, instead of the little ones they used in the Fifties, radioactive fallout would cover half the state."

Craig shaded his eyes. Even with the sunglasses, the bright glare across the desert made him squint. He shuffled his feet, kicking at small stones. "But nothing leaks when you explode them underground?"

Paige's forehead furrowed. "The last time we had an appreciable radioactive release was in 1970, the Baneberry Test. My dad worked on that one." She smiled wistfully. "It was a major turning point for containment technology. Of course now, with the total testing moratorium . . ."

Standing beside the rickety press benches, Craig put his hands on his hips and continued to stare. The vast, open spaces made everything hushed and silent. Far off he could hear the thunder of jet aircraft roaring across the sky, and then a double shotgun crack of a sonic boom.

"This place has a lot of history behind it," Paige said, leading him back toward the truck. "The people who still work here are what you might call Good Old Boys. They used to run everything by the seat of their pants and the backs of envelopes—but over the past few years the rug has been pulled out from under their feet.

"I'll introduce you to my Uncle Mike, who's in charge of the DAF. He's had to open his doors for this Russian disarmament team, showing them all the secrets he'd been told to hide for decades. The Soviets were the reason NTS was formed in the first place, and Uncle Mike—along with a lot of other workers around here—is having a difficult time rolling with the changes."

Back at the truck, Craig walked around to the driver's side and opened the door for her. He heaved himself into the other side of the pickup, then looked sharply at her. "Are you suggesting that one of the old workers might be responsible for the murder of Ambassador Nevsky? Someone who thinks the Cold War is still going on?"

Paige pulled the pickup back onto the long highway and accelerated down the road. "You're the detective, Craig," she said. "I'm just giving you the background you need. None of this stuff happens in a vacuum."

"Nothing ever does," Craig said.

CHAPTER THIRTEEN

Wednesday, October 22
8:05 A.M.

Home of Bryce Connors
Henderson, Nevada

With Craig Kreident pulled away from the militia case, Agents Goldfarb and Jackson approached the small home of Bryce Connors, the Hoover Dam worker who had disappeared sometime the previous day.

They had their search warrants and their suspicions, but nothing tangible to connect Connors with the Eagle's Claw—at least not yet. But if the October 24th deadline could be believed, they could waste no time dismissing possible leads.

Connors's house was a low, one-story suburban home built in the late sixties, painted a burnt-orange color that reminded Goldfarb of baby diarrhea. It did not stand out from the others on the street, an average home in an average residential district.

The area around Henderson had once been a quiet suburb south of Las Vegas, populated by blue-collar families, many of whom worked at the casinos or Nellis Air Force base or the dam itself. Now, though, strip malls had moved in, streets turned into highways—and what had once been a residential neighborhood was now bisected by a busy thoroughfare complete with traffic signals on virtually every corner.

Jackson parked their rental car in front of the house against the curb. Across the street, Goldfarb saw a video rental store, a small coffee and donut shop, a beauty parlor, and a Circle K convenience store. Early-morning customers wandered in the stores, but here on the residential side of the street the homes seemed quiet. Everyone had already gone to work, kids already at school.

Goldfarb stepped onto the sidewalk, brushing a palm over his curly dark hair. Paying attention to every detail, he checked the handgun in its shoulder holster, gripped the search warrant and his badge wallet in hand. "Maybe we'll get lucky and find a hot clue," he said, squinting at the unremarkable house.

Behind the steering wheel, Jackson glanced up into the rear-view mirror, watching carefully for traffic before he climbed out the driver's side. "Sure," he answered. "Maybe Mr. Connors will just confess, and we'll find a nice little manifesto describing everything the Eagle's Claw intends to do."

Goldfarb smiled and shrugged. "Or maybe it'll just be a dead end. But we've got to start somewhere."

They knocked on the front door and waited, but the home greeted them with only silence. "Not surprising," Jackson said. "Mr. García was unable to reach him either."

"My guess is he's skipped town," Goldfarb said. He winked at Jackson. "Hopefully, we can find some trace evidence, at least some residual explosive materials, something to link this guy with the bombs we found at the dam."

After knocking repeatedly, they walked around the house, loudly identifying themselves and following standard procedure. Finally, reaching the side garage door, Jackson removed a pack of locksmith's tools from his inner jacket pocket. "Time to proceed to Plan B," he said.

As Jackson fiddled with the side door, Goldfarb looked around, waiting for the neighbors to come squawking or pointing shotguns at them. He patted the search warrant in his breast pocket, but it didn't console him. No telling who around here might sympathize with Connors. "Can't you hurry it up, Randall?" he said.

"I'm not exactly an expert lockpick," Jackson grunted.

A snap and a *ping* signified either the tumblers finally giving way, or one of the locksmith tools snapping in half. Jackson smiled broadly at his companion, then turned the doorknob, pushing his way into the garage. "Anybody home?" he called.

"FBI," Goldfarb said in a thin voice that carried a distressing squeak. He cleared his throat. That was no way for a Federal agent to sound.

Inside, the garage was dim and smelled of gasoline. Oil stains splattered the floor like old dried blood. Jackson flicked on a light, a bank of crudely wired fluorescents dangling from the wooden rafters.

Goldfarb could see a workbench strewn with tools, an auto-parts calendar tacked onto a two-by-four support beam. With a chilling realization he saw that *Friday, October 24* was circled in red.

"Bingo," Goldfarb said, cautiously withdrawing his Beretta from its shoulder holster. "Time to be prepared, just like the Boy Scout motto says. He might have left us some surprises."

Three gray 55-gallon oil drums sat in a corner. Jackson bent over to sniff. "Fuel oil," he said. "This guy must be gearing up for the next fuel shortage."

Goldfarb gestured to bags of fertilizer stacked against the opposite wall. "Or maybe he's just trying out some chemistry experiments," he said. "He's making ANFO. There must be enough for a hundred pounds of TNT equivalent." He paused. "I think we should be very, very careful, Jackson."

The dark-skinned agent nodded silently, then stood against the entrance into the house. For some odd reason he pressed his ear against the door, heard nothing, then turned the knob, surprised to find it unlocked. He stepped over the threshold, glancing warily from side to side.

Goldfarb followed, his handgun drawn. "FBI," he called out again.

They entered the kitchen. Dishes piled in the sink were caked with dried food. "Not much of a housekeeper," Jackson said.

Goldfarb wrinkled his nose at the old food. "Not much of a cook either."

"I guess blowing up the Free World takes precedence over good housekeeping."

They moved deeper into the house, staying close to each other but separating to cover ground as quickly as possible. The place had a deserted feel to it, but oppressive—as if glinting yellow eyes were watching them from shadowy corners.

"He's long gone," Goldfarb said. "Listen to how quiet it is."

"Yes, but how much of a hurry was he in when he fled, and what did he leave behind?" Jackson answered.

Goldfarb sniffed the air. "This guy must have been nuts to live in here with this chemical stink. Smells like he used rocket fuel for an air freshener."

"Quite the chemist, our Mr. Connors," Jackson said. "But I don't think he'll be making any more bombs in here. Maybe he didn't get time to concoct a surprise for this Friday."

Goldfarb moved down the hallway past a single bathroom. The toilet seat was up, the bathtub stained and cracked, the shower curtains rimmed with mildew. The small single bed in the main bedroom was unmade. Goldfarb frowned, muttering to himself. "I guess the maid hasn't come yet this morning." He continued to snoop around.

• • •

Stepping cautiously into the living room, Jackson found an overstuffed reclining chair, its plaid fabric worn, discolored stuffing poking out like thistledown. Beside it, a metal TV tray held a recent program listing, the kind that came free in the newspaper. The television itself was an old Zenith with vacuum tubes that probably took several minutes to warm up. He saw no cable box, no remote control.

Jackson continued his cursory inspection and went to the front door, where they would have entered had anyone answered the knock. He glanced down at the floor and the hinges—and froze in horror.

Small blocks of the bluish-gray plastic explosive had been mounted along the jamb, rigged to contact points connected to the door, strung to all the front windows. If he and Goldfarb had broken inside, the bombs would have detonated—enough to blow out the front of the house and all the windows. Both agents would have been killed instantly.

Suddenly the house seemed much more sinister around him. Swallowing in his dry throat, Jackson bent over to scrutinize the wires.

At the other end of the house, Goldfarb turned from the bedroom to the opposite side of the hall, some kind of den with a door half closed. He glanced inside, his hand on the doorknob. He saw stacks of books, drawings, maps, leaflets, piled up on and around an old card table. Brown boxes filled with debris, wadded newspapers sat beside the table. "Whoa, jackpot."

On one white wall all the pictures had been removed, but hanging nails still stuck out from the Sheetrock plasterboard. Excited by his discovery, Goldfarb pushed the door open and just had time to hear the faint *tink* as a tripwire popped free. He instantly saw two short words scrawled across the wall in thick black Magic Marker:

DIE FBI!

Jackson yelled from the living room. "Ben, watch out! The place is booby-trapped!"

Before Goldfarb could turn, the inside walls of the den erupted in flames.

CHAPTER FOURTEEN

Wednesday, October 22
8:10 A.M.

Device Assembly Facility
Nevada Test Site

Craig dusted a comb through his chestnut hair as Paige pulled into the DAF parking lot beside other white government pickups. He straightened his tie, glanced at his watch. *Time to look professional,* he thought.

The prisonlike building was as long as a football field. Massive doors provided access in the front, and security personnel patrolled the surrounding area. Hot sunshine and dry heat reflected from the pavement.

Craig shrugged on his jacket and followed Paige through the security checkpoint. Once they were inside the building, a lanky man strode out to meet them. Dressed in a plaid shirt and wearing a narrow rawhide bolo tie, he looked like a scarecrow with thin arms sticking from his short sleeves. "Morning, Paige," he said, giving her a quick hug. "Let's hope it's a better day than yesterday."

Paige held the older man's arm. "Craig, this is Mike Waterloo, the DAF Manager."

Craig stuck out a hand, shaking the other man's firmly, intent on keeping the true nature of his investigation secret. "Hello, sir. I'm Special Agent Kreident, Federal Bureau of Investigation." He brushed a hand down his jacket, anxious to get moving. "I'm required to observe the entire site after such a high-profile accident, check for security breaches. I hope we can get this straightened out quickly, with a minimum of hassles."

Waterloo heaved a sigh of relief. "Just wrap it up by Friday, Agent Kreident. That's all the time we've got."

They entered through a set of double doors. The first closed behind them before the second set opened. "Craig and I worked together on a case at Lawrence Livermore," Paige said.

Craig nodded. "This place seems more . . . rigorous in its security."

Waterloo chuckled as the second door swung open. "Well, you've got to be careful when you have live nukes lying around."

"And you let a team of Russians in to look at everything?" Craig asked.

"Our reciprocal treaty requires it, and the team is even more visible because of this weekend's summit." Waterloo gave a dismissive wave. "Changing times. Not much to bother hiding anymore."

They passed through claustrophobic inner hallways, beyond a series of high bays, construction offices, and storage area boundaries painted clearly on the concrete floor in red, yellow, and blue stripes.

"Regarding Mr. Nevsky's accident, sir," Craig said, pretending he believed the death to be a simple mishap, "could you speculate on why the ambassador was here alone so long after normal working hours?"

The building opened up before them, the far walls a hundred feet away on either side of them. Waterloo wound his way around concrete blocks set up as temporary barricades. "He wasn't supposed to be alone, exactly. Paige shuttled the rest of the inspection team back to Las Vegas, but Ambassador Nevsky insisted on returning to the DAF to check something."

"So you drove the ambassador here yourself?"

Waterloo nodded. "From the cafeteria. I signed him over to PK Dirks, a technician on duty, so I could catch up on some work. But PK, uh, didn't keep very close tabs on him. His negligence is appalling, to say the least."

"What is his excuse for leaving Nevsky alone?" Craig asked.

Waterloo shrugged. "He says the ambassador had to go to the bathroom." He stopped before another set of security doors under a red alarm bell. Waterloo ran his badge through a card reader, punched in a series of numbers, and the door swung open.

Yellow police tape partitioned off a section of the tall storage bays. The remnants of a smashed crate lay spread over the floor, inside the police tape. "PK didn't figure the ambassador would leave the Pit Assembly Area, but instead Nevsky wandered off into the industrial section. What he was looking for, we'll never know."

Craig nodded, but remained dubious about why Nevsky had been left alone. Of course, being inside so many layers of security, with so many alarms and interlocks, workers tended to take certain procedures for granted.

"Carl Jorgenson was in the next corridor, using a forklift to rearrange the top crates," Waterloo said. "We don't have much free space in the DAF, so we stack everything high. We're working three shifts during the disarmament inspection to keep up with the treaty timetable.

"The forklift makes a lot of noise, and the storage area isn't well lit. Jorgenson wasn't careful how he stacked the crates. One of them fell—and Nevsky happened to be in the wrong place at the wrong time."

Waterloo pointed to a red emergency button set head-high into a pillar. "I heard the alarm from my office, and I ran down here to find Carl kneeling, trying to see if Nevsky was still alive. I called an ambulance right after that."

"And where was Mr. Dirks?" Craig continued asking his questions. Out of the corner of his eye, he saw Paige watching him.

"He showed up right after I did," said Waterloo.

"*After* you?" Craig frowned and looked down the narrow passageway. "I thought he was just across the hall in the Pit Assembly Area, and you were up in your office."

Waterloo fumbled nervously with his bolo tie. "PK had to secure the bomb pits. Unless we have a criticality alarm, you can't just run out with plutonium cores unsecured. Number-one priority—and PK did just that. He's sort of a loose cannon, bends the rules a little, and he's well liked. But he didn't forget rule one. He just got sloppy," he paused, "and so did Jorgenson. It's sad."

Craig pursed his lips, pacing back and forth just to keep moving. He ducked under the police tape and stood where brownish stains of dried blood lay inside a chalk outline of the body's position. One arm was up, as if Nevsky had raised his hand to fend off the falling crate.

Or as if it had been strategically placed there.

Someone *knew* Nevsky had been dead long before the crate had crushed him. PK Dirks could not have been innocently "securing the pits" for that long. And how did Jorgenson's "accidentally" dropped crate miraculously manage to hit a motionless body?

Paige knelt beside Craig, but she kept her expression neutral. He knew how tempted she would have been to tell her Uncle Mike about the suspicious nature of the accident. "I'll want to talk to Mr. Jorgenson, as part of wrapping up this investigation," he said.

Waterloo nodded. "He's on administrative leave, but he lives in Pahrump, a town about thirty miles from here."

Craig recalled when he himself had been put on admin

leave after the botched arrest of a NanoWare CEO resulted in the man's panicked suicide. He turned to study the accident scene again, then up to the metal rafters. "What about those security cameras? Did they catch anything?"

Waterloo shook his head. "System malfunction, but not unusual. We got a low-bid contract, but we've been meaning to upgrade. No tapes at all for that night."

Convenient, Craig thought. Waterloo led them to the enclosed area down at the end of the crate alley, far from where Nevsky had been found. "The room on your left is the Pit Assembly Area, where Dirks should have been watching the ambassador."

A voice came from behind them. "But I wasn't, and now we're in this mess." A stocky man stood smoothing his beard. Barrel-chested and solidly built, he carried a slight beer-belly paunch. A stern-looking, ash-blond woman stood beside him, her tanned face solidly serious. Dressed in peach slacks and a loose white blouse, she chewed gum and looked unwaveringly at Craig.

Waterloo blinked in surprise. "Sally? What are you doing here?"

"Just needed to give PK some moral support," she said coolly.

His bearded cheeks flushing pink, Dirks looked at his work boots. "I think the two of us can, ah, clear things up."

Paige quickly added, "Craig, this is PK Dirks, and Sally Montry, Uncle Mike's administrative assistant."

"Just plain 'secretary' is fine," Sally said. "No need for fancy titles."

As Waterloo put his hands on his hips, Sally avoided looking at him. "Okay, what's the story?" He glanced from Sally to PK Dirks.

Dirks swallowed hard, but spoke to Craig, not the DAF Manager. "Uh, is there any way to make sure this doesn't get out?"

"This is an official investigation on federal property, Mr. Dirks," Craig said formally. "I can't promise anything."

Dirks nodded stiffly in defeat. He opened and closed one hand, as if it were difficult for him to talk. "Like Mr. Waterloo said, Sally is his executive secretary. She spends a lot of time here, like everyone else. And she and her husband aren't getting along too well, if you know what I mean." He looked up at Waterloo, as if pleading for understanding. "The only place Sally and I could . . . *meet* was at work. So when Nevsky wanted to putz around in the Pit Assembly Area and asked to be left alone so he could 'concentrate,' it gave me an excuse to see her for a quick—well, you know."

Waterloo turned livid, glaring at Sally and at Dirks. Paige, though, picked up on something else. "The ambassador *wanted* to be left alone?"

"How was I supposed to know he'd go snooping around where he wasn't supposed to be?" Dirks said, clearly upset. "Was he a spy or something? I mean, what *haven't* we shown these guys?"

Craig looked at Sally Montry, who seemed more indignant than embarrassed. "Can you verify that story, ma'am?"

Speaking in a steady voice, she looked straight at him. "I was working late, keying in the disarmament team's report when PK called." She didn't even flick a glance at Waterloo. "We were . . . *together* when we heard the alarm. PK had to leave in a rush, and I hurried back to my station." With a sniff, she spoke again, carrying a trace of defiance now. "Look, we didn't *have* to tell anybody, but we wanted to set the record straight. And if this somehow held up the treaty work with the Russians, all hell would break loose. We've only got until Friday."

"Don't I know it," Craig muttered, then turned to Waterloo. "Any idea what was so hot that Nevsky gave up a night on the town to double-check some numbers? I'd like to try and reconstruct his reasons."

Dirks stepped forward, overly helpful now. "I can show you what he was doing, Agent Kreident."

Waterloo turned to Sally, speaking in a cold voice. "Go back to the office. I'll talk to you later."

Craig followed Dirks deeper into the Pit Assembly Area to three gloveboxes, each containing material samples marked with the three-bladed radiation symbol. Nearby, a table sat piled high with notebooks, computer sheets, inventory tags, and ream after ream of checklist items. Craig's heart sank when he saw the mound of documents.

Paige touched his shoulder. "I can help you go through this stuff later today, Craig. Uncle Mike and I have to take the Russian team up to our tunnel test area at the northern end of the site. It's next on their schedule."

On sudden inspiration, Craig said, "I think I'll go with you. Give me a chance to meet the disarmament team personally, before I go over the paperwork. Mr. Waterloo, you'll be coming along as well?"

Waterloo gave Craig a strange look. "For a while. Then I'll be on my way up to Nellis at the north end of the Site. We're bringing a new shipment of decommissioned warheads out of temporary storage this afternoon. As DAF Manager, I have to be there to fill out the paperwork."

Craig glanced at the table piled high with technical documents. At the moment, he didn't even want to think about paperwork.

Next step was to meet with the Russians.

CHAPTER FIFTEEN

Wednesday, October 22
9:53 A.M.

Nevada Test Site
Pahute Mesa Tunnels

Craig kept a low profile as he joined the seven disarmament inspectors in the white van, watching, keeping his mind open. He wanted to observe personal interactions, witness how NTS personnel treated the Russians, how the Russians responded, and how they reacted to each other. He could learn plenty from a few nuances. The others would wonder exactly why an FBI investigator had come along, and it would make some of them nervous.

Mike Waterloo swung into the driver's seat himself, gesturing for Craig to ride up front with him. Paige sat with the Russian team, politely answering their questions.

Unfolding his list of the inspectors' names, Craig tried to see how the people fit together, who seemed subordinate to whom. Ambassador Nevsky, dead, an academician, the head of the team, replaced by his deputy, the military liaison from the Russian Strategic Rocket Forces, General Gregori Ursov. Then the others: Victor Golitsyn, the geologist; Nikolai Bisovka, the amateur astronomer who smoked Marlboros; Vitali Yakolev, the redhead; Anatoli Voronin, Denis Zagorski, Alexander Novikov. . . . Craig worked hard to put the names to faces.

Ursov said brusquely, as much for the benefit of his team members as for Paige, "I know we have not taken time to mourn our fallen comrade, but Friday is our deadline, and we do not have the luxury of flexibility—despite the criminal lack of safety at your facility."

Apart from his bluster about Nevsky's death, the gruff general seemed interested in their destination—the mountainside tunnels designed to contain small-scale nuclear explosions.

Waterloo accelerated steadily along the open road across the sprawling valley. They headed north into a line of steep mesas that formed the northern boundary of NTS, beyond the even vaster expanse of the Nellis Air Force Range. Craig watched the gaunt man sitting stiffly behind the steering wheel. He seemed to have a thick wall around him.

As the elevation rose, Craig watched the landscape change from crumbly desert to dark-green piñons and junipers, and broad rock faces rippled with colors—white, gray, tan, and maroon. They passed what the map called Pahute Mesa and another boomtown-type settlement of temporary buildings, office trailers, and a big Quonset hut that had been converted to a cafeteria.

Waterloo pulled the van up a steep dirt road to a gated mine-shaft opening in the mountainside. "This is where we do our tunnel shots," Waterloo said, then smiled in embarrassment. "Where we *did* them, I mean. Not much going on here lately."

As they climbed out of the van, the Russians spoke rapidly with each other, but Craig couldn't understand the words. He wondered if they, too, commiserated about their faded glory days.

The brisk mountain air was a good twenty degrees cooler than down in the valley. Craig turned toward the tunnel opening, where a chain of yellow spotlights extended down the shaft, illuminating narrow-gauge tracks for mine cars and personnel transport.

"Seen any suspicious behavior yet?" Paige asked him quietly as the others moved forward.

"I'm still trying to figure out what I should consider suspicious. Everything around here operates under a different set of rules. Do *you* think any of the Russians are suspect?" he asked.

Paige thought for a moment. "There's one, Nikolai Bisovka, who didn't seem to like the ambassador much—he made some crack about Nevsky's drinking. General Ursov didn't take that so well."

"I'll keep that in mind."

As the tiny light of an approaching mine car grew larger inside the tunnel, Waterloo spoke briefly with a guard at the gate, pointing to the group. Turning to them, he raised his voice. "Our teams drilled shafts miles into this mountain, a network of catacombs with twists and turns and branching tunnels for diagnostic equipment, cross-connected to other test chambers."

Rummaging in a set of lockers just inside the tunnel, he removed hard hats, goggles, boot covers, and emergency respirators, handing one set to each person. "Required safety measures," he said.

"Just in case a crate should happen to fall on our heads?" Ursov said stonily. Waterloo looked at him with a flicker of embarrassment, then fumbled with his own outfit. Paige and Craig helped each other secure the respirator fastenings on the hard hat.

Waterloo climbed into the front car on the tracks, motioning for Paige to sit beside him. She smiled, like a little girl asked to sit in the front seat of a car with her favorite uncle. Craig glanced at his watch, then sat beside General Ursov; they maintained an uneasy silence, looking at each other warily.

The mine cars accelerated down the tracks, pulled by a

diesel engine no larger than that of a riding lawnmower. Around them, the tunnels were dark and confining, damp with dripping water like the catacombs inside Hoover Dam. Overhead, metal conduits contained the electrical wires for spotlights and other utilities. Though giant fans kept the air circulating, the atmosphere inside the tunnels stank of chemicals, fuel, and rock dust.

Along the central passage, work crews in hard hats stood in teams, stripping out miles of diagnostic cables from metal troughs mounted to the rock. Laboring together like teams carrying fire hoses, they reeled the extracted cables onto immense spools that would be stacked on trucks and hauled somewhere else.

"Everything's being mothballed," Waterloo called over his shoulder, raising his voice above the rumbling background noise in the tunnel. "No more nuclear testing. Better to recycle it, so a lot of this goes up to Nellis."

When the mine car stopped and they disembarked, Waterloo led them through enormous armored steel doors into a dead-end room—a spherical chamber the size of a small auditorium. The rough walls were studded with sensors, cameras, and fiberoptics that led back through the main tunnel. In the center of the chamber stood a steel pedestal, waiting for test apparatus.

Craig realized with a start that this chamber had been designed to contain an atomic explosion.

Waterloo's voice echoed off the walls. "Tunnel tests are performed to study nuclear *effects,* how military equipment can withstand an atomic war zone. Researchers place objects such as satellites, communications equipment, even missiles at one end of a long tunnel, a thousand feet away." He gestured out the door, down a straight-line corridor to another set of heavy doors.

"Then we set off a small nuclear explosion in here to see how the radiation alone affects the test object. Explosives trigger those doors—a pair of two-foot-thick aluminum slabs—to slam shut at precisely the right moment, within milliseconds of the blast, after the radiation front has passed but before the shock wave and blast debris can get there."

Craig looked around and felt an involuntary shudder, remembering his experience inside the high-tech Virtual Reality lab at Livermore, when he had witnessed such an explosion hands-on.

He knew exactly how one of those test objects would feel.

Finally emerging from the tunnels, taking deep breaths of clean air to flush the stinging diesel exhaust vapors from his throat, Craig turned his gaze upward. He placed his hands on his hips and stared into the fathomless sky, hearing the soaring sound of nearby aircraft.

Startlingly close, a batlike B-2 Stealth bomber cruised over the mesa line. Its black body looked alien as it swept and dove over the mountaintops like a daredevil. Craig's mouth dropped open as he stared in amazement.

"You're lucky," said Waterloo, standing just beside him. "Most of the time they don't fly this far south, into the Test Site. Impressive, isn't it?"

"Where did it come from?" Craig shaded his eyes to get a better look. The Stealth bomber skimmed low and quiet, sleek and creepy. "Nellis?"

"Groom Lake, more likely. The whole base is called the Nellis Air Force Range, but Groom Lake Auxiliary Station is inside, a highly restricted area for the temporary storage of obsolete warheads. I'm heading up there now for a new shipment. Paige will show you our down-hole testing this afternoon."

The Russians had seen the black aircraft, too, and were talking amongst themselves excitedly. Paige stood next to them looking agitated.

Waterloo's voice carried a conspiratorial hush as he spoke

to Craig. "Beyond these mesas is the guard gate into Nellis, and from there, deeper inside, you get to where the Stealth program goes through its paces." He watched as the black craft suddenly accelerated then circled back around the ridgeline, disappearing into Nellis's restricted airspace.

"I don't usually get to see stuff like that," Craig said, watching the B-2 dwindle to a speck against the horizon haze.

"I worry about what you *can't* see." Waterloo lowered his voice. "Think of what else they might be working on way out in the middle of nowhere."

Craig looked at the older man, surprised. "Such as?"

"There's a secret facility, heavily guarded, known as 'Dreamland.' Area 51, the tabloids call it, part of Groom Lake. Plenty of wild speculations about it—alien cadavers, underground survival chambers, biological weapons research . . . Hoffa's body." He laughed. Craig didn't.

"Ever been up there, sir?" Craig asked. "On your way to retrieve nukes?"

Waterloo shook his head, narrowing his eyes. "I can get into Omega Mountain and the stored nuclear warheads without much trouble—but I can't get *near* Dreamland. Gives me the creeps."

Waterloo opened the van doors to let the Russian team climb inside. He leaned closer to Craig. "Think about it, Agent Kreident. They trust me to carry around live nukes . . . what could be so secret, or so dangerous, that even *I* can't take a peek?"

Craig closed the passenger-side door. "I haven't the slightest idea, sir."

CHAPTER SIXTEEN

Wednesday, October 22
8:11 A.M.

Home of Bryce Connors
Henderson, Nevada

Lines of bright orange flame gushed along the den wall like water streaming from a fire hose. With a yell, Goldfarb backed off, covering his eyes as the wash of heat swept over him.

He hadn't triggered an actual bomb, no huge explosion—but the tripwire had set off some kind of incendiary device. Within seconds the enclosed room became blanketed with crepe streamers of blazing fire that raced out into the hall, spilling along weirdly defined pathways.

And now Goldfarb knew that the house's chemical smell, the biting volatile tang in the air, came not from Connors's bomb-making activities in the garage—it was the residue of accelerants, flammable chemicals the militiaman had *painted* on the walls and the floorboards, laying down the ingredients for an instant inferno. He had intended for his house to go up in flames, taking the FBI agents with it.

"Ben!" Jackson yelled. "Get out of there!"

Stacks of papers sitting on the card table curled and singed. With an idiotic numbness that just might have been bravery, he knew he had to retrieve the evidence, some of it at least. It had to be a weapon that would strike the Eagle's Claw where it hurt.

Ducking his head, knowing that untold lives could depend on his snatching information that would prevent this Friday's impending disaster, Goldfarb dashed inside the den and grabbed a handful of the top papers. The flames rushed in, swirling all around him.

"Ben!" Jackson bellowed, sounding close, running down the hall even faster than the flames could spread.

As he lurched back toward the door, toward blessed escape, Goldfarb's hair curled back, crisping; his suit jacket smoldered hot. As he looked at the papers, the boxes, the flammables, he realized that all the records in this room also served as *fuel* for the fire.

"The whole place is rigged!" Jackson said, staggering down the hall and coughing loudly. "It's going to go up." The lean, dark-skinned agent grabbed Goldfarb's elbow and dragged him out of the den, then began pounding his back and shoulders. Goldfarb hadn't even realized he was on fire. Smoke swirled thickly around them.

Goldfarb coughed as they hustled down the hall. The flames followed them like molten dogs lapping at their heels, skirling along the walls, following the lines of chemical accelerants splashed on the walls. Light bulbs exploded overhead, and both agents flinched, covering their heads.

In the kitchen another small explosive device went off, and flames burst from the cupboards. Debris from broken dishes, shattered glass and the smashed window sprayed out onto the floor.

"Here, the front door is closer," Goldfarb said. "Pronto!"

"No!" Jackson yelled, grabbing him. "Plastic explosives! It's booby-trapped."

They staggered past a large window at the side of the living room, but Goldfarb also saw crude wires hooked up to the sill and frame. "Connors must have had altogether *too* much time on his hands," he said, coughing. "Let's go out the same way we came in."

"Get moving, then," Jackson said.

The kitchen was already in flames. Shards of glass and stoneware made the floor an obstacle course. Goldfarb coughed, his eyes watering and stinging. His skin felt raw as if from a severe sunburn, and the chemical smoke from the accelerants and burning paint made his lungs rebel each time he took a breath.

The ravenous flames finally reached the living room, crawling rapidly along the line of flammable chemicals painted in a deadly spiderweb that looped all the walls in the house. Once the FBI agents and tripwire incendiaries provided the spark, Bryce Connors had made sure no scrap would remain, just a pile of ashes.

The two agents staggered toward the garage door where they had entered. Goldfarb looked over his shoulder to see the fire racing toward the front door, licking the flammable chemicals on the Sheetrock—and finally reaching the small blocks of explosive that had been rigged to the door frame.

"Look out!" Goldfarb said.

Jackson saw it just in time. The two of them threw themselves around a corner shielded by the bulk of the refrigerator just as the explosives blew. With a ripping sound that blasted out the front of the house, the bombs took out the door and five feet of structural wall on either side. The windows in the room shattered with the sound of hissing glass.

Where they sat huddled, the overpressure shock wave struck them, making both of Goldfarb's ears pop. His head knocked against the refrigerator, but he got up a moment later, shaking the stars from his vision. He touched his nose, feeling a trickle of blood coming out.

"Let's not wait for all those drums of fuel oil in the garage to blow," Goldfarb said, then sprinted toward the still-open door leading out to the garage. His feet crunched on broken glass and shrapnel scattered across the floor. He slipped, his shoes skittering on the debris, but he caught his balance before he could dive face-first into the stalagmite shards of glass.

Jackson bolted after him. The flames had spread from the kitchen into the garage already, working their destructive lines along the stacked bags of fertilizer, the two-by-fours of the workbench. The calendar curled up, brown at the edges; the red circle around October 24 turned black.

"Get your butt in gear, Jackson!" Goldfarb said as they both dashed out the side door, past the low fence, and ran toward the street.

Moments later, an explosion rocked the house and the rest of the garage collapsed. The blast knocked both of the FBI agents to the sidewalk. Smoke and splintered debris boiled toward the sky like the mushroom cloud from an atomic bomb.

Shaking his head and listening to his ears ring, Goldfarb turned and saw the inferno that was left of the suspect's house. One of the side walls groaned and collapsed.

Goldfarb held up the sheaf of random papers he had snatched from the pile inside the den. "I hope we've got some clues at least," he said with a grin, then brushed a hand across his stinging cheeks. "Oh, boy, what a way to start the day. I could use another cup of coffee. *Strong* coffee."

Jackson stared across the street at crowds that had come out of the little shops in the strip mall. People stood around the coffee and doughnut shop, staring wide-eyed. Traffic had stopped on the street as the blaze continued to roar behind them. The fire department would be on its way but far too late.

Jackson picked himself up and brushed off the front of his suit. Goldfarb did the same. He shook his head with feigned annoyance, narrowing his eyes at all the spectators pointing at them.

"What are they looking at?" he said. "This is Vegas. You'd think by now they'd be use to the light shows."

CHAPTER SEVENTEEN

Wednesday, October 22
1:15 P.M.

Omega Mountain Nuclear Storage Facility Groom Lake Air Force Auxiliary Station

Hours after leaving the nuclear test tunnels behind, Mike Waterloo ducked out of the twin-engine plane that had flown him across Nellis restricted airspace. Holding his black satchel containing a bar-code reader and a portable computer, he scanned the runway for his security escort.

The aircraft had parked at a remote terminus of the desert airstrip, a mile from five ominous hangars clustered at the end of the dry lake bed bordered by rugged mountains. Three huge C-141 Starlifter transport planes sat next to the hangars. The Groom Lake Auxiliary Station provided temporary storage for decommissioned nuclear weapons . . . as well as whatever else the government had hidden in the isolated, secure facility.

Few people ever got to see this place at all—but Mike Waterloo didn't feel terribly lucky. In fact, it made his skin crawl. He had his own suspicions about what was going on up here. The area was partitioned off as the northern part of the Nellis AFB bombing range, deep inside the most isolated portion of the Nevada desert. The town of Tonopah was the only sign of civilization on any map around, outside the base boundary at the junction of Highways 6 and 95.

In 1993 a group of workers had sued the Air Force, the Defense Secretary, and the White House national security advisor, for toxic exposures they had received during top-secret activities taking place at Groom Lake. The suit had progressed for nearly a year while the Air Force flatly denied the existence of Groom Lake. When the President himself had issued an exemption that kept the secrets under wraps because they were "in the paramount interests of the United States," the workers had lost their suit, forbidden even to present their evidence in court. . . .

A blue sedan sat near the aircraft, its engine idling. A trim, black Air Force officer stood next to the car, waiting for him. Everything about the young Air Force officer seemed sculpted, crisp, and right to the point. "Mr. Waterloo? I'm Lieutenant Colonel Terrell, group operations commander." Curt and all business, he handed Waterloo a local area badge: *Escort Required.*

Waterloo shook the man's hand and was not surprised at the rock-hard grip. "What happened to Lieutenant Colonel Felowmate?" Waterloo asked. "He usually escorts me."

"He was transferred, sir. National security reasons."

"Of course," Waterloo said.

"The generals allow Ops Commanders to serve for only two years. Prevents burnout. This tour is classified as a remote assignment—remote from the family, since there's no support facilities for dependents. It's tough for the younger troops."

"I see," Waterloo said. *But at least they still have their wives to go back to,* he thought, pushing away an image of Genny in her last days in the hospital. The times he had spent at the Nevada Test Site in the early years had been considered a "remote" assignment from his home back at Livermore—although the old Atomic Energy Commission had never called it that, never given him credit for the hardships.

The driver opened the back door for him. Waterloo ducked as he climbed in, placing his black satchel beside him. A sign above the driver's windshield read FOR OFFICIAL USE ONLY—USE OF SEAT BELTS IS MANDATORY. The air conditioner hummed on high, and it felt good to relax against the soft seat. LtCol Terrell joined him in the back.

Terrell glanced at his watch. "The transport plane should be here by the time we inventory your devices. We'll get you back to the DAF by late afternoon."

"Good—we've had an incident with one of the Russian inspectors, and I need to ride herd on it." Waterloo leaned forward to look at the C-141s by the isolated hangars. "I hope you're not going to use a Starlifter to transport the devices—we can't land aircraft that big at the strip out by the DAF."

Terrell hesitated. "Those 141s are for another purpose, sir. Sorry, but I can't give you any details. A C-17 is due within the hour. We'll escort the devices from Omega Mountain and set up the convoy in the meantime."

The driver headed east, away from the main complex on a wide two-lane road in immaculate condition. Omega Mountain rose up before them, revealing concrete bunkers with steel doors that dotted the brown foothills every few hundred yards. Waterloo had heard the heavy doors had been salvaged from the sides of old battleships, and could withstand a kiloton blast.

Four concentric electrified fences surrounded the complex. Waterloo remembered the last time he had been here, one of the guards had boasted that more electricity ran through these perimeter fences than powered the entire city of Las Vegas.

As the sedan approached a double-wide gate big enough for a tractor trailer, the driver picked up a microphone.

"Omega Base, this is Ops CC. We are approximately one kilometer from your entrance. Switching off IFF frequencies now."

"That's a rog, Ops CC. We'll look for your blip."

The driver reached to the dashboard, keyed in a number, and flicked a switch on the transmitter box. The green glowing light blinked to red.

"We paint you 10 by 10, Ops CC," the voice said. "Proceed to Omega."

"Rog." The driver flicked the switch back.

Terrell explained, "The Identification Friend or Foe is designed to discriminate between friendlies and hostiles in a combat situation. It's three generations up from what's in our planes."

Waterloo nodded, feigning disinterest. "Oh? How does it work?" He knew the information already from Colonel Felowmate on previous trips, but he listened intently, hoping Terrell would let slip additional details.

"When the IFF box in our vehicle is turned on, it sends a message back to the area security radar and tells the computer to ignore us. Without it, every vehicle on the base would show up on the screen. This way, we detect only unauthorized vehicles."

As they approached the gate, an MP in sand-colored khakis waved for the sedan to stop. The driver rolled down his window as Terrell returned the guard's salute. After checking their badges, the guard signaled for the double-wide gate to swing open. The driver pulled into the sally port and waited between fences as another guard inspected under their car using a mirror attached to a long pole. Security cameras recorded every move.

Waterloo commented, "Since the DAF wasn't built for high-volume work, I'm glad Groom Lake has the temporary storage responsibilities for the stockpile, not us."

Terrell frowned sourly. "Yes, aren't we all." Over the Air

Force's protests, Congress had selected Groom Lake as a staging point for the nation's drawdown of nuclear weapons, a place to store the warheads about to be dismantled at the adjoining Nevada Test Site. It remained a sore point for them.

The second gate finally opened. The driver proceeded slowly into the Omega Mountain fortress as Terrell glanced at a typed checklist. "They're pulling the devices out of bunker 1820 now."

They followed a blacktop road around the nearest foothill, passing two storage bunkers before finally stopping at 1820. A red light in a metal cage gleamed from the top of each bunker; three-pronged yellow and magenta radiation signs prominently marked the front.

The size of the convoy security impressed Waterloo. Two more guards stood in front of the bunker with M-16s at their hips. Behind them nine white drums had been lashed to a flatbed truck while workers hoisted a tenth on top. To the right sat a Bronco bristling with communication antennas. Two Armored Personnel Carriers stood waiting to escort the flatbed.

Terrell opened his door. "Ready, Mr. Waterloo?" Hot, dry air rolled in from the desert.

Grabbing his black satchel, Waterloo followed Terrell to the flatbed. The guard acknowledged them, but did not salute, keeping a wary eye on the two newcomers, as if he did not trust his own commanding officer.

Waterloo glanced into the fortified storage bunker. Yellow lines painted on the concrete floor led deep inside the facility, displaying a transport path to the individual weapons vaults. *Follow the yellow brick road,* he thought. *Maybe it leads to Dreamland. . . .*

A tech sergeant wearing a sidearm jogged up to them. He saluted. "Howdy, Colonel. Everything's on schedule, sir."

Terrell flipped through a sheaf of papers on a clipboard. "You've cleared the devices to transfer to DOE?"

"Yes, sir."

"Let's do it, then."

The sergeant pulled over a small footstool. "Watch your step climbing up." He helped them onto the hot metal top of the flatbed.

Waterloo fumbled in his black satchel, removing the bar-code reader, which he plugged into the hand-held computer crammed with inventory information. He ran the bar-code reader over the top of the first white drum on the truck. Checking the readout, he saw three lines of information appear, listing the previous storage facility, the date assembled, and a short history of maintenance checks performed.

"Ah, a Livermore weapon," he mused. "I probably worked with several of the people who designed this warhead."

Terrell glanced at his watch. "Your plane should be arriving soon, sir—the convoy does have a schedule to keep."

"Right." Waterloo turned to the computer display. "I'll read off the inventory data, and you check it off before you sign each device over to me."

Terrell smoothed his paper on the clipboard as if that were the most obvious fact in the world. "You may ride in the cab on the way to the plane, if you wish to maintain uninterrupted visual surveillance."

"No need," he said. "With all these signatures and all this paperwork, how could anyone accidentally lose track of a warhead?" But deep inside, Waterloo wondered if they truly believed in the infallibility of their security.

It took half an hour for the convoy to make the drive back to the isolated runway and the newly arrived C-17 transport plane. On the way back, Waterloo radioed ahead to the DAF to have Sally Montry finalize the escort vehicles waiting at the receiving airstrip in NTS.

As they approached, the sedan skirted the group of mysterious hangars by a wide margin. Waterloo realized he'd been placed behind the driver's seat, which kept Terrell between him and a good view of the hangars. Intentionally?

Waterloo leaned toward Terrell, still unable to get a good view. "We saw one of your Stealth bombers flying over the NTS a few hours ago. Cruising quite low—everyone was impressed, including the Russian inspectors."

"We're still doing a lot of testing," Terrell said curtly.

"Out here at Groom Lake? I've heard rumors about your Dreamland facility, Colonel. Any chance of getting a tour?"

Terrell flashed a sharp glance over at him. "That request is out of line, sir. Your security clearance does not transfer to our other work here at Groom Lake. Our responsibility for storing nuclear devices is temporary and definitely *not* our primary mission. Beyond that, I am not familiar with the facility you mentioned."

Waterloo didn't pursue the matter further. But the brush-off made him all the more uneasy.

CHAPTER EIGHTEEN

Wednesday, October 22
2:45 P.M.

Yucca Flat
Nevada Test Site

After a cafeteria lunch, Craig was anxious to return to the DAF to begin going over the mounds of paperwork Nevsky had left behind. Time was wasting, and he had gathered about as much background as he considered useful. But he had to accompany the Russian inspectors as they were shown the NTS down-hole testing activities.

The van trundled along a dirt road on Yucca Flat, where hundreds of nuclear tests had taken place underground. Craig could see the dimpled ground, weirdly symmetric circular depressions laid out like a bizarre gardening plot.

"Moon craters," said Nikolai Bisovka, an amateur astronomer and stargazer back in Russia. He fumbled with his pack of Marlboros, sucking on an unlit cigarette, since Paige wouldn't allow him to smoke in the van.

"Subsidence craters," Ursov corrected. "Is that how you say in English?"

"Yes, General," Paige said as the van jounced toward a white tower standing like a sentinel surrounded by trailers and construction cranes. "The explosion forms a subterranean cavity, but the roof collapses, resulting in a subsidence crater at the surface." She swerved around a pothole.

"But all the radioactivity is contained underground, not released to the atmosphere."

Craig adjusted his sunglasses and stared, shifting about to keep comfortable on the van's seat. He felt impatient, eager to be up and making some headway. He glanced at his watch.

"We're going to meet one of our old-timers," Paige said. "Jerome Kostas has worked on underground tests since the 1960s. He even participated in some of the Pacific Island detonations as a young sailor—the Sawtooth Test on Enika Atoll and Castle Bravo on Bikini." She parked the van near the pickup trucks and trailers surrounding the white tower. "I'll bet old Jerome remembers watching most of these craters being made."

Craig climbed out of the van, still watching the Russians and still studying how the Test Site functioned, how various groups worked together. He could see why some hard-liners might have a problem with foreign disarmament inspectors snooping around. For decades, these workers had prepared nuclear warheads for use against the "evil Soviet empire." Now, though, their former enemies were being given a show-and-tell, no more secrets, no more testing, no more reason for a cherished way of life.

Would anyone have been frustrated enough to murder the head of the Russian team?

The inspectors themselves all had alibis, but Craig wondered if there could have been a conspiracy of some kind, two or more of them involved in killing Nevsky so it would look as if one of the Americans had done it. It seemed a good way to rekindle international rivalries, to raise tensions. . . .

A large man sauntered out of the white tower, dressed in painter's pants and wearing a hard hat plastered with faded stickers, team designs for nuclear test shots. He was heavyset, his skin dark brown and leathery, his eyes bright.

"This your team, Miss Mitchell?" Jerome Kostas said. She shook his hand, and Kostas went down the line, methodically gripping each of the inspectors' hands. "We're doing an updated series of benchmark chemical explosions here—no nukes—but the setup is similar. We're gonna have a thunderstorm here tomorrow, Friday at the latest, and we're scrambling to get the prepwork done."

Kostas cocked an eyebrow at Craig, studying his out-of-place jacket and tie, before turning to Paige. "Say, Mike Waterloo says you're Gordy Mitchell's daughter—is that true? I must've done a dozen shots with Gordy."

"My father worked with just about everybody here at one time or another." Paige smiled, glad to know her father was still remembered.

"He retired a while back, didn't he?" Kostas asked.

"Yes, and he died three years ago. Cancer." Her voice became more formal, her words more clipped. Craig felt sorry for her.

"Sad to hear that. Gordy probably never should have retired." Kostas rubbed his leathery hands together, settled his hard hat tighter on his head, then turned to his visitors. "All you get is the canned speech. I've done this too many times to put in any new twists."

Several of the Russians had difficulty with the colloquialisms. Ursov stood listening intently, letting no emotion show on his face.

Kostas said, "A typical underground nuclear test would span a year from conception to the actual shot, involving hundreds of engineers, scientists, technicians, and craftsmen." He gestured to the spools of heavy cable, the tall cranes. Contract workers passed in and out of the trailers, glancing at the group.

"Look at all the craters," the old engineer said. "Before drilling, we take into account the predicted yield of the device, the local geological medium, and separation from other test sites. A lot of factors, and a lot of paperwork." He blew air through his lips. "After grading the surface, we bring in support structures, bogey towers, diagnostic trailers, construction cranes—and offices, so we can fill out the damned paperwork."

The Russians commiserated with him. Craig looked over at Paige, but she seemed lost in thought, perhaps reminded of her father. Out in the open air, Nikolai Bisovka lit up his Marlboro.

"We put two canisters down-hole," Kostas said, "the nuke itself, plus an instrumentation canister seven feet in diameter, fifty feet long, four hundred thousand pounds once you add all the radiation shielding to protect the delicate diagnostics." Kostas wiped a hand across his brow.

"See, we field very precise instruments in a hostile desert environment. They get left down-hole for a month or so while we pour dirt and concrete on top of them. Usually these instruments are one-of-a-kind designs concocted by some engineer with too much computer time and not enough common sense. *I* have to guarantee they'll work. The sensors are vaporized in a few thousandths of a second, but the signals travel faster than that, so we get the data we need."

Kostas crunched toward the tall tower in his heavy work boots. One of the construction cranes rotated away, dangling cables like bullwhips from its peak. "The instrumentation canister and the device canister get hooked together, then hung from the bogey tower for final assembly and checkout. That's where we christen it, usually with a little message written on the side. *Another Superior Product of the MFWBB.*" Kostas laughed at a private joke.

Craig grew suddenly interested, thinking of the words on the bomb he'd found at Hoover Dam. "You write messages on the sides of the device canister?" he said. "What is MFWBB? One of your engineering groups?"

Kostas looked abashed. "Well, you see, the last three letters stand for, uh, 'Who Build Bombs.' I'll let you guess what the 'MF' means. Just a little Test Site humor . . . although once some general found out, we had to cease and desist immediately." He frowned at Ursov in his general's uniform, as if the Russian had been responsible. "Some people just can't take a joke."

Standing inside the white tower, Kostas pointed to a weathered steel disk like a ten-foot-wide manhole cover over a deep shaft. "Those cranes lower the canister to the desired depth, and then we stem the hole with sand and gravel, layered in such a way as to ensure proper density and compaction. Some epoxy, then plugs of sanded gypsum to block the flow of radioactive gas up the column."

He removed his hard hat. "When everything checks out, we set off the test—then we get ready for the next shot." Kostas put his hands on his hips and looked up into the tower, squinting until the crow's-feet scrunched together in a network of wrinkles. "At least that's what we used to do. Now we pretty much sit around and bullshit about our golden age."

"Excuse me," said Victor Golitsyn, the geologist, who had expertise in using sensitive seismic instruments to detect surreptitious underground nuclear tests. "Drilling these holes a thousand feet deep . . . do you experience any particular difficulties—?"

Kostas kicked the toe of his work boot against the steel lid covering the shaft. "We're cutting eight- to ten-foot diameter holes. The whole job takes weeks to months, depending on the size of the hole. We keep those lids on them to make sure nobody else falls down inside." The engineer grimaced.

"Nobody *else*?" Craig said.

"Only happened once, far as I know. Two guys lifting the steel plate stepped forward when they should have stepped sideways. *Zip*, there one kid went, straight down to hell. We lowered cameras, grappling hooks, cables, but never did manage to recover the body."

Kostas placed his hands on his hips and rocked backward in his boots. "Had to drill a new damn hole for the test, cause they sealed that one right up. It was reported as an 'industrial accident,' and the news media never made a big deal out of it. Never even caught on, far as I know."

Craig frowned, not sure whether to believe the old engineer's tall tale. Yet another death called an "industrial accident."

"I am not impressed with your safety records." Ursov's voice dripped scorn as he looked at the hole cover. "But at least it is a better death than having a crate dropped on your head."

CHAPTER NINETEEN

Wednesday, October 22
4:18 P.M.

Device Assembly Facility
Nevada Test Site

When the van finally returned to the DAF in the late afternoon, Paige had to stop on the access road and wait for a heavy convoy to go first. Craig tapped his fingers on the armrest, adjusting his sunglasses, anxious to get back inside so he could start the nitty-gritty part of the murder investigation.

The guard's M-16 looked big to Craig, but the Armored Personnel Carrier looked even bigger as it leveled its huge weapon at the van, much to the consternation of the Russian VIPs. Other guards held their weapons at port arms, protecting the convoy toiling from the airstrip out to the DAF. Craig realized that these vehicles must be carrying the nuclear weapons Waterloo had retrieved from Omega Mountain.

A pilot truck with a flashing blue light led the line, followed by the APC and a communications Bronco. Two flatbed trucks crawled along, each bearing five white barrels lashed as far from each other as was geometrically possible. After the flatbeds came another APC, more guards, and finally a DOE staff car. Two Air Force helicopters sliced through the sky overhead.

Paige raised her voice above the Russians' excited chatter. "These warheads were flown from a classified storage location to a nearby airstrip, and now they're being taken to the Device Assembly Facility. After DAF personnel place these devices into inventory, you will be able to inspect the parts as the warheads are disassembled, per treaty. We need to finish it by Friday, when you must make your final report to both our governments."

Craig pushed his sunglasses back into place to watch. Unable to sit still, he tapped a quiet, random drumbeat with his fingertips on the seat. Everything was heating up, and the Friday deadline seemed to be hurtling toward him, though he had nothing so far to show for it.

The cell phone at his side gave out a shrill bleep, and Craig grabbed it as the Russians divided their attention between eavesdropping on his conversation and watching the high-security convoy.

"Craig, this is Jackson—and boy, do I have a report for you." He listened as Jackson described the ordeal at the booby-trapped home of Bryce Connors. The papers Goldfarb had rescued from the blaze offered scant clues, but confirmed that the Eagle's Claw intended something spectacular for Friday, October 24.

"Second item," Jackson said. "The autopsy of Bill Maguire came through, confirming that he was indeed murdered, given some chemical substance I can't pronounce—it caused his coronary arrest."

Craig felt cold as he listened. He had stopped fidgeting entirely, turning into a statue as the sick feeling fought with his anger at the Eagle's Claw.

"Third item—and this one's the jackpot, Craig. Just got a message from the FBI crime lab. We've got an ID on our dead militia bomber out at the dam. Got his prints on file. Turns out he's a local. Warren P. Shelby."

"Good work!" Craig exclaimed. "Any other information about him? What was he booked for?"

"Never arrested," said Jackson. "His record's clean."

"Then how do we have his prints on file?"

"Drum roll," Jackson said. "He had a *security clearance*. The guy was a contractor for the government—until recently, he was working out at the *Nevada Test Site*."

"Here?" Craig said, trying to keep his voice down. "Well, thousands of people work out at the Test Site."

"Since when did you start believing in coincidences?" Jackson asked. "Anyway, Goldfarb's gone to the library to do some digging. I'm here at the Las Vegas FBI office, looking over some blueprints. I've . . . got a hunch."

"Since when did you start having hunches?" Craig asked with a smile.

"Learned it from you. Look, I'll call if we get any additional information. Give us some time here."

Feeling drained and exhausted, Craig flipped the antenna down and pushed the cell phone back in the pocket of his suit jacket.

Meanwhile in the back of the van, General Ursov straightened the sleeves of his brown uniform shirt, staring as the last of the warhead-hauling convoy rumbled past. The stars on his shoulders reflected the light.

The second APC swung its turret and ground its gears as it rolled to take the rear guard of the convoy. A guard snapped up his M-16 and jogged to the Bronco waiting on the side of the road as the DOE staff car pulled to a stop, its blue light flashing.

A gaunt, short-sleeved man stepped out of the car. Paige rolled down the driver's side window and waved. "Uncle Mike!"

Hot, dry air spilled into the van, and Craig smelled diesel exhaust and dust. Waterloo frowned as he came over to the white van, glancing across at Craig in the passenger seat.

"Agent Kreident, I thought you'd be back inside by now, poring over all the paperwork Ambassador Nevsky left behind."

Craig brushed off his suit jacket. "It seems we've been in sort of a traffic jam, sir."

Waterloo slapped the side of the van. "Come on up with me, we'll get you right inside. Sally can escort you while Paige finishes up here. Myself, I've got to log in all the inventory paperwork for moving these devices."

Craig readily agreed and joined Waterloo back at the DOE staff car. Climbing inside, he watched the DAF Manager carefully. "I guess I can understand why you need such tight security, given recent events."

Waterloo's brow furrowed. "How's that? Because of Nevsky's death?"

"No, the Eagle's Claw. Does that mean anything to you?"

"Isn't that a ski area in New Mexico?" Waterloo shook his head. "No, I'm thinking of Eagle Nest."

Craig took off his sunglasses and wiped sweat from his forehead. Waterloo hadn't turned on the staff car's air conditioning. "I just learned that the saboteur killed at Hoover Dam yesterday was a former NTS employee. Warren Shelby, a contract worker here. Did you know him, sir?"

Waterloo pursed his lips as he considered. "Agent Kreident, a lot of people work here, especially contractors, who get hired on a job-by-job basis. You saw those people stripping cables out of the test tunnels up on the mesa. If you're suggesting the militia had anything to do with the accident that killed Ambassador Nevsky . . ."

Craig sidestepped the question, curious, since he had made no such suggestion. "Doesn't it worry you that a member of a terrorist group was working right under your nose, with a security clearance? Given their agenda, isn't it possible the militia might want to stop the Russian disarmament team from doing their work?"

Waterloo adjusted his bolo tie. "I won't kid you that we have a lot of rednecks working here, good old boys, like me, who can't read a liberal agenda without laughing out loud. But so what? By its very nature NTS is a pretty patriotic place to work. We're all about freedom and democracy—freedom to be what you want, even if it means joining a protest group. No one is granted a clearance if he's considered to be a threat."

"Well, you missed one," Craig said.

Waterloo drove into the fenced compound as more guards swarmed around the flatbed trucks. "Just look at our security—nobody can sneak in here and slip away with a bomb in his car trunk, no matter what radical organization he belongs to."

"But isn't it possible," Craig persisted, "if they got into the right place at the right time?"

"You don't understand, Agent Kreident," Waterloo said. "We've got technological and administrative fail-safes on every weapon. Regulations require three signatures to transport any component of a nuclear device, and work crews are rotated at random. Every part is documented, inspected, and certified. *Three signatures,* Mr. Kreident, by important people in the process."

Craig put his sunglasses back on and glanced up at the DAF, drumming his fingers on the seat. The security helicopter thundered overhead.

"Occupational hazard," he said as they waited for the guards to motion them inside. "It's part of my job to be suspicious of everything."

CHAPTER TWENTY

Wednesday, October 22
4:23 P.M.

Public Library
Las Vegas, Nevada

Goldfarb removed the plastic lid, and the smell of freshly brewed coffee wafted from his Starbucks cup as he settled behind the microfilm reader at the Las Vegas library. At least the reference librarian had given him a special dispensation to bring the coffee inside, once he'd shown her his badge. This late in the afternoon, grimy and exhausted, Goldfarb needed the caffeine just to keep himself going—and with their time dwindling minute by minute, he couldn't afford to relax.

The Eagle's Claw meant to strike on the day after tomorrow.

From the burning den, Goldfarb had rescued handwritten notes filled with random numbers, a tourist brochure with a map of all the casinos in Las Vegas (several of which had been circled), discolored work orders from a slot-machine repair shop, photocopied articles from underground publications about the excesses of the United Nations, yellow pages torn from the phone book with ads for various airlines, Amtrak trains, and Greyhound buses.

Scattered clues, but no obvious answers. The next step required digging.

Goldfarb glanced at his dot-matrix printout and inserted a microfilm cassette into the reader. Under the headings MILITIA and EAGLE'S CLAW he found a series of newspaper dates and page numbers. Most would make only passing reference to extremist groups, but he just might find the one clue that could break the case wide open. He had already read the field reports of covert agent Maguire, now deceased.

Maguire had left his wife and thirteen-year-old daughter behind in Sacramento to pose undercover as a Clark County highway worker who hung out in redneck bars. He made his fabricated political views known and eventually worked his way into the militia. His regular reports provided much background on the violent organization.

In the best tradition of clandestine groups, the Eagle's Claw was divided into compact cells, each with its own mission, each reporting to a single superior. But the Eagle's Claw had somehow discovered that Maguire worked for the FBI. And they had drugged him, murdered him—but not before he managed to leave his warning note about Hoover Dam. . . .

Goldfarb had met Maguire's wife once at a Bureau function. He remembered that the man's daughter was extremely tall for her age and played basketball on the junior high team. Goldfarb felt burning anger as he thought of how the woman and her daughter would no longer see Bill Maguire, how he would never again show up for his daughter's games.

Goldfarb thought of how his own wife Julene and their two children could just as easily suffer the same fate, if he wasn't careful.

He turned the microfilm dial, and blurry newspaper pages raced across the screen. He zoomed past the first date on his list and had to back up to read a letter to the editor from the Western States Militia: a complaint about the United Nations making a power grab, which led into a screed against gun control, then liberals in general. Goldfarb noted the organization on a sheet of yellow legal paper, just in case he spotted a pattern.

Checking off the first item on his printout, he moved to the second.

And the third. . . .

He took another sip of hot coffee, feeling the bitter taste glide down his throat like a depth charge. He stared at the barely legible, negative copies of newspapers on the screen, but no amount of caffeine seemed able to force connections in his mind. He cranked to the next article; the microfilm whirred and rattled as the days flew by.

With the noise of the machine, Goldfarb didn't hear the man come up behind him. He sensed rather than heard the presence, smelled the pungent whiff of aftershave, a strong dose of Old Spice—a brand he had worn himself as a younger man, believing that it made him rugged and sexy to women, until Julene had talked him out of that notion.

"You're invading my right of privacy," said a man's gruff voice. "As an American citizen I find that offensive."

Goldfarb started to turn in his chair, but the loud *snick* of a spring-loaded knife popping out of its hilt made him freeze. The blade pressed against his throat.

"Now, now, Mr. FBI," the man said, "gotta keep quiet in the library. Can't you read the signs?"

Goldfarb swallowed but made no abrupt moves. He looked up, saw the broad shoulders, the close-cropped dark hair, and square jaw bearing a shadow of dark whiskers. The man wore a lightweight, billowy khaki jacket.

The knife point poked the corner of his jaw under his ear, within instant reach of his jugular. The tall shelves, the microfilm reader, and the bulk of the man himself shielded them from view of the library's other patrons.

"I hope you know automatic knives are illegal in the United States," Goldfarb said calmly.

The burly man grunted; the sound might have been a quiet laugh. "I bought it in Mexico. And you're going to *buy it* right here."

"In the Reference Section?" The sarcasm caused the man to push the knife in closer. Goldfarb winced and decided that humor might not be the best way to resolve this situation. "Bryce Connors, I presume?" he said. "I recognize you from your picture in the employee file. It's about the only thing in there that wasn't faked."

"You all know too damn much," Connors said. A high school student carrying a backpack sauntered by, glanced at them, but saw nothing more than an intense, private conversation. She moved back toward the magazines.

"We already know who you are, Connors, and we have plenty of leads," Goldfarb said. "If you do anything to me, we'll hunt you down in no time."

The militiaman remained unimpressed. "All I need is to keep out of your reach until Friday. That's only two more days, no sweat." The point of the switchblade did not waver against Goldfarb's neck. A warm, syrupy drop of perspiration trickled from his curly hair down his temple and in front of his ear. "After Friday, nothing's going to be the same anyway."

"I can't wait," Goldfarb said.

"Sorry, Mr. FBI," Connors whispered, "but you won't be there to see the show."

"So give me a sneak preview. What's going to happen?" Goldfarb hoped it could be so simple.

"They won't even tell *me* exactly what's going to happen—but you can bet it'll be spectacular. The first bombs were my work. Somebody else is in charge of the festivities on the 24th."

"So how did you find me?" Goldfarb asked, trying to draw the man out.

Connors smiled, his thick lips curling upward but not parting to reveal any teeth. "I've been watching you ever since you left the fire." He gave a rude snort. "I don't know what took you guys so long to get to my house. If I'd known you were going to wait all night and half the morning, I would've had time to clean out the place instead of rigging it to burn down."

At the far end of the stacks, one of the assistant librarians rolled a heavy metal cart laden with books toward the private offices in the back.

"Now get up," Connors said. "We're going to walk out to my truck, where we can continue this conversation in private." The man hissed into his ear, "Slowly—no sudden moves."

Goldfarb had no desire to continue the conversation with Bryce Connors, in private or otherwise. Feeling the knife against his throat, he swiveled counterclockwise, rising from the chair in the opposite direction from what the militiaman expected. It was a little thing, nothing Connors could fault him for—but the instant of confusion was enough to draw the knife point slightly away from his skin. Goldfarb reacted with spring-tight reflexes, jerking his head backward as he snatched his cup of hot coffee and flung it over his shoulder into Bryce Connors's face.

The man yowled and raised his hands as Goldfarb dove out of the way. Connors immediately regained enough of his thoughts and reflexes to slash downward with the knife. The razor-sharp blade ripped open the sleeve of Goldfarb's jacket but did not cut the skin.

Connors lunged again blindly, and Goldfarb smashed into the microfilm reader, upsetting the table and knocking the machine over with a loud crash. The militiaman bellowed, clawing at his scalded eyes. Goldfarb ripped his handgun from the shoulder holster, thrusting it close to Bryce Connors. "Freeze!"

Several of the readers and students in the library cried out; a few ran for the exit but most stared, captivated by the tableau. At the checkout counter, the librarians stepped back, wide-eyed.

Connors gripped his face and moaned loudly as Goldfarb pressed closer, holding the handgun steady. "My eyes!"

Goldfarb had just enough time for a flicker of suspicion—the coffee hadn't been *that* hot—but he was unprepared for the lashing cowboy boot that swept at his leg with the force of a wrecking ball. The stone-hard heel caught him directly on the shin and Goldfarb shouted his pain as he fell over like a toppled matchstick.

Connors, his eyes unharmed after all, bolted.

Goldfarb howled and then limped after the man as Connors dashed between two long bookshelves in the stacks. Every step sent a cannonball of pain up his leg.

He stepped around one of the shelves, ducking as he scanned down the long corridor of books. He saw Connors for just an instant as the militiaman whirled, gripping a genuine cowboy-style Colt revolver he had pulled from the pocket of his khaki jacket. The man fired twice, and the gunshots sounded like explosions in the library. A loud ricochet struck the metal shelves within a foot of Goldfarb's head, and the other bullet struck the books. He toppled backward out of the way.

The people in the library screamed and finally began to run for the exits.

"Should've known he'd come prepared with more than just a little knife," Goldfarb muttered, then he raised his voice to a shout. "Everyone, listen! I am a Federal agent. Please evacuate the library. Call for help. 9-1-1. Get backup here right now." Goldfarb hoped that at least one of the librarians would maintain enough wits to call in the emergency.

He slid around the corner, but Connors had vanished, diving down a side aisle. Where did the burly man think he could go? Goldfarb limped down the stacks as quietly as he could, his handgun drawn. His gaze flicked from side to side, waiting for motion.

He heard people running toward the exits, then a librarian shouted. "The police and the FBI are on their way with full backup. They'll be here in less than two minutes." No backup could arrive so quickly, but Goldfarb suspected the woman had used that as a ploy, a weapon to make Connors panic. He hoped it might work.

Goldfarb could not respond, because that would give away his position. He crept along, then slid to the next section of shelves, one aisle at a time. He heard no sound, no one moving along the line of books. The fluorescent lights overhead cast murky shadows.

His heart pounding, his breath ragged, he glanced from side to side. His Beretta extended, he turned to the right, praying that Connors hadn't doubled back, wasn't slipping around behind him—

Then suddenly to his left a section of books tumbled off an upper shelf as Bryce Connors shoved them. Heavy encyclopedias thumped down, raining on Goldfarb's shoulders—but it was a surprise and a distraction more than an actual injury.

Ignoring the bruises, Goldfarb dashed over to where the militiaman had been. Connors whirled, firing once more behind him, but he took no time to aim. Smoldering confetti showered from bullet-damaged books.

Connors dashed into the library's back offices, and Goldfarb charged after him.

As he passed through the door, his head low and his attention focused, Bryce Connors popped out from the side, rolling a heavy cart full of books, smashing it into Goldfarb like a locomotive. The metal cart tipped over, and Goldfarb sprawled to the floor as more books tumbled around him.

Connors dashed deeper into the offices where three young library assistants worked at repairing books, every one of them wearing earphones plugged into Walkman cassette players. Two of them wrapped plastic protective coverings over new arrivals while the third keyed in entries in the computer. All three leaped to their feet, confused and astonished, yanking earphones away from their head.

Connors pointed his revolver and fired point-blank at the glowing computer screen. The cathode-ray tube exploded like a bomb, a spectacular distraction, and the three assistants dove to the floor for cover, screaming. Sparks and smoke sprayed from the ruined computer.

Goldfarb scrambled to his feet, crawling over the piles of loose books and the metal cart. He slipped and stumbled, trying to regain his balance. "Hold it!" he yelled.

Connors ignored him. He reached the back emergency exit door and crashed through it, setting off fire alarms. Loud bells rang, adding to the chaos. The militiaman dove outside into the slice of sunlight.

Goldfarb scrambled across the back room, still in hot pursuit. The three assistant librarians were terrified, picking themselves up. Goldfarb took a second to glance at them. "Are you all right? Did he shoot you? Are you injured?" He saw three stunned faces look at him blankly. All shook their heads.

Goldfarb ran to the still-closing door, crashing his way out. His battered shin stung and burned. He didn't think the bone was broken, but he could think of various tortures that would have felt more pleasant at the moment.

To his dismay, the rear of the library butted up against a busy parking lot filled with cars and trucks, pedestrians, shoppers. He focused quickly on the pickups, since Bryce

Connors had mentioned his truck—but then he saw a dark blue Galaxie 500 roar off down the street, and he knew that the man's words must have been a decoy.

He felt the energy drain out of him like water, replaced with suffocating dismay. The man responsible for creating the Hoover Dam bomb—a bona fide connection to the Eagle's Claw—had slipped right through his fingers! Connors would probably ditch the car within the hour.

"Jackson's never going to let me forget this," Goldfarb groaned, then used his good leg to kick his heel in frustration against the library wall.

Within moments, far too late of course, he heard sirens approaching in the distance.

CHAPTER TWENTY-ONE

Wednesday, October 22
4:51 P.M.

Device Assembly Facility
Nevada Test Site

The mountain of paperwork in front of him had become a blur in his eyes. Craig shook his head. He had spent the last hour just trying to figure out *what* the forms signified before he could unravel any discrepancies. But the thought of skimming it all—not to mention understanding it—by Friday seemed an insurmountable task.

"Boy, that stuff must be fascinating," Paige said, startling him. She stood behind him in the Pit Assembly Area.

"You sure are a welcome sight." Craig sat up straight, rubbing his sore back. He gave her a warm smile, then glanced at his watch. "Are the Russians still here?"

"Uncle Mike took them back to the Rio and out to dinner. He's got a meeting in Las Vegas tomorrow morning, so I volunteered to stay and help you for an hour or so, if you'd like." Paige bent over to glance at the top layer of papers.

Craig sighed in relief. "I'd like that a lot. The pieces are in here somewhere, but I have to let them fall into place."

Now, without General Ursov and the other Russians eavesdropping, he told her what Jackson had said on the cellular phone about the dead militiaman at the Hoover Dam being a former NTS employee.

Paige remained quiet for a moment. "Why don't we double-check Warren Shelby's records? We can get them from the administration building in Mercury. His clearance would have been denied if anything showed up during the background check, but security reinvestigation is done only every five to ten years—a lot of things change."

Craig groaned. "More papers . . ." He pushed stacks of Nevsky's notes aside, rubbing his temples. So many numbers, signatures, dates, cross-references to other forms, specific listings of nuclear weapons components. "But that's a really good idea. I also want to get the file on Jorgenson, the forklift driver. And while you're at it, let's check out PK Dirks. I know Sally Montry gave him an alibi, but he could have coerced her somehow."

Paige gave an impish smile. "I'm not sure *anybody* could coerce Sally."

"I can't give out employee addresses," said Sally Montry. Her short blond hair was perfectly cut, laying straight against her tanned forehead. A stack of memos lay on her desk awaiting Mike Waterloo's signature. "That's confidential information." She seemed rigid and uncooperative, and Craig wondered if she was trying to protect her boss out of some sense of loyalty.

He drummed his fingers on Sally's government-issue, gray metal desk, pacing the floor. A matted photograph of a nighttime atomic blast hung behind the desk, autographed by numerous people. He saw no family pictures, none of her estranged husband, none of PK Dirks, only a button stenciled with **I ♥ NUCLEAR WEAPONS.**

"Look, Mrs. Montry," Craig said. "I need to speak with Mr. Jorgenson as part of this investigation. I'm sorry if I humiliated you in front of your boss this morning, but the alibi you provided for Mr. Dirks was crucial for determining exactly what occurred Monday night. This is just as important."

She started to retort, but seemed to think better of it. Sullenly, she opened a drawer that held a row of hanging files. She flipped through a file marked PERSONAL and withdrew a sheet of paper. "He lives at 26 Antelope Trail, in Pahrump. You'll have to drive a ways. Carl won't be home, though—he likes to hang out in the local bars. Best bet would be to wait until morning, stop by on your way in to the site."

Craig jotted down the address. "Thanks. And tomorrow I may also need your help deciphering the paperwork Nevsky left behind. Mr. Waterloo tells me you're good at that."

"The best," Sally said, without seeming to brag at all.

Kill her with kindness, Craig thought, *if that's what it takes.*

CHAPTER TWENTY-TWO

Wednesday, October 22
6:15 P.M.

Las Vegas Strip

During their long drive back from the Test Site, the desert sky opened up like a black vault filled with diamond stars. The night wind curled through Paige's half-open window, nudging scents from her pine air freshener.

Sitting beside her, Craig felt reluctant to talk about anything other than safe topics. He avoided talking about his ex-girlfriend Trish, knowing how boring it was for another woman to hear of a man's previous loves. Instead, he told her about his early work for the Bureau, his training at Quantico and certification as a field agent . . . and before that, his year and a half working for a small private-eye firm, where he had spent days in a stakeout van to watch people suspected of committing insurance fraud.

Paige, in turn, talked about her father's career at the old Livermore Radiation Laboratory. Like so many others involved with nuclear testing, he had died of cancer, but she refused to be bitter or vindictive, merely chalked up the tragedies to a grim learning curve for working with dangerous technology.

Traffic picked up when they entered the north end of Las Vegas, off the freeway and down the Strip. Craig watched the swarms of pedestrians moving down the sidewalks from casino to casino as flickering light bulbs cascaded like shooting stars. The city's exuberance at all hours of the day and night amazed him.

Paige interrupted his thoughts, getting down to business. "Since we know the ambassador's death was no accident, I see two primary possibilities. Either somebody caught *Nevsky* doing something he shouldn't have been doing—or *he* caught someone else, and they murdered him for it."

Craig nodded. "If Nevsky was really spying, he picked a very suspicious time to do it. At that late hour, he would have stuck out like a sore thumb. In fact, the hardest part to swallow is that PK Dirks just wandered off and left him alone in the DAF."

The streetlight turned red in front of Paige, but several cars roared through the intersection anyway. "What if PK himself was engaged in illegal activities, expecting no one would see him at that hour, and Nevsky caught him? Remember, the security cameras were conveniently on the blink—PK could have arranged that."

Craig shook his head. "No, I think Nevsky found something well before he was murdered. That's why he wanted to come back to the DAF after everyone else had left." He shuddered to think of all the documents. "Whatever it is, he probably buried it in that mound of paperwork."

"No more tours for you tomorrow," she said dryly.

Craig glanced at his watch. "I know. Time's running out, and the coroner's report is due to be released soon—if I don't have something by then, the crap is really going to hit the fan." He paused, exhausted just from the thought of all the work he still had to do. "I think I'll go out to find Jorgenson tonight anyway, so I can spend Thursday hitting the books."

Paige accelerated as the light turned green. They passed the Mirage, whose facsimile volcano erupted with lights and color. Extravagant fountains gurgled around atolls of rock.

A block away, crowds gathered in front of Treasure Island to see a battle between mock pirate ships.

"How about dinner?" Craig said impulsively. "I'm starved."

"You always seem to be starved." She laughed. "How about some good prime rib this time? At least *I've* got a per diem."

In the medieval spirit of Excalibur, the prime rib house was called *Sir Galahad's*. Coats of arms, lances, and colorful pennants hung on the walls above suits of armor. The waitresses wore medieval costumes, their hair done up in conical hats.

Craig and Paige each had a thick cut of prime rib served on a pewter plate with creamed spinach and Yorkshire pudding. Craig dug into the meal, ravenous, as Paige watched him, amused.

"Well, well," came a woman's rough voice behind them, "I didn't think you'd be alone for long, Sweetie." Craig turned to see Maggie the Mind Reader dressed in her court jester's getup and holding a small parakeet on her finger. She looked appraisingly at Paige.

"I'm surprised you remember me," Craig said.

Maggie snorted. "I'm psychic, if you'll recall." Then she leaned over the back of the booth, speaking conspiratorially to Paige. "And I see that while you two should be having fun, enjoying Vegas, all you think of is work." Her breath carried the perfumy smell of scotch.

"When people aren't here to have fun, they look different, feel different." She raised her eyebrows, scrutinizing Craig. "Hey, are you with the DEA? I sense . . ." She let her eyes fall half closed. "Wait! The *FBI*."

Paige laughed, and Maggie's eyes sparkled, knowing she had guessed right. "Now do you believe I'm psychic?" she said, petting her parakeet.

"I, uh, never doubted you," Craig said, the tone of his voice stating exactly the opposite. He tried to remember how much he had explained to her last night.

She focused her attention on Paige, drawing a deep breath, concentrating. "And you, young lady . . . you're worried about someone. Someone close to you. Yes, I can sense the concern in your thoughts, but you're trying to cover it up."

Embarrassed, Paige turned away, her cheeks flushing. "Yes, I am concerned about someone." She looked at Craig. "It's Uncle Mike. He's really withdrawn since he lost his wife . . . and when my dad died a year later, he lost his best friend, too. Maybe he just doesn't know what to do, now that he's all alone." Paige shook her head, then glanced up at Maggie, blinking her blue eyes. "You sure scored a point with me," she said.

Craig smiled. "Maggie does seem to be an astute judge of character."

"Damn straight," Maggie said with an amused expression on her face. "I think you're just skeptical about everything, Sweetie. Is that the reason your old girlfriend . . ." She held her hand out, concentrating again. "*Trish,* was that her name? Is that why she left you?"

Craig blinked in astonishment, and Paige laughed. "Even *I* haven't been able to get him to talk about that."

"Well, Maggie, to tell you the truth, I *am* with the FBI," Craig said, wanting to divert the subject away from Trish. "And we're here on a case."

Maggie seemed intensely interested. She lowered her voice. "Is it a gambling investigation, a sting operation for money laundering? Can I help? We hear about those things all the time in the casinos."

Craig decided to take a chance; maybe he could at least help Goldfarb and Jackson. "In truth, Maggie, maybe we could use your help. Do you know about the bomb planted at Hoover Dam Tuesday?" Craig asked. Paige looked over at him, perplexed.

The wrinkles deepened around Maggie's lips. "If those militia morons think they're going to gain public support like that, they don't understand human psychology at all."

"But *you* understand human psychology, Maggie—probably as well as a professional psychiatrist does. I've watched how you read people." She beamed at the compliment. "You also keep your eyes open."

"It's my job," she said firmly. "I spend my whole day listening, reading faces, checking how they dress, how they act. You can draw a lot of inferences."

Craig nodded. "And you pick up on things nobody else knows you've even noticed."

"Damn straight," she said.

Craig looked over at Paige with a shrug. "At this point, I don't suppose we've got anything to lose."

He gave her a bit of background, just what had been on the news—then Maggie told him what she knew.

CHAPTER TWENTY-THREE

Wednesday, October 22
9:10 P.M.

Jorgenson's Home
Pahrump, Nevada

Craig drove down the unpaved road in the dark. The turnoff to Antelope Trail had taken him a good twenty minutes off the main highway, but the moonlit view was worth every minute of the drive.

The mountains bounding the beautiful valley were black bulwarks in the night, siege walls thrown up against the lights of Las Vegas. Pahrump was a small town that had burst its seams with burgeoning housing developments and strip malls. Fast-food restaurants replaced old diners that had been called simply "EAT."

He planned to meet Goldfarb and Jackson early the next morning to exchange information, but before then he hoped to have a long talk with the forklift driver, Carl Jorgenson.

Following the address Sally Montry had given him, he found a dirty mailbox with the number 26. Craig had tried to call Jorgenson first, rather than showing up unannounced, but the phone had rung and rung. Maybe Jorgenson was asleep—or drunk, as Sally had suggested.

Craig turned into a rutted driveway that led to a white house trailer. A red pickup was parked at the front next to a pile of discarded tires. POSTED: KEEP OUT signs were tacked to a ragged split-rail fence; an old posthole digger, rakes, and uncut firewood lay scattered in the yard. A porch light looked like a sullen yellow eye over the front door, while a mercury yard light blazed from an old telephone pole at the corner of the trailer.

Around back Craig could see a rotting wooden storage shed and a homemade shooting range, bales of straw with paper targets—human silhouettes rather than simple bulls-eye circles. Apparently, Jorgenson could sit inside his living room and practice with a rifle.

Craig could see the winking streetlights of Pahrump in the valley below, but they served only to point out how isolated he found himself up here. The night remained silent, smelling faintly of ozone—he remembered the old-timer Jerome Kostas and his prediction of an impending thunderstorm in the next day or so.

He heard nothing, not even night insects. Jorgenson's place gave him the creeps. Pulling out his cellular phone, he saw the indicator blinking red—out of signal range.

He suddenly wished he had called Goldfarb or Jackson for backup. Paige might not remember he had gone out, since he had mentioned it only briefly. No one else knew he had driven out here. Bad idea. Even Sally Montry hadn't expected him to speak with Jorgenson until the following day.

He wondered if the man was watching him even now, peeking through a gap in the curtain, readying his rifle to shoot a nighttime trespasser.

Recalling the booby-trapped home of Bryce Connors, how his two partners had nearly perished in the blaze, Craig felt a gnawing pain in the pit of his stomach. The man who lived alone in this isolated trailer had already admitted to causing the "accident" that had crushed Nevsky. But only Craig, Paige, and the killer himself knew the accident had actually been a murder.

He stood by his rental car and considered returning to Las Vegas. He could come back with Goldfarb and Jackson the next morning. As he had originally planned to do.

But the other two agents were busily crunching through the Eagle's Claw case, working against their own intense deadline. Two more days until October 24—Craig couldn't pull them away from their work because he heard a bump in the night. Besides, just because one contract worker out of thousands at NTS had been a member of the Eagle's Claw, he had no real reason to connect a DAF forklift driver with the violent militia group. Craig couldn't waste time either—he had his own deadline to meet.

Focusing his concentration, vowing to keep on his toes, Craig remembered lessons he'd learned while shadowing people as a stringer for Elliot Lang, Private Investigator. One time, while watching a mark's apartment to catch him cheating on his wife, the man's lover showed up and caught on to Craig immediately, scuffling with him, succeeding in dumping the film in his camera. From that embarrassing incident, Craig had learned that *anything* could happen in a high-pressure situation.

He patted his shoulder holster, comforted by the Beretta's weight. He didn't dare draw the handgun as he approached. He didn't want to look suspicious. Late-night visitors already carried their own baggage of distrust.

He slammed the car door, careful to make plenty of noise to announce his arrival. "Mr. Jorgenson? Hello, sir? This is Agent Kreident, FBI." He walked past the posthole digger toward the front door. "I'm investigating the accident at the DAF. I have a few questions to ask you before I close out this case—just some things to clear up."

Craig scanned the area as he spoke, taking in the trailer's drawn curtains, the piles of debris around the outside. The bright mercury light washed out the colors, sharpened the shadows. He heard nothing louder than the soft whir of a refrigerator from inside, no TV, radio or phone.

He rapped sharply on the front door. "Mr. Jorgenson? Are you there?" He knocked again, then moved to the side, trying to peek through a curtain slit. He dreaded that Jorgenson might have skipped town.

With the passing seconds he felt the increasing sourness in the pit of his stomach. Since he hadn't obtained a search warrant, he couldn't just force his way in. The forklift driver was probably out bar-hopping, as Sally Montry had suggested. All this way for nothing—and his time was running shorter and shorter. Now he would have to waste part of Thursday conducting the interview as well.

Craig pounded on the door one last time, then stepped to the left, standing on his tiptoes to take a quick peek through another small window. In the darkened trailer, it took Craig a moment to realize he was looking into the bathroom.

A dark form lay slumped by the small shower stall—a body fallen just inside the door.

Craig's nervous system snapped into high gear. He tried the trailer's flimsy door, but it was locked; then he pulled out his weapon and stood back to kick out with his foot. The heel of his black wing tip smashed the aluminum doorknob, and the plywood door splintered open.

Craig burst inside at a crouch, sweeping his weapon from side to side. "Federal agent! Mr. Jorgenson, I'm here to assist you, sir." His heart yammered at the back of his throat. He hoped no trigger-happy militiaman would go nuts, thinking that the government was invading—

Craig trotted down the darkened hallway, searching for a light switch. An American flag was draped on the wall in the far bedroom. He kept his handgun moving, tracking anticipated targets as he expected someone to jump out from a bedroom, but nothing happened. Silence filled the trailer.

Reaching the cramped bathroom, Craig bashed the door

open with his elbow, glanced in to see the body by the shower, then backed into the small toilet area. He clicked the light, blinking as the harsh bulb dazzled him.

Keeping his weapon leveled at the door, listening, Craig reached down to pull the body around. A man in his late forties, with close-cropped salt-and-pepper hair, rough face, slack mouth—and skin cold with death. His expression was a grimace of pain, like a rubber mask distorted and twisted.

Craig checked for a pulse, reaching up to touch Jorgenson's neck. He bent down and put his ear by the man's mouth, but felt no warm exhalation. Cold sweat soaked Craig's clothes.

He quickly searched the rest of the trailer to convince himself that no one else was around. Craig thrust his handgun back in its shoulder holster and returned to the bathroom.

Jorgenson could have slipped and struck his head. But Craig could see no bruise on his face, no cracked skull, nothing obviously fatal. Had he died of something else instead? Another "convenient" heart attack?

Like Maguire's?

CHAPTER TWENTY-FOUR

Thursday, October 23
7:35 A.M.

FBI Satellite Office
Las Vegas

Craig didn't sleep late, nor did he sleep well. Finding the dead body of a prime suspect spoiled his ability to rest comfortably. Everything would come to a head tomorrow, not only the inspection team's deadline, and the President's visit, but also the fatal countdown from the Eagle's Claw. He didn't have time to sleep anyway.

Before he headed out to the Nevada Test Site on a last, desperate search of the records, Craig drove bleary-eyed to the FBI Satellite Office where Goldfarb and Jackson had set up shop.

Even at this early hour, telephones rang, photocopiers whirred, people in suits moved up and down the halls. It could have been a commercial bank in any large city, but here the file cabinets contained dossiers of every con man, high roller, or drug dealer who had crossed state lines and fallen under their jurisdiction.

Jackson had draped his suit jacket on a chair; a paperback Western peeked out of the pocket, though Craig didn't suppose the other agent would have much free reading time at lunch. Goldfarb looked up from his second cup of coffee. In front of him on the desk lay a manila folder crammed with photocopied faxes. "You missed the excitement this morning. June Atwood called—she's sending another dozen field agents out here to help."

"Great," Craig said. "Just as long as they help and don't take up any of my time. We've got less than twenty-four hours to go."

"So, what time did you get to bed last night, Craig?"

"After midnight," he said with a yawn. "Once I found Jorgenson's body, I had to wait for the local law enforcement and the coroner, then fill out a bunch of forms, make my statement, add to the sheriff's report."

Goldfarb shook his head. "I called Julene and the girls at nine and got to sleep by ten. After almost being barbecued, stabbed, and shot in the same day, I needed my beauty sleep."

"Good. After all that rest, you two can go check out Jorgenson's trailer yourselves. Have those new field agents take over for you here." Craig rubbed his eyes. "I've already applied for the search warrant, and it should be ready by lunchtime."

Jackson sat stiffly, intent on Craig. "How does that connect to our case? Tomorrow's the 24th, and, like you said, we don't have a lot of extra time on our hands."

"I've asked the ME to check for the same chemical substance they found in Maguire's autopsy. Jorgenson's convenient death sounds a bit too similar. And since Warren Shelby was a militia member and an NTS worker . . ."

Jackson cleared his throat, all business now. "We think along the same lines, Craig. Remember that hunch I had yesterday?" He slid open the center drawer of the desk, shuffling aside sticky notes, paper clips, pens, and a yellow legal tablet. "I was also wondering if the dam incident had any connection to the murder of your Russian inspector."

He pulled out sectional topographic maps of southern Nevada showing power lines and railroad tracks. He had used a lime-green highlighter to draw lines, circling electrical substations. "Look at these power substations and electrical lines. A carefully placed explosion at the hydroelectric plant would have cut off power not only to parts of California and Arizona, *but also to all of the Test Site*."

"That's a big area and a big assumption," Craig said.

Goldfarb leaned forward eagerly. "Remember, Craig, these guys are militant separatists who don't want our country dabbling in foreign affairs. That high-visibility Russian inspection team is a vital part of what the two presidents will be discussing about at their summit meeting. A total power blackout would have sabotaged the disarmament activities, thrown a wrench into the works, mucked everything up before Saturday's big show. Quite a statement for the cause, don't you think?"

Craig stared at the map as the ideas converged around him. "I can't seem to get away from the militia even when I'm investigating my own case." He turned to the door, anxious to be on his way to dig through Nevsky's paperwork.

He had to stop back at the Excalibur to pick up his notes on his way out to the Test Site. This was his last day to solve everything. "Oh, let me pass along another tip I got last night," he said, suddenly remembering what Maggie the Mind Reader had suggested. "Could just be a false alarm, but you can decide for yourselves.

"Somebody spotted suspicious activity in one of the casinos, frequent surreptitious meetings on the crowded slot-machine floors. Often the people wear service uniforms from a slot-machine repair shop called Dennisons—but the odd thing is that Dennisons apparently doesn't service the equipment in the Excalibur, so why they'd be there at all is a mystery to her."

Jackson nodded, running a finger along his smooth chin. "We had assumed the militia group meets in local bars, but if they hang out in busy tourist places, like the Excalibur, they'd never be noticed."

Goldfarb rubbed down his hair, still frizzy from his close call with the fire yesterday. "Hey, Jackson—wasn't there a work order or a receipt from some slot-machine repair in the papers I rescued yesterday?"

"Dennisons. We'll check it out later this morning," Jackson said matter-of-factly, scribbling a note down on his yellow legal pad.

CHAPTER TWENTY-FIVE

Thursday, October 23
8:31 A.M.

Sedan Crater
Nevada Test Site

Another day of touring, but without Craig this time. Paige had to complete her protocol obligations with the Russian team, salvage the success of their mission, and hope the spirit of disarmament and international cooperation survived the debacle of Nevsky's death.

Even after all the other places Paige had shown the Russians, nothing could have prepared them for the sheer size of Sedan Crater. She watched the look of amazement on their faces as they stepped to the edge and looked down, *down* into the enormous parabolic bowl scooped out of the sand.

"This was *intentional,* yes?" Anatoli Voronin said, puffing his large lips.

"It's our largest nuclear excavation, three hundred kilotons," Paige said. "Some of the original test engineers thought the crater would be a good site to hold the Super Bowl."

The wind picked up, whispering around them. The inspectors crept close—but not too close—to the edge. Down at the crater bottom, discarded tires bespoke of carefree amusements, NTS workers rolling tires down the long slope. Now, though, warning signs had been posted: *Danger—Ra-*

dioactive Area. No Digging. A yellow-painted wooden fence blocked off the observation stand; its peeling and weathered appearance implied that Sedan Crater was no longer much of a tourist attraction.

General Ursov locked his hands behind his back and stood simmering with undirected anger, the frustration and unease he had exhibited since the morning of Nevsky's death. Paige couldn't blame him—this was now his inspection team, his responsibility. No doubt his own superiors had roundly chewed him out for the disaster, and Ursov had no way to defend himself against the charges.

Paige had been stonewalling the general about the autopsy results, and she knew it could not go on much longer. The coroner's report declaring that Nevsky's death had been murder, not a simple accident, would be issued tomorrow—just in time to throw the entire disarmament process into chaos.

Unless Craig could wrap up the investigation before then.

Though Paige tried to maintain her helpful, professional appearance around the inspection team, the State Department had been pestering her, anxious to keep the situation under control; DOE Undersecretary Madeleine Jenkins had been personally calling Paige for updates.

Now, Paige reeled with the news of Jorgenson's death. Although the forklift driver had admitted to dropping the crate on Nevsky, she wondered if he had killed the Russian in the first place, for whatever reason, then tried to cover up the murder as an industrial accident. Though that would have wrapped up the case, she knew Craig didn't believe it was so simple. Jorgenson's heart attack seemed too convenient—and Paige was chilled just thinking about it. Somebody else might have murdered Jorgenson. . . .

After his late night, Craig planned to drive out to the Test Site himself to spend the morning ransacking Nevsky's records at the DAF. While Uncle Mike was at his DOE meeting at the Las Vegas Operations Office, Craig would work with Sally Montry to check part numbers, track down transportation forms and receipts. If anyone could make sense of the morass of forms, Sally could. Meanwhile, Paige was on her own with the Russians.

The group peered down into Sedan Crater. "You planned to use nuclear weapons for civil engineering purposes, did you not?" said Victor Golitsyn, the geologist. "This was a test for that program?"

"Project Plowshare," Paige said, concentrating on her job. As if drawn, she stared into the huge crater herself. "From 1957 until 1974, we considered using nuclear explosives for excavating canals and roadbeds, creating freshwater reservoirs, even making parabolic craters for radio telescopes."

"We too had such plans years ago. Beating swords into plowshares," Ursov muttered. Paige was surprised the Russian general would catch the biblical reference.

"Radiation releases?" asked the redhead, Vitali Yakolev. "How much did it contaminate surrounding area?" He looked meaningfully at the warning signs still posted decades after the blast.

"More than would be acceptable today," she admitted. Paige placed her hands on the new jeans snug against her hips. "At the time, we weren't so careful about containment—nobody was. But public opinion changes. Our Plowshare work faded away in the 1970s. Our citizens are now too sensitive to environmental contamination to allow nuclear blasting."

"Yes, we know Chernobyl too well," Ursov said. "And that was merely a fire. Even out here in desert, a surface blast would spread deadly fallout far and wide."

"That's why we do them underground, General, where they are contained," Paige said, not glancing at the gaping crater's evidence to the contrary.

Bisovka puffed on another one of his Marlboros, then tossed the butt over the crater rim. Everyone watched it tumble, carried on the wind, bouncing along the steep sand. "And how do you ensure there are no leakages from your underground tests?" he said icily. "Accidents happen."

Paige knew about this, not just from her briefings for this protocol assignment, but also because her father had worked on Baneberry—the 1970 test that had been the last significant radioactive release.

"We can't afford accidents," she said. "We make worst-case calculations to guarantee that nobody anywhere would receive anything above negligible radiation levels. The calculations assume a hypothetical person stands naked in a field twenty-four hours a day for a full year—extremely conservative assumptions, I might point out."

"Yes, very conservative," Ursov growled. "Just as it's conservative that you take four days for a simple autopsy. What have you learned about Ambassador Nevsky's death?"

Paige swallowed, taken aback at the abrupt change of subject. "I'm sorry, General. We have been promised the full report by tomorrow."

The general's face turned blotchy. "My team leader is dead, and I need to know what you have learned—or perhaps I should ask your president myself. You are hiding something, I can tell."

Bisovka turned away from the group and lit another Marlboro, seemingly uninterested in the exchange.

"General," she said, drawing upon all her experience and skill to keep her emotions in check, as she tried to turn the tables on him, "if I might ask, is there something you expect us to find in this autopsy? Your request was rather unusual, since the apparent cause of death was so . . . obvious. Do you know something the rest of us don't?"

The other Russians looked at her uneasily, but she kept her gaze locked on Ursov. He was the one who mattered at the moment. Her heart pounded. Was he involved somehow?

"I know why you are stalling us, what you don't want anyone to know." Paige felt her blood freeze, dreading what he might say. Ursov's face seemed ready to slump. "Just tell me if Nevsky was drunk at the time!" His fists clenched and unclenched. "I must know—because if I allowed him to smuggle vodka into the DAF and drink himself into a stupor, then get himself killed—then I am partially to blame."

"It was probably bourbon, not vodka," Bisovka said scornfully, standing away from the others as he smoked.

Paige looked at him, startled, giddy with relief. She had to work hard to keep herself from laughing.

Ursov continued, "I filed repeated formal complaints, but he always loved his drink. I never took it seriously enough. Now Nevsky is dead." Ursov gripped her arm, leaning closer. "Tell me—*was he drunk?* Is that why you are so embarrassed to give me your coroner's report?"

She shook her head emphatically. "No, General. He wasn't drunk. I can tell you that much for certain."

Ursov seemed relieved for a moment, then glanced up, wearing a suspicious look. "Then what else are you hiding from us?"

CHAPTER TWENTY-SIX

Thursday, October 23
8:32 A.M.

Las Vegas

Craig rushed back to his hotel room, intending to stop for only a few minutes before heading out to the Test Site. After picking up some papers in preparation for a long day, he would get to NTS in an hour or so, and stay there all night if he had to. He could get all the sleep he wanted after he had solved the murder.

Already his temples pounded and his skull ached because he had crammed it so full of numbers and forms, reports, and minor memos from the previous day. And with the discovery of Jorgenson's body last night, he felt the tension tightening around him like a vise.

Tomorrow was October 24.

Craig popped in the plastic key and pushed his door open. His room smelled strongly of months-deep layers of cigarette smoke that no amount of air freshener would obliterate.

On the red carpeting he saw a scrap of paper, a white note shoved through the crack under the door. He snatched it up, wondering who wanted him now. Maybe June Atwood had left a message pulling him from the Russian murder investigation after all and sending him off chasing casino fraud or some other equally exciting case.

The note was torn from one of the message pads found

throughout the casino, written in thin lines either from a mechanical pencil or an extremely sharp point, in careful block letters.

AMTRAK MESA ZEPHYR

- CROSSES COLORADO RIVER BRIDGE NEAR LAUGHLIN NV AT 10:56 A.M.
- EAGLE'S CLAW WILL BLOW UP BRIDGE.
- SAVE THOSE PEOPLE!

Craig stared at the paper to convince himself the words said exactly what he thought they did. He wasn't even on the militia case any more—yet someone had known to give him the note, known how to find his hotel room.

Heart pounding, Craig carefully set the scrap of paper on the courtesy table, hoping against hope that it might retain residual fingerprints. Then he looked at his watch, seeing how little time remained before 10:56. He raced for the phone in his room.

Ducking down, holding his sunglasses in place, Craig leaped out of the government car and ran across the airport tarmac. His tie flopped back over his shoulder, his chestnut hair ruffled in the wind. Overhead, a 737 took off from McCarran Field, thundering as it lumbered up from the runway.

Not far away, the FBI helicopter's rotors spun faster as the pilot completed his preflight checklist. Jackson sat in the cockpit, already in position. Over the chattering drone of the helicopter blades, he gestured for Craig to hurry.

"Come on, Ben," Craig shouted to Goldfarb, and the smaller, dark-haired man sprinted beside him, his dress shoes slapping the pavement. Craig scrambled in the back of the helicopter and extended a hand to help Goldfarb up. "Let's move it!" Craig said.

The pilot adjusted his headphones, then requested clearance over the radio. Within seconds, he pulled back on the stick and raised the chopper, fighting thermal updrafts as he headed low and to the south.

"Thanks for getting out here so fast," Craig said, raising his voice so the pilot could hear him. "We couldn't possibly make it in time by car."

"That's what I'm here for," the pilot said. "What's the emergency?"

"Militia threatening to blow up the railroad bridge near Laughlin."

The pilot shook his head. "Again? What is it with these bozos? What are they trying to prove?"

Craig turned to Jackson, who had finished buckling himself in. "Guess you'll have to follow up that lead at Dennisons later. Did you contact Amtrak HQ?" he said. "Pass along the warning?"

"I got bounced up the telephone chain pretty fast," Jackson said. "I spoke to a manager senior enough to halt the train, and he said they'd radio the train operator."

"But did they get through to the engineer?"

"Not while I was on the phone. They thought the train had just left Silverpan, the last stop before crossing the Colorado River, but they were going to keep trying. Sounded like they were having some problem with the radio."

"Terrific," Craig said.

Goldfarb spoke up. "The *Mesa Zephyr* is perennially late, so we might have some leeway."

Craig fidgeted as he looked out the curved Plexiglas window of the helicopter. Beyond the city limits the marks of civilization vanished quickly, leaving only arrow-straight roads across the desert like ancient Inca tracks. "I don't care if the train is an hour late, we've got to make sure it doesn't cross that bridge." He looked at his watch. Twenty-five minutes to go.

"It's going to be tight," the pilot said. "But we've got a tailwind and smooth flying. I won't slow down for any stoplights."

Bleak desert scenery streaked below them, banded with color, wrinkled and furrowed into petrified rivulets like the refuse from some insane potter's kiln. But Craig looked at his watch more than the scenery.

Jackson touched his headset, frowning grimly. He sent an acknowledgment into the microphone, then turned to Craig. "Still no word from the train. The engineer's radio is out of order somehow, though it was working just fine before their last stop."

"More sabotage?" Goldfarb asked. "These guys are pretty thorough."

"How much farther?" Craig said, staring at his watch. "We've got twenty minutes if that thing is set to blow at 10:56."

"We're making good time and following the river," the pilot said. "It shouldn't be too hard to find a railroad track across this desert."

Laughlin, a gambling town by the river, was situated at the bottom-most knifepoint of the state of Nevada, nestled against the Colorado River and Lake Mead. Amtrak's *Mesa Zephyr* was an express train that traveled from Albuquerque to Los Angeles, departing twice daily, carrying a load of passengers and crossing a bridge in a remote desert area north of Laughlin.

As Craig scanned the landscape, he realized that the Colorado River bridge made an excellent target, isolated enough that the Eagle's Claw could set up their explosives in private, and the regular schedule of the train would allow them to stage a disaster that would make the world news.

Jackson squinted ahead out the front. "There it is—see the silver line?" he announced, pointing.

Craig saw only the glare from the sun on his sensitive

eyes. He snugged the sunglasses up closer, blinking, trying to focus. As the sun glinted across the desert, he did make out gleaming parallel tracks. The river flowed below, blue-green with muddy brown edges against the rocky canyons.

He glanced at his watch again. Fifteen minutes. "Come on, come on," he said.

Goldfarb peered out the side window using his pair of pocket binoculars. His face looked ruddy and raw from his exposure to the previous day's roaring fire. "Let's hope the train isn't on time," he said.

"Just our luck that they'll be right on the money today." Craig wiped sweat from his forehead and drummed his fingertips on the seat beside him. The second hand on his watch swept around with astonishing speed, minute after minute. "Even if it isn't, the bridge might be blown right before the train comes in. The engineer might not be able to stop in time."

The helicopter thundered low to the ground. Rocks and scrub streaked by in a nauseating blur. Craig watched the silvery tracks, saw where the arched steel bridge crossed the bottleneck canyon. The sweeping metal arches looked like a portion of the Eiffel Tower laid on its side.

Once, on a Colorado vacation he'd taken with Trish, the two of them had gone out to cross Royal Gorge on the world's highest suspension bridge. He remembered the breathtaking drop into a sheer-edged canyon. Some people practiced hang gliding or parasailing off the bridge. Craig couldn't imagine being that daring . . . or "foolish," Trish had said.

She had refused to walk up to the edge and lean over, instead standing back with her arms crossed, the wind ruffling her short brunette hair. Craig had approached the rail, moving in front of his girlfriend, and she had asked him nervously to step back as he stared down at the incredible height.

At the time he hadn't recognized a chasm equally deep and widening that already separated their lives and their interests. Their relationship of five years had simply not proved strong enough to bridge that gap.

The railroad bridge over the Colorado River was not nearly as spectacular or as breathtaking as the span across Royal Gorge, but this one might soon be the site of a deadly explosion.

Goldfarb adjusted his pocket binoculars. "Here comes the train, right on time. Lucky us."

"Why isn't the engineer stopping?" Craig said.

Jackson leaned into the cockpit window, his voice maddeningly calm. "He's not slowing down at all."

Craig glanced around inside the cockpit. "Give me the loudspeaker mike. If his radio's not working, we'll try to get the engineer's attention some other way."

"Aren't you going to contact Amtrak again?" asked Goldfarb.

"No time. We're going to have to head them off." Craig leaned forward to the pilot. "Fly down the tracks right in front of the train."

The pilot twisted around in his seat and looked at Craig in disbelief. "You want me to play chicken with a train?"

"I want you to play law-enforcement officer," Craig said. He leaned forward, his face flushed, his expression earnest. "When he sees our FBI helicopter, he'll stop. I'm sure he'll stop."

"I'm glad *you're* sure," the pilot said. "That gives me all the confidence I need." He adjusted course so that the helicopter roared down with the tracks beneath him like white lines in the center of a highway.

Directly in front of them they saw the oncoming silver train, its circular white beacon like a cyclopean eye streaking toward them. "Do you think he'll blink first, or should I?" the pilot said, zooming forward on a collision course.

"You've got to be kidding," muttered Goldfarb. "We

wouldn't stand a chance against that train." The curly-haired agent grasped the seat in front of him.

Smoke sizzled up as the train's brakes began to squeal. Craig could see sparks rising from the tracks.

"We've got his attention," Craig said. "Now don't get us killed."

With the slightest upturn of his lips, proving that he actually enjoyed this stunt flying, the pilot swerved to the left at the last instant, like a matador taunting a bull. He circled the helicopter around the train, coming parallel to the engineer's compartment in the front locomotive. The train's brakes continued to squeal as the *Mesa Zephyr* attempted to force an emergency stop before it reached the bridge.

Craig grabbed the loudspeaker microphone and shouted into it. His voice boomed out like a god from Mount Olympus. "This is the FBI. Stop the train immediately. Danger ahead."

The train squealed and shook, shuddering as it slowed. It seemed to take forever. Gray-white smoke boiled from the metal wheels as the brakes fought against the massive momentum. Craig heard a deep, grinding sound even over the incessant chopping of the helicopter blades. On and on the train went as it ground slower and slower, closer to the bridge.

The train finally groaned to a shuddering stop a hundred yards from the high suspended trestles.

"Set us down next to the tracks," Craig said.

The pilot glanced around. "Sure. Plenty of flat space." The skids touched the baked desert floor.

Craig glanced at his watch. "Six minutes to spare." He unbuckled his seat belt and lurched for the helicopter door.

"We'll find out in a few minutes if we've made a big mistake, Craig," Goldfarb said.

"Better safe than sorry."

Goldfarb snorted. "I see you took that course in clichés at Quantico."

"We know the Eagle's Claw isn't much for kidding around," Jackson said.

The three agents tumbled out of the helicopter and ran toward the train. The engineer had already climbed out of the front locomotive, gripping the handbar. He stared across at them, his face florid, his expression a combination of fear and anger.

Craig fished out his ID and badge wallet as he marched toward the train, his shoes crunching in the rough soil. "Federal agent," he announced. "You should have received our warnings about possible sabotage to the bridge ahead, sir. You did not acknowledge our radio transmissions."

The engineer looked flustered, turning to glare at someone unseen in the locomotive compartment with him. "Sabotage? What the hell are you talking about?"

"You didn't get a radio call about a possible bomb on the bridge?"

A fellow engineer walked up, wiping his hands on a towel. "What's this about a bomb? Are you people serious? There wasn't anything over the radio—we just had it checked at Silverpan."

Jackson leaned over and said quietly to Craig, "I think somebody did more than *check* the radio in Silverpan."

"Is there a bomb? Is this for real?" The first engineer had a blond moustache, dark eyes closely set with heavy folds of skin around his eyelids. His skin had a rough texture as if it had been sunburned beyond repair many times.

"We received a threatening message, sir," Craig said. "We felt it best to be cautious."

"Another 'threatening message,' awww jeez! Tenth time in two months. Didn't you read the story about the boy who cried wolf?" the engineer said. "We haven't heard jack from HQ."

Craig looked at his watch. "We'll know in a minute," he

said. "Actually a minute, thirty seconds . . . if my time is right."

"All right," the engineer said, hands on his hips. "But my passengers won't take too kindly to a delay—we were on schedule for once, too."

Goldfarb and Jackson stood on either side of Craig, nervously glancing at their own wristwatches. The helicopter pilot remained in his craft. The rotor blades continued to whirl as he kept the engines powered up and ready for instant departure.

The sunburned engineer turned to his companion. "Use the intercom, Paul. Tell the passengers we'll be on our way momentarily. Sorry for the delay . . . all that crap. Make it sound nice. And call HQ. Find out what the hell is going on. Why didn't we hear anything over the radio?"

Craig didn't speak, but stared at his watch. The second hand swept around the dial. Forty-five seconds. Thirty seconds.

Fifteen seconds.

His heart pounded. His throat grew dry and sweat broke out on his forehead as the mid-morning sun shone down. Around him, he could hear the sounds of the Amtrak train groaning, ticking, making settling noises from its violent and sudden stop. The smell of burned lubricants hung in the air.

Craig couldn't decide whether he wanted the explosion to take place, just to vindicate him for sounding the alarm . . . or for nothing to happen so that the Eagle's Claw would not have any sort of victory. That bridge was an expensive piece of real estate.

Five seconds.

Zero seconds. Time 10:56.

Craig tensed, looked across the span of the railroad bridge. The second hand continued around his watch dial. He waited, then looked up at Jackson and Goldfarb.

"Maybe the militia group didn't set their watches right," Goldfarb said.

They waited another thirty seconds. The engineer stood beside his train, wearing a bored look on his florid face. He stared down the length of silver cars, looking ready to explode even if the bomb didn't. "Surprise, surprise, surprise," the engineer grumbled. "Another false alarm."

Jackson said it first. "Might have been a hoax after all, Craig."

"Guess we got lucky today," Goldfarb said. "But why didn't this train get any message from Amtrak?"

Both of the other agents looked to Craig for his admission of failure. Craig knew his expression could not be read behind his sunglasses. But all he could think of was the note he had found in his hotel room. Someone had put it there specifically, maliciously. For him. He could not believe it was a mere accident or a prank.

In order to find out his hotel room, *his* room, the whistleblower had to know that he, Craig Kreident, had been personally connected with the Hoover Dam investigation. That took more than the bluster of an anonymous phone call to a newspaper or a radio station.

He himself had been a specific target. Had somebody meant to discredit him personally? Yet another in their series of crying wolf?

The engineer looked at his watch. "How much longer will this take? Do you really think there's anything to this? We're on a timetable, you know."

Craig looked up, took a deep breath—and suddenly froze. "The *Mesa Zephyr* had a habit of missing its schedule, right?" He whirled to look at Jackson and Goldfarb. "If the Eagle's Claw wanted to blow up this bridge with the train on it, and this train never manages to be on time, they wouldn't bother to set a timed explosive, would they?"

Jackson scratched his cheek. "Not if they were trying to catch it that closely."

"The only way they could make sure they got the train and all the people on board," Craig said, his words picking up speed as he paced next to the locomotive, "would be to station a man in view, probably hidden in the canyon wall! He could be watching, ready to push the button. And if that's the case—*the man must still be there!*"

Craig, Jackson, and Goldfarb all sprinted down the tracks toward the railroad bridge.

CHAPTER TWENTY-SEVEN

Thursday, October 23
10:03 A.M.

Nevada Test Site

As Paige drove the van back from Sedan Crater, her cellular phone rang shrilly at her side. She excused herself from polite conversation with the Russians and used her thumb to punch the RECEIVE button.

She recognized the crisp, reedy voice of Dr. Adams, the Nye County ME who had discovered Nevsky had been murdered and who had promised his final report on the autopsy no later than today. "Ms. Mitchell, could you come down to the Medical Examiner's office as soon as possible? I have disturbing news, and I think we should discuss this in person."

She immediately became wary, knowing the Russians would be eavesdropping. "Certainly, sir. I'll get there as soon as possible," she said, not asking for additional details.

"You might want to bring your FBI friend, too."

She felt suddenly cold. Had he found something else about Nevsky? Something must be terribly wrong. "I'll try to get in touch with him. Can I ask what this is regarding?"

"It concerns some . . . unexpected results he asked me to check," Adams said evasively. "Have a pleasant drive."

Paige returned the phone to her side as she felt eyes boring into her as conversation faded. She looked over to see

Ursov staring at her expectantly. "A message from your coroner, Ms. Mitchell? Can we finally have the analysis of Ambassador Nevsky's death? Or has someone else suffered an unpleasant accident?"

Paige turned to face the Russian general, unwilling to let him bully her. "I promised you that report as soon as it's available, General."

"My government is getting extremely impatient," Ursov said. "Our scheduled inspection activities end tomorrow, and I must submit a final briefing upon our return to Moscow. It will look very bad for the summit meeting if we must end our mission with such difficulties."

Nikolai Bisovka spoke tightly, leaning back and holding an unlit cigarette between his fingers. "This reminds me of times before fall of former Soviet Union." She found his supercilious tone highly annoying. "Or, as some say, back in the good old days."

Paige pulled the government pickup into the Nye County offices. The main civic building was a two-story stucco structure set off from the street, as if the city wanted to hide its administrative functions from Main Street traffic.

Uncle Mike dislodged his gangly legs from the front of the pickup, swinging down. Since Craig had been whisked off on some sort of emergency call, Paige had decided to take the DAF Manager along instead, since this concerned him as well. Mike ran a hand through his thinning hair. "I bet you miss your MG sports car back in Livermore," he said.

She smiled warmly at him. "Oh, a red convertible or a big ugly government pickup—gee, I hardly notice the difference."

The county administration building was a cool relief from the noon sun. A building directory stood near an indoor planter of prickly pear cactus that extended along the wall.

Somewhere in back a fountain splashed. Running her finger down the list, Paige saw what she needed. Room 127, third door down.

As they walked along the hall, Uncle Mike spoke quietly, as if afraid his voice would echo throughout the building. "Did the ME give you any hint of what he learned about Nevsky when he called this morning?"

Paige rapped on the door of Room 127. "He only said he wanted Craig to be present. I didn't ask any questions, since our friend General Ursov was listening in."

The heavy door swung open, pushed by a policeman dressed in a short-sleeved black uniform. Another policeman stood inside with two men in white lab coats and another man in a suit.

"Ah, Miss Mitchell?" A short, angular man wearing a white lab coat looked up from a table, putting down a clipboard. "Please come in." His reedy voice seemed very loud in the room. Dr. Adams made quick introductions of his staff.

"Mr. Waterloo is the Device Assembly Facility manager," Paige said. "Is this about releasing the report on Ambassador Nevsky's death?"

Adams looked taken back. "The Russian? I'm sorry, Miss Mitchell—we're waiting for the State Department to clear our final report. I'm glad Mr. Waterloo came along, though, since he's the NTS representative. We've completed a preliminary chemistry analysis on Mr. Carl Jorgenson, and that's why these officers are here. Thanks to a suggestion from Agent Kreident, we checked for a certain drug known to cause cardiac arrest. Usually fatal in a large enough dose."

Paige and Uncle Mike both looked at each other.

Adams raised his eyebrows. "You see, Jorgenson's death was not accidental—far from it. He may have caused the death himself by ingesting this drug, or it could have been murder. It's not my place to make that determination."

Uncle Mike's expression sickened, his skin tone turned grayish. "Why would Agent Kreident ask you to check for that specific drug? Why did he suspect Jorgenson might have . . . not died from natural causes?"

The coroner looked at the police detective, then at his lab assistant. "Because an FBI undercover agent connected to this case was murdered in the same fashion. According to my counterpart in the Clark County Medical Examiner's office, the chemicals are identical."

Alarmed, Uncle Mike looked at Paige. "Clark County? An agent connected to this case? What are you talking about? I thought Mr. Kreident was just investigating an accident in the DAF."

"That death wasn't an accident either, Mr. Waterloo," the coroner said.

Uncle Mike reeled, and when Paige looked at him, she felt her cheeks burning. "I had to keep it from you for the past few days, Uncle Mike. We know that Ambassador Nevsky was dead for half an hour before the crate crushed his body," she said. "He was murdered, and Jorgenson must have been involved somehow. Now we know Jorgenson's been murdered, too."

Uncle Mike looked from one person to another in the sterile room, speechless in his surprise. He looked down at the floor, shaking his head. "Carl—*murdered*? It doesn't make sense. There was no reason for this to happen."

Paige slipped an arm around the older man's waist, knowing how much he had been through. "There's no reason for any of it."

Uncle Mike opened his mouth as if to say something, but all he could do was to shake his head.

CHAPTER TWENTY-EIGHT

Thursday, October 23
11:01 A.M.

Colorado River Bridge
Near Laughlin, Nevada

Running along the railroad tracks on the baked hardpan, Craig approached the edge of the Colorado River gorge. He could smell the creosote-covered railroad ties, the metallic tang of the hot sun glinting off the steel rails.

Goldfarb and Jackson followed close, approaching with all senses alert. Goldfarb kept his gaze down, studying the railroad tracks as if looking for a land mine or some sort of tripwire. After triggering the incendiaries that had set Connors's house on fire, he seemed overly conscious of booby traps.

Craig stood at the top, staring along the rim of the gorge and seeing numerous cracks and shadows where a person could hide. The canyon walls dropped off like a knife edge, but the erosion had left a steep but terraced slope to the winding, sluggish river below.

Jackson put a hand on his shoulder, startling him. "Keep down, Craig. You make too good a target up here."

Realizing that he stood silhouetted and exposed for any hidden sniper, he crouched quickly. Momentarily angry at himself, he tried to calm down. He had too many things on his mind but couldn't afford to slip up on the basics. Staying low, he continued to scan the patchwork of shadows along the multicolored rocks. "Goldfarb, you have those field glasses?"

"Remember they're only five power," the other agent said. He reached into his jacket pocket and withdrew a small pair of pocket binoculars.

In a careful search pattern, Craig worked his gaze back and forth down the cliff, starting just under the railroad bridge and moving out, scanning for any movement, any sign of tampering, or a human figure.

In the desert behind them, the motionless Amtrak train hissed and creaked as it baked in the mid-morning heat. The passengers would be angry, or panicked, or confused. But he focused his entire attention on the cliff itself, on the bridge, on the framework of girders, on the attachment points and support pilings. He then scanned across the chasm.

He saw nothing. He felt a terrible fear that he might be wrong again. If the mysterious whistle-blower had meant only to discredit Craig, he seemed to be doing a good job.

The other two agents squatted beside him, shading their eyes and squinting. Craig pressed the small binoculars against his sunglasses, then finally removed his dark lenses to stare through the field glasses directly, trying to focus in the glare.

After five minutes of silence, Goldfarb finally cleared his throat and stood into a half crouch. "Uh, what do you think? Maybe they were just trying to distract us so we couldn't spend time on the real investigation."

But Craig kept scanning, moving his field of view farther from the bridge—knowing that if a member of the Eagle's Claw had intended to sit here and trigger the explosive, he would have taken shelter some distance from the bridge, not right under it.

Then Craig saw the man, a silhouette crouching between two large boulders about a hundred yards away from the bridge and halfway down the canyon wall. He sat hunched over like a predator, not moving—a spider waiting for the fly to come just an inch closer. . . .

Craig stood up and drew his handgun. The Beretta felt cold to his grip.

"Where?" Jackson whispered, still crouching. Craig pointed, and both other agents saw the militiaman in the place where he attempted to keep an eye on what was going on above. The silhouette froze, as if he couldn't believe he had been spotted, and then he ducked back behind the boulder.

Goldfarb and Jackson both drew their weapons. "We can box him in," Jackson said. "Just like a Quantico exercise."

The militiaman scrambled away behind the boulders, working his way down the rugged terraced wall toward the river at the bottom of the canyon, hoping to get away unseen.

"Well, so much for simple solutions," Jackson said.

"My shin still hurts from yesterday, and I wish I'd brought my rock boots," Goldfarb muttered. "How are your climbing skills, Craig?"

"Certified by the FBI," Craig said and picked his way down the steep slope. He tried to divide his attention equally between watching the fleeing suspect, keeping his gun ready, and maintaining his footing on the rough rock wall.

"He's coming to the right," Jackson said, "working back toward the bridge."

"I don't know where he thinks he's going to go," Goldfarb said, then gasped as his foot slipped. Rocks broke, pattering on other boulders along the cliffside in a hard rain.

"Keep steady," Jackson said, grabbing his partner's arm. "It's going to be tough scraping you off the bottom and catching the bad guy at the same time."

"Gee, thanks," Goldfarb said. "Just don't let him get away."

"I don't see any direct path over there," Craig said. "Let's split up, come at him from three sides."

Then a thin gunshot rang out like a tiny firecracker. A rock near Craig's head burst into a spray of fragments. Two more shots echoed as the three FBI agents scrambled for cover.

"Why can't anyone just surrender?" Goldfarb muttered.

"He's trying to distract us," Jackson called.

"Okay, I'm distracted," Goldfarb said, ducking.

Craig peered around his meager shelter and saw a wiry man clad in military camouflage nimbly moving along a path that would have made a mountain goat nervous.

Jackson steadied his own handgun and fired carefully, striking the rocks above and to the right of the fleeing suspect. The militiaman ducked and bent low, grasping for cover.

"That should slow him down," Jackson said.

Craig gestured for Goldfarb to continue the direct pursuit, while he himself cut straight across the top, heading toward the bridge girders. He only hoped he could find some way down once he reached the terrorist's position.

The terrorist tried to move; Jackson fired twice more, keeping the camouflaged man under cover.

Craig made good progress, finding a narrow ledge where he could pick up speed, so long as he didn't look down the steep side to the muddy river far below.

The rocks became larger, jutting up in shards of red, brown, and tan as he approached where the bridge clung to the sides of the gorge. Craig stumbled upon a narrow fissure that allowed him to work his way straight down toward the crouching militiaman. He could see the figure taking shelter below him as Goldfarb and Jackson both fired harassing shots to keep the wiry man down.

"Federal agents," Jackson bellowed. "You must surrender, sir. Throw down your weapon."

As Craig approached as quietly as he could, a ricochet from one of Jackson's shots spanged close to his own foot. Craig froze, feeling a wash of cold sweat, but he did not dare shout for his partners to be careful. The militiaman did not seem aware of his approach.

"Hey, you heard the man!" Goldfarb shouted. "Throw down your weapon—now." He continued more quietly. "We've got a good look at your face, you idiot. Why don't you just give up and save us all a lot of time? You wouldn't believe my list of things to do today."

The militiaman popped out from behind his large rock and fired two shots toward Goldfarb. He and Jackson scrambled out of the way from the ricochets—and then Craig leaped down the last few feet, his Beretta drawn. He landed firmly, handgun aimed squarely at the man's torso as the terrorist swiveled around.

The world slowed, and Craig tensed, ready to shoot—but the militiaman thought just as quickly, recognized the weapon in Craig's hand, saw the FBI agent's readiness to fire.

"If you're a smart guy, you'll know you don't have a chance in hell," Craig said quietly.

The militiaman paused for a moment, half turned toward Craig, his own gun pointing toward the opposite canyon wall. He became a statue. Craig saw a young man, short sandy blond hair, freckled cheeks, pale blue eyes. His demeanor bespoke feral meanness, an utterly solid conviction—but Craig did not think the man was willing to die at the moment. The suicidal bomber at Hoover Dam had risked everything to keep his explosives from being discovered, but this terrorist had no such hope. His plan had already been foiled.

"It would be a good idea for you to drop your weapon," Craig said, keeping his Beretta steady, his eyes locked. "A very good idea."

Craig saw the gun waver in the militiaman's hands, saw his arm drop slightly, his fingers loosen around the trigger guard. The handgun dropped to the dirt, a military-issue sidearm . . . but Craig saw absolutely no surrender in the man's eyes. As the weapon dropped, clanking on the rocky ground, the militiaman moved his other hand—and suddenly Craig noticed the small box he held.

A detonator box.

The man pushed the button just as Craig launched himself forward. "No!"

Explosives planted beneath the support girders of the bridge detonated, blasting rock and steel. A plume of fire and debris erupted into the sky.

Craig ducked, covering his head and protecting his eyes as metal shrapnel flew all around him. Sand, then gravel pelted him. Rocks struck around him, tumbling toward the distant water in a building avalanche. Boulders sloughed down the canyon wall, picking up speed and bouncing. The reverberating echoes deafened him as the thunder continued.

Groaning and grinding, the bridge began to fall, heavy steel girders shrieking, twisting, dragged down by gravity.

As the boulders began to slide and Craig clung desperately to his own precarious balance, the blond militiaman dove away, recklessly tumbling down the terraced wall of the gorge, skidding away toward the river as part of the avalanche.

Craig scrabbled for cover and balance, trying to keep his head clear. He dropped his pistol but didn't bother to grab for it as the ground shifted beneath his feet. More rocks fell. A chunk of granite the size of a Volkswagen careened beside him and hurtled into the roiling, muddy water with a huge splash as if a depth charge had gone off in the river.

The militiaman disappeared in the debris as the bridge continued to fall, one section after another torn from its moorings. Rivets and tie-downs ripped from their sockets; steel girders twisted. Railroad pilings tumbled like spent firecrackers down into the canyon.

Craig found a sturdy shelf of rock, grabbed it, and held on. Dust sprayed into the air. He coughed, unable to see.

The bridge finally ceased its chain reaction of destruction, hanging limp in the middle of the canyon, dangling with torn stumps of girders. Thunderheads of smoke boiled all around.

His pulse pounding, his vision ragged, his sunglasses scored and scratched, Craig gradually came back to his senses. Shaking himself, he toiled upward to reach the top of the canyon wall. He glanced frantically from side to side, searching for his two partners. "Ben!" he croaked. "Jackson!"

Up above, the Amtrak engineer and the helicopter pilot stood at the rim, awestruck, amazed to see Craig emerging from the debris. The pilot reached down to help him up, while the engineer stood with his mouth opening and closing like a stranded fish.

"Where are . . . the other two?" Craig panted, brushing himself off. The dust clung to his clothes, his skin. He flicked blood from his cheek where a sharp rock fragment had scratched him.

"They're on their way up," the helicopter pilot said. "There! I see them."

The engineer shook his head as if to clear cobwebs from his brain. "Didn't see where that other guy went," he said. "I think he's down in the river."

Jackson came up, supporting Goldfarb by the elbow. The curly-haired agent held out his left hand, which dripped blood. "Injury in the line of duty. My little finger's broken in two places, I think." He winced, then sighed. "Suspect blows up a railroad bridge, and I get my pinkie broken. Imagine how that's going to look on our report!"

Craig stood, trying to keep himself from degenerating into shakes after the disaster. At least he had managed to keep the train and its passengers from being destroyed. For what it was worth.

He thought of the bombs planted at Hoover Dam, and now this explosion—and it wasn't even the deadline given by the Eagle's Claw! He swallowed hard and looked down to the churning Colorado River as the remnants of smoke and debris continued to settle.

"What are they going to do for an encore tomorrow?" he said, panting.

CHAPTER TWENTY-NINE

Thursday, October 23
2:04 P.M.

Nevada Test Site
DAF Helicopter Pad

Feeling as if he had been run over by a truck, Craig climbed stiffly out of the FBI helicopter as it bumped to a landing at the pad two miles from the DAF. After barely surviving an avalanche, even looking at piles of Nevsky's papers sounded enjoyable.

Pushing his scratched sunglasses back into place, more out of habit than because they did any good, Craig carried his jacket over his arm. His shoulder holster slapped against his side as he jogged painfully away from the helicopter. Though he'd cleaned himself off, he hadn't the luxury of a shower, or a change of clothes, or a decent lunch. Three aspirins and a cup of lukewarm tap water had been all he could manage, and now it was time to get back to work.

He spotted Paige standing by her white pickup, waving to him. He called out, but the FBI helicopter drowned out his words as it took off behind him, slowly rotated, and tipped its nose. The pilot streaked back for Las Vegas.

Paige had already contacted him about the coroner's report on Jorgenson, and he had told her about the bridge explosion. He wondered if all potential couples had such charming conversations. . . . Now Craig had another murder to investigate, one day left to wrap up the Nevsky case before the Russian delegation went critical, and a ticking clock on the Eagle's Claw threat for the following day.

However, the scenario had changed dramatically because of one little detail—since Jorgenson had been murdered with the same obscure drug that had killed Bill Maguire, Craig knew for certain Nevsky's death was connected with the Eagle's Claw. Somehow.

Without a moment to recuperate or gather their thoughts, Goldfarb and Jackson had obtained their search warrant after the pilot dropped them off at the Las Vegas airport. After a quick stop by the hospital to take care of Goldfarb's finger they raced out to Jorgenson's house trailer, hoping to find other evidence (without burning the place down this time), while Craig came to concentrate on the paperwork at the DAF.

He trotted toward Paige's truck, feeling his adrenaline running low. But he didn't have time to rest. He had already lost half a day of his own investigation because of the Amtrak explosion, as had Goldfarb and Jackson. Could that be what the Eagle's Claw had intended? He had to be in five places at once, with a dozen leads—every one of which seemed to go in opposite directions . . . and if none of them could make sense of the mess within twenty-four hours, a lot of people could die.

Craig touched the stinging cut on his cheek as he approached Paige. "Thanks for the ride. I was afraid Waterloo was going to send his moat dragon to pick me up."

Paige laughed, arching her eyebrows. "Between Sally and Maggie the Mind Reader, I thought you were getting the hots for older women."

Craig groaned and put his head back on the headrest, closing his eyes as she shifted into gear. "If Sally helps me figure out all that paperwork, I'll give her a big kiss. We've got to make sense of what Nevsky could have been looking for, and why the militia wanted to kill him."

With the tires humming beneath the truck, Paige gave him a few moments of blessed quiet, which worked wonders. He hadn't realized it, but when he and Trish were together he'd always felt drained afterward. She needed constant conversation, emotional contact, sharing every thought. At least he and Paige could sit in comfortable silence.

Craig sat up straighter. "Maybe we'd better go over a few things. We already knew the Eagle's Claw was connected with NTS, and now we can be sure the militia even had connections inside the DAF itself. But somebody wanted to make sure we never got a chance to talk to Jorgenson."

"PK Dirks?" asked Paige while looking straight ahead at the road.

"I've always thought the timing of that fling he had with Sally was a little too convenient," Craig said. "He might have used it to obtain an alibi. Maybe he set Nevsky up, left him alone to tempt him into snooping around." He thought for a moment. "But you've already gone through his file?"

"Nothing suspicious. Average performance, some commendations, some complaints. Not a star player, but not a nuisance either."

"Of course, I'd be more suspicious if the guy seemed *too* clean," said Craig. He tried to fidget, but his body hurt too much. "Let's see what Goldfarb and Jackson turn up when they comb through Jorgenson's place."

Paige drove to the DAF security post. "Meanwhile, you and I have the easy task—a couple tons of paperwork to wade through in one afternoon."

CHAPTER THIRTY

Thursday, October 23
2:43 P.M.

Jorgenson's Home
Pahrump, Nevada

"How did Craig ever find this place in the dark?" said Goldfarb from the passenger seat as Jackson turned off at Antelope Trail. "It's a wonder the place hasn't been condemned."

The rental car bounced on the ruts in the dirt driveway, and Goldfarb winced, cradling his newly bandaged hand. The broken little finger seemed more a wound to his pride than a serious injury.

"People out here like to do things their own way, I suppose," Jackson replied, pulling the car to a stop. A Nye County Sheriff's car was already parked in front of the trailer. "Looks like we've got company."

"I'm glad somebody's on the ball. We were a bit late picking up our own search warrant." He climbed out of the car, frowning at the dilapidated fence, the clutter in the yard, the run-down appearance of the homestead. "I can't believe Craig came out here alone at night, especially after what happened to us at Connors's house."

Jackson slammed his car door, carefully stuffing the keys in his pocket. "At the time Craig had no reason to suspect the militia was involved in his murder case."

Goldfarb shaded his eyes to stare at the makeshift firing range in Jorgenson's back yard. "The guy was a serious sportsman. From the looks of the holes in those targets, he used bigger ammunition than .22 caliber. What do you want to bet we'll find some automatic weapon cartridges?"

"I don't bet," Jackson said, standing next to the shorter agent. "Especially in Las Vegas."

They walked up to the trailer entrance, which had been draped with yellow POLICE LINE tape. Goldfarb straightened his tie, scanning the area. Jackson strolled around back, studying the exterior of the trailer.

Goldfarb knocked at the half-open front door and called loudly. "Hello? This is the FBI, with a search warrant. Anybody home?" He didn't want to surprise the local law enforcement officers, especially if they were the "Ready, Fire, Aim" type.

After an uncomfortably long pause, a muffled voice came from inside. "In back. Come on in—just don't touch anything."

Goldfarb stepped inside and peered around in disgust at Jorgenson's sloppy quarters. Of course, he himself had been a bachelor once, but Julene had cured him of those habits. In the cramped living room, magazines lay strewn on the floor next to an easy chair—*Soldier of Fortune* lay on top. A bowl of pretzels sat in the kitchen, a pile of dirty clothes thrown next to an empty laundry basket with one white sock dangling over the top. The odor of disinfectant filled the trailer.

"Back here," came a man's voice down the hallway. It sounded familiar somehow. . . .

Hanging from the walls were pictures of men standing in groups, around a table at a restaurant, in front of an NTS drilling bit as big as a house. As Goldfarb glanced at the photos, he noticed no family pictures, no children, no women, no parents, not even a photo of Carl Jorgenson himself.

The bathroom door stood halfway open. The naked lightbulb splashed yellow-white light on the linoleum, where Craig had found the forklift driver's body late last night. Goldfarb slipped his badge from his jacket and rapped lightly on the door. "Hello? Are you the sheriff? I'm Ben Goldfarb, FBI."

"Agent Goldfarb—how ya doing?" A gruff voice came from behind the door, and the smell of disinfectant came strongly from the tiny room. Was the guy cleaning the toilet with a toothbrush? "Anyone else out there besides you?"

"What's going on?" Goldfarb pushed against the door, but the sheriff must have been standing right behind it. "You shouldn't be altering a possible crime scene—"

A sharp click echoed down the hall, the unmistakable sound of a cartridge being chambered in a rifle. Goldfarb whirled to see a long steel barrel poking out of the single bedroom down the hall.

His system instantly went into overdrive. He slammed forward into the bathroom door while reaching under his jacket for his shoulder harness. "Jackson—they're armed!"

He heard an "oof" from within the cramped bathroom as he drove the door into the man inside. A crack of gunfire erupted down the hall; a bullet splintered the flimsy paneling of the trailer walls.

Goldfarb tried to push his way into the meager shelter of the bathroom, trapping the other man inside. The door smashed the stranger between the sink and the wall. The trapped man cried out in pain.

"Drop your weapons! Federal agents!" Jackson yelled from the trailer's cluttered living room as he charged through the screen patio door. A spray of bullets thudded against the far trailer wall as Jackson dashed back outside to cover.

Pressing his only advantage, Goldfarb kept pushing against the door, grinding the other man inside as he tried to squeeze himself out of the line of fire. His feet slipped on the bathroom linoleum, but he was partially inside, hidden from the sniper in the bedroom.

He heard the sound of glass breaking from down the hall, then a crash and more gunshots. Jackson's voice was loud but in cool control. "Drop it, now! You heard me—surrender your weapon!" He must have run around the side of the old trailer and broken the sliding glass door into the bedroom.

The shooting stopped, but the man Goldfarb had trapped still struggled to get free, spewing a string of curses laced with anger and pain. Goldfarb finally got his head inside the door to peer down at a broad-shouldered man with close-cropped dark hair and a swarthy complexion, showing the heavy shadow of beard stubble.

"Why, Mr. Bryce Connors! How good it is to see you again!" Goldfarb smiled. "I see you've given up hanging out in libraries to take up a new career as a house cleaner."

Using his weight, Goldfarb smashed against the bathroom door, jamming Connors inside against the sink and wall. "Oww! You're breaking my ribs!"

Jamming his handgun into the back of his prisoner, Jackson marched out of the bedroom. The sniper was a thin, leather-faced man with a crewcut. He wore the outfit of a deputy sheriff. His eyes were small, dark, and darting in panic.

As Jackson and the sniper clumped down the hallway, their heavy shoes caused the flimsy trailer to reverberate. "You all right?" Jackson asked Goldfarb, looking from side to side.

"I'm just dandy," he said. "I believe the other prisoner's secure. I'd like you to meet Mr. Connors, up close and personal."

He drew his handgun from the shoulder holster and squeezed into the tiny bathroom. But Connors crumpled over in pain and nausea, caught between the sink and the bathroom door, where a corner of the vanity had pushed into his testicles. His face had been pressed, as though in a vise, against the medicine cabinet that jutted from the wall. His can of disinfectant spray lay next to three blue rags on the floor. The place had been thoroughly scrubbed—not only of dirt, but of fingerprints, bloodstains, or any other evidence.

"Looks like somebody's been doing a cleanup job," Jackson said, still keeping his weapon on the dark-haired gunman.

"Not the kind of work I'd expect a deputy to be doing at a crime scene," Goldfarb said. "We'd better get the sheriff on the line."

When Goldfarb released the door, Bryce Connors slumped to the linoleum floor. He closed his eyes as his face contorted in a grimace. He cradled his genitals, but offered no resistance as Goldfarb cuffed him. Then, while Jackson held the handgun on the sniper, Goldfarb put handcuffs on the man in the deputy's uniform.

Goldfarb pulled a wallet from the man's back pocket. "Deputy Sheriff Mahon. Hey, Jackson, I bet if you look closely enough, you'll spot his ugly mug in one of Jorgenson's photos on the wall."

Jackson turned the sniper around. "Let's make a phone call. The real sheriff should be interested to know one of his deputies is engaged in extracurricular activities."

With the two handcuffed men lying on the living room floor, Goldfarb frisked them for other identification. Unfortunately, from his tense conversation with Bryce Connors yesterday, Goldfarb suspected that the militia bomber did not know exactly what the Eagle's Claw intended to do on October 24. But he supposed they would enjoy interrogating him anyway.

Jackson came down the hall, where he had found a box of

materials the sniper had been trying to remove from behind a false wall in the bedroom closet. “Look at this.”

Goldfarb glanced at one of the self-published pamphlets, all bearing the image of an eagle with an upraised claw. “Don’t you just hate junk mail?”

CHAPTER THIRTY-ONE

Thursday, October 23
3:12 P.M.

Device Assembly Facility
Nevada Test Site

After Goldfarb and Jackson telephoned him about the arrests at Jorgenson's trailer, Craig tried to get his mind into the dizzying paperwork Nevsky had left behind—but now the problem had been magnified immensely.

Although Bryce Connors had been involved in the Hoover Dam threat and had burned down his own home to destroy evidence, the Eagle's Claw kept its members isolated in individual cells. Neither Connors nor Mahon seemed to know many details about the "main event" set for the following day.

And that made Craig even more nervous—the threat must be something spectacularly destructive indeed. If June Atwood wasn't pushing so hard for the President to keep his schedule, he'd recommend calling it off.

And why had Ambassador Nevsky been murdered in the first place, even before the Hoover Dam incident? What did the militia have to gain by the Russian's death? *What had he found?*

Perhaps Nevsky had stumbled onto something related to their plans for the UN anniversary. Jorgenson had needed to silence the Russian before he could sound the alarm, and now someone had silenced Jorgenson as well. Had the forklift driver and PK Dirks killed the ambassador together, then staged the accident? That still left Dirks. . . .

It was late afternoon already; Craig had lost most of a day down at the railroad bridge. He had to gamble that the bearded technician was involved, because that gave him a chance to put the pieces together . . . if he could just figure out *what* Nevsky might have seen.

And that answer lay buried somewhere in these papers.

For the past hour he had studied logbook after logbook, looking for some connection. Sally Montry kept track of his work, answering questions, making photocopies, bringing him a cold soda when he asked for it.

Paige sat beside him, her eyes red from too little sleep and too much migraine-causing concentration on the complex accountability forms. "I never thought I'd prefer spending time with General Ursov to *anything,* but I'm beginning to wonder."

As he sat staring at the mess of forms, logbooks, and accountability sheets, Paige handed him a new report. "You might find this interesting."

Craig studied the paper, saw the stamped words CLOSE HOLD. He scanned the sheet. "An old background dossier on PK Dirks? I thought you already checked him out."

"This time I dug all the way back in his files, not just from his last security reinvestigation. These background checks go pretty deep, especially for anyone with hands-on responsibility for nuclear weapons. Still clean as a whistle, though. You'd think *something* about the militia would show up."

Around them the DAF high bay hummed and echoed with intercom announcements and growling forklift engines. Two technicians lounged by the side of a two-story concrete wall; a worker pushed a metal cart into one of the small vaults. Craig lowered his voice. "Unless the people who interviewed them are also mixed up in the militia."

Paige raised her eyebrows. "You're starting to sound paranoid."

Craig shook his head. "It's not paranoia if you have good reason to suspect something. We've already got the deaths of an FBI undercover man, a Russian ambassador, and a DAF forklift driver, and the suicide of another NTS contractor—not to mention the arrests of a Hoover Dam worker and a deputy sheriff." He glanced at his watch. "With the President showing up in less than twenty-four hours, I'd say I'm entitled to a little paranoia."

Attempting some method of organization, Paige started stacking Nevsky's papers into piles. She drew a long, deep breath, then scanned the top sheet of one pile before moving to the next.

Craig picked up a stack of sheets bearing a series of arrows and serial numbers, seemingly a timeline for warhead dismantling. It showed delivery dates for various components, manufacturing sites, cross-correlated code numbers, reliability figures, and shipping destinations. "Remember that old saying—if you can't give them the facts, baffle them with paperwork?" he said with a laugh. "I'm certainly baffled."

He stepped over to the wall where a poster showed the schematic of a generic nuclear weapon. The drawing had been declassified for the disarmament team, the words SECRET CRITICAL NUCLEAR WEAPONS DESIGN INFORMATION scratched out on the red borders. Using the poster as a road map, Craig started checking the entries on the dismantlement timeline. He followed each component beginning with its removal from the actual warhead to its final delivery site for storage. He traced each part, taking care to ensure full accountability.

One page after another, Craig tracked the destruction of obsolete stockpile weapons. Some parts were shipped to the Pantex plant in Texas, back east to Oak Ridge in Tennessee, to Hanford up in Washington state, or to Savannah River in Georgia.

As far as Craig could tell, the inventory was correctly logged out, each verified by three different levels of authority, approved by the three signatures Waterloo had promised. But the corresponding pieces rarely went to the same places—and never more than one piece per warhead.

Rubbing his eyes, he picked up a paper that held his notes. "Why can't DOE follow normal accounting procedures? Is it just meant to be confusing?"

Paige set aside a stack of accountability forms. "The dismantling procedures are clearly defined—we've been doing it this way for years. Everything's detailed by treaty as well."

Craig handed her items from the stack of forms. "Look. Most of these components were 'administratively destroyed'—that is, not physically taken apart, but spread to the four winds. And they're always one number off the inventory schedule. Like these Permissive Action Links—they were transferred from Sandia Albuquerque to Rocky Flats and then to Oak Ridge. But for some reason, *one* PAL was transferred to Pantex instead. Only one."

Craig shuffled to another sheet of paper. Paige pulled her blond hair back as she leaned over the paper to see. "And over here, the PAL is recorded in a different column. The *total* seems to work out right, but only if you add up all the other columns. Or here—a listing of the plutonium pits from a series of dismantled warheads. Every one is still here at the DAF—except for *one,* and that one was shipped off to Oak Ridge in Tennessee."

"Oak Ridge? They're authorized to receive nuclear components, but why would NTS do that?" Frowning, Paige followed the entry across the page with a finger. "Oak Ridge isn't actively assembling—" She studied the inventory pages again.

Craig tossed the sheets down on the desk. "They don't even pull separate components off the same warhead." A gnawing worry grew at the back of his mind. "Unless . . ." He tapped a finger on the desk, fidgeting more furiously than usual.

He looked at the declassified poster that showed a cutaway of a nuclear weapon. It listed all components the inspectors would have verified. He started checking off items: PAL, pit, explosives, timer, initiators. . . . Craig frowned. "Paige, grab that sheet and start reading off the oddball components I marked, the ones not shipped with the majority of pieces."

Raising her eyebrows, but not questioning his reasons, Paige started reading. "Casing."

"Got it. Next." He made a checkmark on the poster.

"Initiator."

"Okay, go ahead."

"Explosive lenses . . ."

"Check."

After thirty-four items, Craig stopped her. "Good God, look at this. Every item I've marked is different." He sucked in a cold breath. "And it adds up to an entire weapon."

Paige studied the poster, and her face turned pale. "This can't happen."

"Enough parts have been diverted to build a separate nuclear warhead!" A tune ran through Craig's head, an old Johnny Cash song, "One Piece at a Time," in which the singer had cobbled together an automobile from parts smuggled off the assembly line over many years, one piece at a time.

Given the knowledge and all the right pieces, could the Eagle's Claw have assembled a functional thermonuclear weapon?

"Craig, building a warhead is more complex than slapping parts together in an Erector set," Paige said cautiously.

Sweat sparkled on her forehead, though, and she breathed heavily. "It's impossible to put these things together without a huge technical support cast and precision equipment to handle the radioactive parts. The tolerances are extreme."

He pressed his lips together and studied the poster on the wall. There were hundreds of components still left to be marked, and yards of paperwork to wade through. "Okay then, let's go back to square one. Ambassador Nevsky was an expert in the subject, not just bumbling investigators like us. Maybe he came to the same conclusion."

"And Jorgenson killed him for it, since we know *he* was involved in the militia plot from what your partners found at his trailer," Paige said slowly. She looked up from her accounting sheet.

Craig moved back to where Paige still sat perched on the desk. "What did your Uncle Mike say—that each time any component of a nuke is moved, it requires three signatures for verification? Then why go to all this trouble to divert various parts? If they could get the required signatures, why not just move the whole warhead itself? It would be a lot easier."

Paige blinked in surprise and disbelief as Craig strode back to the poster. "How would they ever get the three signatures?"

"So pretend there's a conspiracy. You've already told me I'm being paranoid—I may as well live up to the billing. As long as the inventory *paperwork* shows that the nuke was dismantled and all components are accounted for, although distributed across the country where nobody can readily check on them—who's to know if they just kept the whole thing together in the first place? It only *looks* as if the weapon's been dismantled, on paper. Tell me I'm crazy."

Paige's bright blue eyes widened. "You're crazy—but that doesn't mean you're wrong."

Craig wasted no time. "We'll have to assume a nuclear warhead is actually missing—and the Eagle's Claw has threatened to do something really spectacular . . . tomorrow! Hoover Dam and the railroad bridge were just warmup acts." He felt suddenly tired, the last four days catching up with him. But he had to keep going, keep his head clear.

Paige stood quickly from the desk. "Didn't your partner find some papers involving Las Vegas before the suspect's house burned down?"

Craig picked up the inventory sheets, as if hoping the part numbers had changed in the last few moments. "Yes, a map of the Strip showing all the casinos. And it makes sense—where else would the Eagle's Claw want to blow up the bomb? Las Vegas has the people, the NTS history, and even the Russians. If they can make a splash while the President is here, then what else could they want? We can't wait on this—if I'm right, we are already running down to the wire!"

"I'll let DOE know right away," Paige said. "The Secret Service is going to go ape."

"It's time to stop screwing around and call in the NEST experts. Nuclear Emergency Search Team. Not a minute to lose!"

CHAPTER THIRTY-TWO

Thursday, October 23
7:53 P.M.

Nuclear Emergency Search Team Headquarters
Las Vegas

Taking Craig's theory with the utmost seriousness, the FBI joined with the DOE, the Department of Defense, the Secret Service, and the Federal Emergency Management Agency to launch a prompt NEST response. June Atwood was instrumental in convincing the FBI Director of the validity of Craig's conjecture. The Secret Service immediately wanted to veto having the President stop over—but the DoD insisted that any change of plans would be tantamount to announcing to the entire urban area that a nuclear bomb might be hidden somewhere on the streets. Air Force One remained on schedule, but ready to divert straight to Los Angeles at a moment's notice.

The Nuclear Emergency Search Team catapulted into motion with its on-call equipment already loaded onto aircraft. Once the team was activated, they flew in immediately from California, New Mexico, and military bases in Nevada. It took less than three hours for the group to converge on Las Vegas: volunteer experts, scientists, security forces, Explosives Ordnance Disposal, and tactical commanders. They had no room for mistakes.

From the Las Vegas FBI Satellite Office, Jackson made numerous phone calls, finally securing an abandoned textile warehouse on the city outskirts to use as the NEST command center. Dozens of technicians swarmed through the building, hooking up phone lines, computer monitors, electrical connections, modems, and four satellite dishes. Rental cars and vans drove up to the warehouse.

In the eye of the storm, Craig stood outside the tall receiving door. Ryder trucks loaded with equipment ground up to the bays, while unmarked white vans and specially outfitted RVs pulled inside the warehouse. NEST workers rapidly stripped out the back seats of the vehicles, added monitoring devices, and rigged up the communications gear.

The commander of the operation, an Air Force major named Braden, stood with his arms crossed over his broad chest. He was a cool, hard-eyed man with a boyish freckled face, milk-white skin, and shockingly red hair. He never raised his voice, yet always managed to get the job done. Braden stood with a clipboard, using a red felt-tip pen as he looked over computer printouts, circling groups of names to be assigned together as teams.

"We've got a city to comb, Agent Kreident," Braden said. "Normally, we'd plan for a dirty homemade fission device, but if your speculation is correct we're looking for a bona fide warhead from the U.S. arsenal. And that makes me very nervous indeed. Given a terrorist weapon, there's a better-than-even chance they've screwed up the assembly, and all we'd get is a big dud. But in this case, if it's real—it's real."

"Are you going to evacuate the city?" Craig asked.

"Not just on circumstantial evidence. You caused one hell of a debate back in Washington. Right now my orders are to take your claim seriously."

"Then should I hope I'm wrong?" Craig said.

Major Braden's sea-green eyes looked at him strangely.

"Of course not," he said. "You should hope our team finds the device in time."

Goldfarb rode in one of the unmarked NEST vans, cruising down the Las Vegas Strip, waiting for the sensitive radiation detectors to sound an alarm. The flickering lights of casino after casino dazzled the night. Tourists and gamblers streamed past the pirate ships of Treasure Island, beyond the Stardust, the Imperial Palace, the Gold Coast.

He leaned over to peer out the small porthole window of the nondescript van. Other team members scrutinized readouts from the gamma sensors that protruded from the van's side walls.

Beside him an Army sergeant, a young Asian woman with short straight black hair, checked off their progress on the street map, tracing their search path with a yellow highlighter marker.

An Air Force lieutenant sat on one of the padded chairs in back of the darkened van, studying nuclear cross-section profiles, squiggly lines that danced across the screen of his laptop. Geiger counters sampled the ambient gamma levels every five seconds, but so far the lieutenant had seen no spike.

The vehicle cruised from block to block down the crowded Strip, which Major Braden had designated a likely hiding place for the militia weapon. Bryce Connors had kept a map of the casinos in Las Vegas—even though he claimed to know nothing about the militia's October 24 strike.

NEST's most likely scenario assumed that members of the Eagle's Claw had somehow lugged the stolen device to a hotel room suite and locked the doors . . . or else they had parked it in a van in a long-term lot, much as the terrorists had done in the World Trade Center bombing.

The lieutenant continued to stare at his computer screen, blinking, obviously nervous but trying to maintain his composure. He looked up at Goldfarb. "Just like one of our exercises," he said. "We do NEST wargames every year or so—and I always dreaded it ever happening for real."

Goldfarb raised his eyebrows. One of the NEST first-aid techs had rebandaged his hand, but the broken little finger still throbbed. "So how does reality match with the exercises?"

"Similar, so far," the lieutenant said. "The last one I did was called Mirage Gold, about a terrorist nuclear device hidden somewhere in New Orleans. We had three days to find and disarm the bomb, and we didn't have many clues about where it might be. We received a red herring that it might be in the big sports stadium, you know, where the Saints play—but that turned out to be a dead end. Finally, in the last few hours, we tracked it down to a small shed near a runway in one of the smaller airports."

"Did you win?" Goldfarb asked as the van continued along. "Did the bomb get defused?"

"Oh, sure, we had thirty minutes to spare. Covered the shed with a containment tent, pumped the whole area full of foam, then we waded in with anti-C clothing to x-ray and defuse the device."

Goldfarb considered this, his confidence dropping. "So you found it with half an hour to spare, but that was just a simulation. What would've happened if you'd had no leads?"

The lieutenant glanced at his computer screen, but still saw no change in the background spectrum. "The exercise controllers kept track of the time frame and provided us with various clues and information as they deemed it necessary."

"This time nobody's going to give us free hints," Goldfarb said.

The lieutenant didn't answer as he continued to stare at his screen. Still nothing. Absolutely nothing.

The van drove on down the Strip, turning left onto Tropicana past the giant gold-and-emerald lion of the MGM Grand. The radiation spectra remained flat, showing no indication of a covert nuclear warhead.

If the terrorists had hidden it in Las Vegas, they had hidden it well.

Jackson carried one of the unmarked NEST briefcases, trying to look like a first-time conventioneer in Las Vegas. Unfortunately, Jackson's demeanor carried an aura of formality that pegged him as a government official, no matter what he wore. Most of the time he reveled in the knowledge of his professionalism, but he did not know how to shut off that attitude when it became necessary to do so.

The hard lump of the radio earphone rested in his ear. He walked through the McCarran Airport terminal at a brisk pace, as fast as the detectors could analyze data. He and seven other NEST members carried identical briefcases loaded with sensing equipment. Voice-synthesis chips would speak into his earphone should he encounter background radiation that matched the anticipated signature of the diverted warhead.

But the earphone remained silent.

Jackson walked casually past the lockers, expecting, hoping, dreading that he might encounter such a pulse. Other inspectors worked the baggage claim areas, while additional teams walked at random up and down the terminals, the waiting areas by the gates, the line of restaurants and gift shops.

One of the NEST physicists who had ridden with him out to the airport had described an exercise dubbed "Busy Force I," which had simulated a weapon-carrying aircraft crash near Salina, Kansas. Four fake warheads had been downed—one destroyed and scattered across the landscape, three damaged but intact in the burning wreckage of the plane.

"Afterward we knew just how many mistakes we'd made, how many things didn't work the way they should have," the physicist had said. "And we didn't have to *find* anything—we could see the burning wreckage, and it still took us days to get everything under control." He looked exasperated. "This time we don't know where the damned thing is, and we don't even know how much time is on the clock. It could go off at any moment."

Back in the converted textile warehouse on the fringes of the city, FEMA experts had already marked urban-scale evacuation routes, checking on available medical facilities and emergency care—in the event they did not find the device in time. They got ready to help the tens of thousands, perhaps hundreds of thousands, who would become victims.

Back in Washington the debate raged on, voices raised against causing an unwarranted panic versus those who took Craig's assessment at face value.

NEST Health Physicists had sent up weather balloons linked to computer models from ARAC, the Atmosphere Release and Advisory Capability; they would use the data to project distribution patterns of radioactive fallout, should the bomb explode. With the weather brooding, the thunderstorm gathering, the winds stirring up, the warhead detonation would not only wipe out Las Vegas, but would spread a swath of contamination over the southwestern United States.

Jackson continued to pace up and down the airport corridors, continuing his relentless search. He squeezed the handle of the briefcase again to send a test signal to his earphone. Everything functioned properly.

The airport had seemed a likely target for planting the bomb, but as Jackson covered his search pattern for a third time, he still found no indication of the hidden doomsday weapon.

CHAPTER THIRTY-THREE

Thursday, October 23
8:06 P.M.

Las Vegas

When Craig and his team launched the frantic NEST response, searching for a nuclear weapon hidden somewhere in Las Vegas, Paige found herself left alone in her room at the Rio with too much time . . . too much time to think about everything that had happened. And too much time alone to ponder the craziness of it all.

Like Craig, she had looked at the numbers, at the part identification codes, at the complex forms. The forest of documents could have hidden any number of conspiracies. *Plans within plans within plans. . . .* If all the separate pieces of a missing warhead had indeed been covered up in a labyrinth of paperwork, buried under shifting signatures and complex serial numbers, any such plan would have required the active participation of someone very important, someone near the top of the chain.

PK Dirks must certainly be involved. And she could see how Carl Jorgenson had been enlisted to help. But still, there *had* to be someone else. Someone with knowledge of the overall workings of the Device Assembly Facility. . . .

She refused to think of the inevitable, and instead forced herself to race through the other options. *Any* other option.

Could it be a contractor like Warren P. Shelby, someone who had infiltrated the DAF? Or what about the Russian Nikolai Bisovka—he certainly knew a lot about the DAF, and his obvious feelings about "the good old days" implied he might want the disarmament process to fall apart. Sabotage from inside the disarmament team itself? Now that would be a weird alliance, a radical militia group and a Soviet sore loser.

But none of those people had proper access to the security codes, and the time frame was all wrong.

Paige kept coming up with the same answer, again and again. It had to be someone above reproach. Someone even the FBI wouldn't suspect.

Someone like Mike Waterloo, Manager of the Device Assembly Facility.

She couldn't believe it. Paige had known Uncle Mike her entire life. He and her father had worked together, taken vacations together. He was one of the most patriotic people she knew. Mike was a "regular guy," not a violent terrorist, not an anarchist, and certainly not a bloodthirsty militia commando.

Of course not.

She picked up her cellular phone and started to call Craig. It was crazy for her even to think Uncle Mike was involved, but she couldn't shake it from her mind. Craig would give her a "sanity check" on the idea.

But then again, he was in the middle of the NEST investigation, which had the absolute highest priority. Was she allowing the pressure of the last week to cloud her judgment? Perhaps some of Craig's paranoia had rubbed off on her. She had to know first.

Paige flipped shut her phone. She was a big girl. She could do this herself, straighten it all out.

Despite all her efforts to block such thoughts as she drove over to Uncle Mike's home, she considered how he had changed over the past several years, as if a part of him had died along with Genny. Paige *had* to look him in the eye and ask him if he knew anything more. She owed that much to him at least. She would know if he was lying. Lying to her.

She accelerated through a yellow traffic light, paying little heed to the other cars. The evergreen air freshener hanging from her rear-view mirror smelled old and stale. She kept driving, blinking back disbelieving tears until she found the Waterloo residence.

Scrubby weeds had grown up in the yard of the modest ranch house, and most of the grass had died. Newspapers lay scattered on the driveway, though she knew he went home regularly. Uncle Mike just hadn't bothered to pick them up.

No lights shone from the house windows, though it was long after dark. She looked at her watch and frowned. No one seemed to be home, but she rang the doorbell anyway.

Her stomach clenched with ice. What would she say to him if he answered? "Excuse me, Uncle Mike—are you by any chance a member of the Eagle's Claw? Did you help plant the bomb at Hoover Dam on Tuesday? Did you plan to blow up all those people on the Amtrak train this morning? Say, what are your plans for tomorrow?"

She rang the bell again and again, but the place remained silent, like a haunted house. She realized that if he wasn't home, Uncle Mike was probably working late at the DAF. As usual.

Now that she had set herself in motion, Paige had to find him. Craig was distracted with his NEST response—but he would soon make the connection himself, and she needed to talk to Uncle Mike before the FBI arrested him. . . .

Distances in the desert seemed hypnotic. At night, with only the stars and the headlights of oncoming traffic to keep her company, she had nothing to do but concentrate on the highway ahead of her.

She kept daydreaming about all the Christmases when Uncle Mike and Aunt Genny had come over, exchanging presents. Uncle Mike always gave Paige something special—a Hope bracelet, a gold Thai *baut* chain, even a St. Christopher's medal for her sixteenth birthday.

Three years ago he had delivered a broken-voiced eulogy at her father's funeral, talking about the times they had spent together, fishing trips they had taken, backpacking sojourns in the Sierra Nevadas.

She drove on, staring at the long ribbon of moonlit highway.

Uncle Mike had given her colorful streamers for her first bike, and he had figured out that she no longer wanted to play with dolls well before her parents did. Paige had loved him so much for that. . . .

But now Mike Waterloo might be at the heart of a conspiracy to detonate a stolen nuclear weapon.

She swallowed hard and tried to keep her face expressionless as she passed through the Mercury guard gate into the Test Site. The long road across Frenchman Flat and Yucca Flat passed by in a blur to where the Device Assembly Facility stood like a prisoner-of-war camp bathed in harsh white spotlights and surrounded by tall guard towers.

Several vehicles sat in the parking lot, those of third-shift security guards as well as late-night technicians and custodians. NTS shut down primary operations on Fridays, but the place never emptied entirely—especially not now. With the Russian disarmament team visiting, DAF personnel spent twice as much time keeping the facility up and running, everything neat and tidy.

The Russians would come in the next morning for their final closeout ceremonies, finish the rest of their mandated work—and receive their copies of the official autopsy report where they would learn that Nevsky had been murdered. Then it would really hit the fan.

Craig had already put many of the pieces together, but there was no telling how Ursov and the rest of the team would react to the news. The delicate disarmament summit might crash and burn—

But then, if a stolen atomic bomb obliterated downtown Las Vegas, any news of the presidential summit would definitely be bumped to page two.

She parked her truck and passed rapidly through the security procedures. With her Protocol Escort pass, Paige did not require an escort of her own or prior permission to enter the facility. She did not want to inform Uncle Mike that she was coming.

She felt her knees trembling and her heart pounding as she strode down the linoleum-tiled hallway from the high bays and the main warehouse area into the wing containing the offices. This late at night, every office remained dark and closed . . . except for one at the end of the hall, the administrative suite of the DAF Manager.

She'd known he would be here.

Paige swallowed hard and thought seriously of just backing away, ignoring her suspicions, what she needed to say to him. Uncle Mike would never realize she had come here at all.

She thought again of riding her bike with its lavender streamers flaring from the handlebars, Dad and Uncle Mike at the end of the blacktop driveway cheering as she wobbled but did not fall off because she had sworn she was going to keep her balance *this time* without training wheels. . . .

No, she could not turn him in to Craig. She could not believe this man was a monster bent on terrorist destruction. Not Uncle Mike.

But given what she knew, how could she *not* believe it?

She stepped into the front office where Sally would normally sit answering the phone, making photocopies, typing on her word processor. But the secretary's station was empty, though the computer was on.

Uncle Mike was in his office, out of sight. A file drawer

rolled shut, banging heavily. She could hear him moving around by his desk. Paige hesitated again, wondering what to say—and then she was in the middle of it, because Mike Waterloo stepped out of his office, a folder in his hand.

He stopped, startled to see her. "Paige! What are you doing here?" He flushed, seemingly with guilt, then pushed the folder under his arm, clumsily trying to hide it.

She kept her gaze locked on his face. Her lips trembled, and she balled her fists at her sides. She had to be strong, she had to make it clear . . . she could not let him see her waver.

"Paige, are you all right?" He took a step toward her.

"I came to tell you . . . tell you that we *know,* Uncle Mike. We know about the missing warhead, we know about the militia connections. It's all clear now—*everything's* clear. But I need to know something else before the FBI comes for you."

Her voice was stretched taut with fear. What would he say? What would he do? Would he laugh at her? Or would he smile and gently explain everything, as he had so many times when she was a little girl. She prayed she was wrong. . . .

But Paige could tell instantly by the wiry man's reaction that she had guessed right. Mike Waterloo didn't even try to deny it. His sad eyes flicked down.

"Where is the bomb, Uncle Mike? Tell me where it's hidden. Save us the grief, and save a lot of lives." Time seemed to draw out forever.

"Oh, Paige, Paige," he whispered, shaking his head, his face turning gray and sweaty. She watched him, waiting.

His shoulders slumped. "I shouldn't keep thinking of you as Gordon's little girl. You always were smart as a whip and not afraid to speak your mind." He turned to go back into his office. "Your father would've been proud of you," he said.

That comment made her anger flare brighter than her deep sadness. "And what would my father have thought of *you?*" she said, stepping after him. He retreated to the back of the office and settled slowly in his chair, as if in great pain. He looked down at his desk, a vacant expression on his face.

Paige placed both hands on his desk and leaned over, her voice accusing. "After everything you two did together—and now you're engaged in a maniac's campaign of sabotage and murder?"

"Part of the campaign, not all of it," he whispered.

"How could you?" Paige felt her face grow flush.

He hesitated, then leaned forward and opened a drawer. "It's quite complicated, and if there were time, I'm sure you'd understand." His voice sounded tired, as if he were lost in thought, debating something . . . and he pulled a revolver from his bottom desk drawer. He pointed it at her, but he didn't seem to know what to do with it.

Paige stood like a statue, too stunned from everything else she had discovered about Uncle Mike for this final act of betrayal to matter much. "I guess you can stoop even lower than I expected," she whispered.

He held the revolver out, but he was sweating. "I knew Gordon better than you ever could, Paige. Friends talk about things that a father would never tell his daughter. Your dad would have been sickened by what I happen to know is going on in this world. There comes a time when you have to take a stand, when you can't put up with it any longer . . . when you've got nothing else to lose."

Still aiming the revolver at her, he picked up the phone on his desk, punched in several numbers, and cradled the handset against his ear. The gun didn't waver. Paige felt numb and detached, not exactly fearing for her life, just unable to believe what she had stumbled into.

Uncle Mike listened to the phone ring and ring. His face became grim, impatient. Finally, someone answered. "It's me," he said tiredly. "Problems. Paige Mitchell is here. The

FBI has figured it out. They know about the warhead. They know about my involvement."

He listened intently, and Paige could see the anguish on his face. He nodded absently. "We'll move out tonight, then. I thought you'd suggest that." Then he swallowed hard, growing angrier. "No! I won't do it. There has to be another alternative."

He listened. "No, I'll take her with me. After a while it won't matter." He paused. "Well, I'm sorry, but that's the best I can do. You know where to find me." He hung up, his sunken face blotchy as emotions roiled beneath his skin. He looked toward Paige, at a loss for words.

"What?" she said. "You're supposed to kill me where I stand?"

"There are some things I refuse to do, even for the Eagle's Claw," he said. "You probably despise me already, but I do have my own sense of honor. I was the one who tipped off Agent Kreident about the Amtrak explosion. I didn't mind wrecking the railroad bridge, but I didn't want to see all those people killed."

"How admirable," Paige said. "But if you're so concerned about people, how can you let a warhead go off in Las Vegas?"

"Las Vegas?" He blinked at her in surprise. "What are you talking about?"

"Isn't that your obvious target? You've smuggled out a functional nuclear warhead, and you're going to set it off to make your insane point . . . whatever it is. What better target than Las Vegas? Even the President will be here—what more could you want? You can't tell me you're hiding an atomic bomb in *Pahrump* or some other little town. The FBI found a map of the casinos in Bryce Connors's house, with some of them circled."

"That map just indicated where the Eagle's Claw would meet." Uncle Mike looked at her, absolutely appalled. "We would never harm a major American city full of civilians. My God, and certainly not the President! This is my country. I love the United States—but I'm fighting the biggest threat to freedom our nation has ever known."

He came back around the desk and gestured with his revolver for her to precede him out the office and down the hall. "You'll go with me until it's all over with, tomorrow morning."

Paige walked stiffly ahead of him.

"After that, I don't care what happens to me," he said.

CHAPTER THIRTY-FOUR

Thursday, October 23
9:17 P.M.

Home of PK Dirks
Las Vegas

The squad cars pulled up, three of them, their lights flashing. Las Vegas police jumped out of the vehicles. Craig emerged from his own car, drawing the 9-mm Beretta from his shoulder holster. With his other hand he clutched the folded search warrant and arrest warrant.

Two officers pounded on the door, while Craig stepped back in full view, holding out the warrants as if they were weapons, passing them from hand to hand, shuffling his feet as he waited impatiently. He glanced at his watch.

The officers pounded again, and Craig was just ready to tell them to break the door down when the lock clicked and the door popped open.

PK Dirks stood in a T-shirt and baggy Bermuda shorts, scratching his beard and blinking. His eyes looked bleary, and from the smell of his breath, Craig suspected Dirks had recently put away most of a six-pack of beer.

"Yo, Agent Kreident," Dirks said, then finally focused on the squad cars, the flashing lights, the policemen. "Something happen? Where's the Russians?"

Craig extended the folded papers. "Mr. Dirks, I have a warrant here for your arrest and authorization to search your premises for suspected involvement in the Eagle's Claw and for the murder of Ambassador Kosimo Nevsky."

Craig had insufficient evidence to arrest PK Dirks under normal circumstances, but the laid-back technician was one of the only men who could have been involved in both the diversion of a nuclear weapon as well as the Russian's death. After receiving special phone calls from June Atwood as well as personnel from State, DoD, the Secret Service, the Defense Special Weapons Agency, and FEMA, the judge had given Craig greater leeway in questioning potential suspects. They didn't have much time left.

"The Eagle's Claw?" Dirks spluttered. "Those buttheads! Why would I have anything to do with them? And Nevsky—I already explained that." Then the rest of the news finally sank in. "You're *arresting* me?" It took him a moment to gather his wits. Finally, he growled, "Shoot, let me change my shirt." He staggered back inside while the policemen swarmed into the building to begin their search.

Hour after hour, past midnight and into the darkness of early morning, PK Dirks raggedly insisted on his innocence and protested that if they found anything at all that connected him to the militia group, then they'd better show him first.

Judging from the pile of aluminum cans stacked in a wobbly pyramid beside his lounge chair, Dirks had been drinking one Coors after another while watching *Lost in Space* reruns on the Sci-Fi Channel. The man had been settling in for a long night of doing nothing . . . which concerned Craig.

Those were not the actions of someone who knew a nuclear device was soon set to go off somewhere in the city.

At the same time, in a different interrogation chamber, Bryce Connors and Deputy Mahon pleaded ignorance as well.

After the other agents took Dirks away for questioning, Craig had stayed behind to help ransack the place, desperately hoping to find some clue. But the man's cluttered apartment showed no evidence of anything except perhaps criminal lack of housekeeping. . . .

Craig had been working nonstop since their arrival—but by three o'clock in the morning they had found nothing. And it was already Friday, October 24th. Deadline day. Time was running out.

Back in the warehouse command center, he rubbed his temples, knuckled his burning and bloodshot eyes, and hung his head with a sigh. If only he had gone to the DAF early the morning before, spent hours going through the paperwork as he had intended to, he might have made the connection about the nuclear weapon *then,* which would have given NEST another entire day to find the stolen device.

At least he had accomplished something during the diversion yesterday. He had saved the passengers on the Amtrak train—he could not ignore that.

He thought about calling Paige—he had not seen her since that afternoon, when he had initiated the nuclear search. If it hadn't been for her help, he would never have gotten this far on the case. Glancing at his watch, though, he saw what time it was. She must already be back in her room at the Rio, sound asleep.

Alone, he paced the bustling NEST command post, past the maps and tables, telephones that did not ring nearly often enough. Search teams continued to comb the streets, but so far they had found nothing. Nothing. His head ached, his temples pounded, spinning wheels in his brain.

What if he was wrong about PK Dirks? What if the technician was not a member of the militia cell after all? Then who else could divulge the location of the warhead?

His mind ran through all the possibilities. Who else had access to the weapons and knew the authorizing procedures cold? Who else could have been in the signature loop? Craig had seen the list of personnel, and only a few people were in critical positions at the Test Site, critical enough to know how to go about diverting a nuclear weapon.

He kept coming up with another possible connection, and he didn't like the answer—DAF Manager Mike Waterloo. It was the only idea he had left.

Grabbing one of the command center phones, Craig attempted to call Waterloo—but the DAF Manager wasn't at home, nor did he answer his pager. Of course, at 3:30 A.M. any sensible person would have his pager shut off, and maybe even the ringer on the phone disengaged.

Or perhaps he wasn't there. Perhaps he had run . . . fleeing an impending nuclear detonation. Craig couldn't afford to pass up any possibility. Not now.

No possibility at all.

Suddenly remembering, he turned to Goldfarb, who sat red-eyed, gulping what must have been his thirtieth cup of coffee for the day. "Hey, Ben, did you and Jackson follow up on that lead I gave you yesterday morning—Dennisons Machine Repair?"

The short, curly-haired agent snapped up in surprise. "Oh, cripes. No, we never got there, Craig. With the Laughlin bridge explosion and getting shot at in Jorgenson's trailer and now this NEST exercise, it got shuffled to the bottom of the stack." He jumped to his feet, angry at himself for letting the task go undone. "Should we head over there now?"

Craig pulled his own jacket back on. "Have Major Braden drive one of their detector vans by the repair shop to check if the weapon is there. You and Jackson get a warrant and be prepared to make an armed entry."

"An armed entry?" Goldfarb said skeptically. "Are you sure about this?"

"Am I sure? Hardly!" Craig didn't want to bring up the fact that so far they had not managed to confirm that a warhead was even *missing,* much less set for imminent detonation. The NEST team and the FBI response had swung into action, the President's stopover had been placed on hold, all on Craig's call because he had made a convincing case. He had been right about the Amtrak bridge explosion—just barely—and he hoped this whole incident wasn't another example of crying wolf. "But we don't have time to do things cautiously anymore. Today is the day!"

"Okay, you've got the intuition—I'm not going to argue with it. We're grasping at straws, so we may as well grab with all we've got." Goldfarb slid his arms into his jacket, gingerly keeping his bandaged little finger from bumping against anything. "What are you going to do in the meantime?"

"Mike Waterloo doesn't answer his home phone, so I'm going to go over there and wake him up. Besides telling him we've arrested PK Dirks, I want to poke around. Something's just a little fishy."

Goldfarb went looking for Jackson, but tossed a glance over his shoulder. "You keep having these hunches, Craig, sooner or later you're going to be right."

CHAPTER THIRTY-FIVE

Friday, October 24
2:10 A.M.

Land Rover
Far Northeastern Border,
Nevada Test Site

Sitting helplessly in the passenger seat of the camouflaged land rover, Paige pressed her lips together to trap her despair and anger inside. She didn't want to grant Mike Waterloo the benefit of conversation, and her coldness disturbed him greatly.

They'd headed overland in his car from the DAF, driving north across the darkened flats, using abandoned dirt roads that had been carved for test shots completed in years past. Pulling up to an old ammo bunker that had been abandoned in place, Mike had held the gun on her as they switched to a hidden land rover. They left his car inside the old bunker and drove the rover out of the musty-smelling storage place, off to their grim destination.

He kept the land rover's headlights switched off as he crept across the broken land. Overhead, the soup of storm clouds made the desert a murky wasteland. The rugged vehicle bounced and rattled. Paige felt her internal organs jostling, her teeth chattering—but she stared ahead, not wanting to look at Mike and his grim expression, not wanting to look in the back of the rover.

The missing nuclear device lay in the rear cargo bed.

Mike risked the paved roads again as he drove up into the mesas, where only two days earlier he had taken the Russian team on a casual tour of the tunnel tests. He had been such a hypocrite, informative and chatty, when all the while he had been arranging a wave of violence and nuclear destruction. *How long had the warhead been hidden in the old bunker, waiting for the Eagle's Claw to decide how best to use it?*

Mike wound up into the higher lands that separated the Nevada Test Site from the vast spaces of the Nellis Air Force Range. Once he descended out of the mountains and down to the open basin of Gold Flat, Mike veered away from the roads and struck out overland again. The land rover didn't mind the lack of pavement, but once the storm broke and desert rain sheeted down, the ground would become a quagmire.

Upon crossing into Nellis, he reached over to a squarish box he had installed next to the four-wheel-drive shift lever. He flicked on the gadget, some kind of transmitter, and lights winked green on its panel. Though Paige heard nothing, noticed no difference, Mike visibly relaxed.

"I don't suppose you just came to your senses and surrendered to the authorities," Paige said coldly.

Desperate to engage her in conversation, Mike looked at the blinking lights on the box. "That's an IFF transmitter—Identification Friend or Foe. We've just passed into Nellis's security net, but now their sensors will ignore us. Every motion detector, sonic transducer, and microwave relay they have won't matter anymore. The computers will log our entry but won't raise any alarms. We can thank another friend of the Eagle's Claw, a Staff Sergeant Marlo, for this marvel of technology. Our members can be found all over the area—in NTS, in Las Vegas, even in some parts of Nellis."

"You sure know how to be sneaky in the name of mass destruction," Paige said bitterly. "I always admired you for being so smart, but this whole militia thing is so preposterous."

Mike frowned, taken aback. "The evidence is there for anyone to see, Paige—but they all refuse. *I* have seen reality, and I've got to do what's necessary. My conscience demands it."

Paige rolled her eyes, making it clear she did not believe him.

He drove across Gold Flat, picking up speed. Paige hoped he would strike a sharp rock and damage the vehicle, leaving them stranded with no hope of reaching his target, whatever it was. Lost in the desert with a flat tire and a stolen nuclear warhead in back!

They drove for hours and hours through the darkest part of the night, after the moon set. Paige had no idea where they were, but she would not give Mike any satisfaction by asking him. She had not seen so much as a dirt road in some time. She recalled how the band of hippie protesters had wandered into NTS on Tuesday, aimlessly hiking around the desert looking for the warehouses that hid UFOs. Now Uncle Mike was chasing his own elusive phantom.

"We're almost there, Paige, and then you'll see what I mean. I love my country. Your dad loved it, and my wife loved it as well." Uncle Mike checked his notes, a Magellan GPS indicator, a map, then a sheaf of aerial photographs in a three-ring folder.

"Genny and I planned to join those caravans of retirees with large RVs driving around to see the country. We wanted to spend our golden years being gypsies, visiting the mountains, the plains, all the things American anthems are about." His hands tensed on the steering wheel, gripping it tightly. "But she died first, and I don't want to see America all alone. So instead I'll help to preserve it for future generations."

"By spreading a cloud of radioactive fallout across four or five states," she said with an angry snort.

Mike's face wore a grim but passionate expression. "My heart is good, Paige. You know that." He reached over to touch her arm, but she drew away. "Remember the bicycle? Remember the coloring book I gave you when you were sick getting your tonsils out in the hospital?" His voice carried an edge of desperation. "Remember how I helped you with your math because you wanted to go to college and make something of your life?"

Paige's lips trembled as the memories flooded past her. "A different man did those things. Not you. You're not the Uncle Mike I knew and loved. He's as dead as my Aunt Genny."

Mike drove farther on, looking as if she had just stabbed him.

Predawn light began to seep into the eastern sky, turning the stormclouds a watery greenish gray. Paige could make out twinkling lights, some sort of security complex at the base of rugged mountains. The pale expanse of a dry lake bed extended for miles, etched with long runways. Mike drove toward the most remote set of buildings, following the bottom of a wide gully, keeping them low and unseen.

She could discern a thick perimeter fence, double chain-link topped with razor wire, probably electrified. RESTRICTED AREA and NO TRESPASSING signs alternated with GUARDS ARE AUTHORIZED TO USE DEADLY FORCE BY ORDER OF THE COMMANDER.

"Welcome to Area 51," he whispered. "A sight not many citizens get to see."

Picking his way along in the scant light, Mike approached from the rear of the facility. The gully narrowed and deepened as it ran behind the nearest massive building. Finally he pulled the camouflaged land rover to a stop as close as he could get to the fence, still more than a hundred yards away from the restricted complex. Their vehicle was hidden from sight deep in the gully.

The main structure covered acres and acres, like a gigantic warehouse, larger even than the DAF. Paige saw no windows, only air vents on the rooftop, big roll-up metal doors sealed shut.

Even skeptical, she recognized that this building was no simple hangar, no bunker or supply warehouse, no Wal-Mart in the middle of the desert. The featureless contours looked sinister to her—she could almost believe the paranoid fears Mike had voiced.

This place was not *right*. It housed something terrible and deadly.

Mike glanced over his shoulder at the stolen nuclear device filling the back of the land rover, then he stared forward again as dawn began to break over the desert. The giant structure fascinated as well as horrified him. One word came from his mouth in a quiet whisper.

"Dreamland," he said.

CHAPTER THIRTY-SIX

Friday, October 24
4:17 A.M.

Residence of Mike Waterloo
North Las Vegas

Feeling as if he hadn't slept in a month, Craig kept moving. His head pounded, his body ached from the ordeal at the Laughlin railroad bridge, from the frantic chaos of the fruitless NEST search.

He wondered when, or if, Major Braden would decide to announce an all-out evacuation of the city. But he also knew the final decision would be made in Washington—and there was no telling what they might decide.

Craig thought of Paige, hoping she was getting a good night's rest at the Rio. For now, he thought it was best if she didn't know he wanted to question her Uncle Mike. While Jackson and Goldfarb checked out Dennisons repair shop, Craig thought Waterloo was his last, best hope.

Though it was just a little after four in the morning, Craig rapped again on the front door of the DAF Manager's house. The doorbell didn't seem to work, so he pounded loudly enough to wake anyone in the bedroom, as well as several neighbors.

Finally giving up, he crunched across the nugget-sized lava rock spread throughout Waterloo's front yard. Cholla, prickly pear, and bristly yucca had been meticulously arranged in a landscape with larger rocks and scrub oak, but much of it had gone to weeds, untended for some time. He wondered if Waterloo's wife Genny had been the gardener in the family. He wondered why Waterloo hadn't at least bothered to pick up the newspapers tossed in his driveway.

Letting himself through the fence gate, he walked around back to where he could peer through the bedroom windows. Pressing his face against the glass, he discerned shadowy details by the light of a glowing clock radio.

With a chill down his spine, he thought of Carl Jorgenson lying dead inside his bathroom, poisoned by the Eagle's Claw. He hoped the same thing hadn't happened to Waterloo.

Instead, he found the bed empty, neatly made. Apparently, the DAF Manager had never even come home the night before. He glanced at his watch again to confirm the time. Something was wrong.

Craig didn't have much time. He took a deep breath, pacing back and forth in front of the bedroom window, wondering what to do, impatient to make a decision. He had wanted to use a little more finesse instead of breaking the door down—but he remembered again what had happened at Jorgenson's trailer, at Hoover Dam, at the Laughlin railroad crossing, at the home of Bryce Connors.

And he thought again of the missing nuclear weapon.

Waterloo had run, just as Craig had expected PK Dirks to do—perhaps he had fingered the wrong man.

He found a sliding glass door at the patio; the cheap lock popped open easily when Craig pushed against it. He called out again, identifying himself, but heard no sound from inside.

Waterloo either wasn't home—or he was lurking in the shadows with a loaded rifle. Once again, Craig wished he had brought his backup with him—but even now Goldfarb and Jackson would be mounting their investigation of the slot-machine repair shop. . . .

In a hurry but also cautious, Craig began to look around, switching on only one or two small lights at a time.

It took him no more than ten minutes to find an appalling collection spread across the dining room table, as if Waterloo just didn't care anymore: a dozen Eagle's Claw leaflets, maps of southern Nevada, the Test Site, Nellis Air Force Range, and a hand-drawn sketch of Groom Lake with topographical lines penciled in. Waterloo had scattered the papers on tables, next to notepads, as if frantically making plans, double-checking his destination, throwing supplies together.

Getting ready.

In a cardboard box by the coffee table, Craig found booklets with alarming titles: *Unarmed Combat to Kill, The Political Sellout of America,* and *The ANFO Solution—Ammonia Nitrate Fuel Explosives.* With ice in his stomach, he flipped through the documents.

Craig felt as if the wind had been knocked out of him. All this time he had been working with Waterloo, feeding him information on Nevsky's "accident" investigation. "We have found the enemy, and he is us," he muttered.

Feeling sick to his stomach, he found a telephone in the kitchen, looked up the Rio in the phone book, and dialed the number with leaden fingers. He had to tell Paige.

But she didn't answer. The phone in her room rang a dozen times.

"I'm sorry, sir. Your party isn't available." The Rio operator seemed too perky for so early in the morning. "May I leave a message?"

"No, uh, no thanks."

"Thank you, and have a wonderful day."

Where could Paige be at 4:30 in the morning? Why didn't she pick up the phone? He had convinced himself that Waterloo might have switched off his pager and disconnected his home phone—but Paige would never do that, not in her hotel room.

He swallowed hard, knowing her devotion to "Uncle Mike" and her concern for him.

What if she had stumbled upon his militia activities? Waterloo had disappeared, and now Paige seemed to have vanished as well. What had she gotten herself into?

He ran for the door and his car, roaring off into the predawn stillness toward the Rio.

CHAPTER THIRTY-SEVEN

Friday, October 24
4:47 A.M.

Dennisons Machine Repair
Las Vegas

With tension clenching his abdomen, Goldfarb stood beside his rental car under the streetlights, looking across at the warehouses. He hated putting himself in situations like this, and here he had done it several times this week alone. Julene would lose sleep for a month once she found out about it.

Dennisons slot-machine repair shop was located in an industrial area not far from the Strip—close enough, he supposed, for a nuclear device to devastate the entire area, but far enough for the Eagle's Claw to operate freely outside the crowds of tourists and gamblers.

Major Braden had rushed his nuclear surveillance vans over to the machine repair warehouse, driving by with gamma counters in search of an incriminating background trace that would be evidence of the smuggled nuclear device. But the initial sweeps had turned up nothing, not even a blip.

Having no other leads, Goldfarb and Jackson decided to go in, regardless. It was better than returning helplessly to the command center, where they would twiddle their thumbs and wait for something else to turn up.

Unless they found something, and soon, NEST would be forced to call for an evacuation of the entire city.

Goldfarb sipped his sour, cold coffee, holding the foam cup clumsily in his bandaged hand. He had reversed his shoulder holster to put the Beretta within reach of his left hand, but he didn't know if he'd be able to shoot straight. He hoped it wouldn't come to that.

They had no real reason to believe this would turn out to be anything other than one more wild-goose chase—but Craig himself had suggested the agents prepare for an armed response.

As he waited by the car for the rest of the backup to arrive, a few splatters of rain drifted down. The wind picked up, carrying a metallic smell of ozone as the precursor to the storm. Goldfarb wondered where Craig had gone, what he had learned at Mike Waterloo's house. He just hoped their own search here would uncover *something*.

Jackson and two other Las Vegas agents—Rheinski and Holden—took up positions on the other side of the street, bracketing the darkened storefront with DENNISONS MACHINE REPAIR stenciled in a half circle on the glass. The agents wore black windbreakers with the letters FBI stenciled boldly in white on their backs; if the situation turned hot, the distinctive garb would help them tell the good guys from the bad guys.

Old pickup trucks lined the backstreet, each one displaying a prominent gunrack. Two converted Oldsmobile "low rider" cars sat on bald tires in the parking lot of the pawn shop next to them.

A white van rolled down the street from the opposite direction, its engine idling, and parked a block away. Goldfarb knew the white van contained SWAT backup forces, just in case the FBI men should need help. Major Braden was taking no chances.

Goldfarb took the last swallow of his coffee and tossed the empty cup inside the car. His own bulletproof vest pinched him, and he adjusted it, feeling like one of the Excalibur's knights in armor.

"Does the SWAT team have ears on the building yet?" he said into the small microphone at his collar.

A thin voice came through his earphone from the communications officer inside the white covert van. "They're using both the sonic horn and a laser Doppler on the window, sir. Getting ragged background sounds, like snoring, possibly from two people, but I get no movement from inside. Uh, one moment, Agent Goldfarb, Major Braden wishes to say something."

The redheaded NEST commander said, "Agent Goldfarb—since we're not picking up any special nuclear material inside, I'll let the FBI run the entry. We'll move back to an assist mode."

Goldfarb felt a surge of adrenaline and second thoughts. In many ways he had secretly hoped the NEST team would take the lead in the raid— with the enormous consequences of surprising someone holding a nuclear weapon, the assault team would be empowered to shoot first and ask questions later.

But with the responsibility now relinquished to the FBI, Goldfarb had to follow conventional "rules of engagement" for a legal raid. He would have to give fair warning, identify himself before charging in—he hoped the militia wouldn't start shooting the minute he rapped on the door.

"Just keep the SWAT team handy, Major," he cautioned. "We don't know exactly what we're expecting in here." Raising his hand, he signaled Jackson and the two other agents. All four moved together, converging toward the door.

"No sound from inside," Jackson said.

"It's still pretty early in the morning," Goldfarb said.

"Not too early for a warehouse shift." The tall black agent tugged on his Kevlar vest beneath his windbreaker. "Maybe the militia already pulled out."

Even when coupled with the scraps of work orders from Connors's house, Craig's lead had not seemed too definite in the first place, and now the Dennisons tip was a day old, thanks to the bomb on the railroad bridge. Goldfarb should have followed up the lead earlier . . . and Craig should have spent the day scouring DAF paperwork, and the NEST response should have been launched by noon Thursday. . . .

Now, their time was running out—unless the Eagle's Claw was bluffing. And he doubted that, after the militia had already rigged high-powered bombs and murdered several people.

With his bandaged hand Goldfarb checked his pocket to make sure he had the warrant. *Play by the rules.* And hope the other guys did too. He wanted to make sure he came back home to Julene and the kids.

He wished he would have at least called his wife back in Oakland this morning . . . for nothing else but to reassure her. It made him even more nervous to be thinking about such things right now.

"I'll take the lead," said Goldfarb. "Jackson, you and Rheinski fan out. Holden, back me up. We'll enter through the back. The SWAT team will cover the front, just in case. Any questions?" They shook their heads. "All right. Nobody screws up, nobody gets hurt. Let's go."

Goldfarb trotted around behind the building, keeping to the shadows. He motioned his team to the side, back by the warehouse doors. No sense raising a ruckus and going in through the front, giving the bad guys a good thirty seconds' warning as they made their way to the back. He hoped the SWAT team was right about only two people being inside.

Goldfarb searched the shadows, clumsily holding his Beretta upright in his left hand. Jackson pointed at him and gave the high sign. Drawing in a breath, Goldfarb motioned with his head. He fought back a sudden wild urge to pee. Nerves. And too much coffee. Worry about that later.

He slammed his hand against the door. "Federal agents! We have a warrant to enter and search the premises." He waited long seconds. "FBI—if you do not open up immediately, we will break it down."

After a moment of silence, Holden bashed into the door, which bent but did not buckle. They had full locksmith equipment in the van, but that would take too much time. Still holding his handgun high, Goldfarb stepped back and kicked the doorknob. Wood cracked, and the side of the door splintered.

Holden threw himself against the door, and it finally crashed inward. A loud bell began clanging as they set off Dennisons' built-in alarms.

Flushed and breathing hard, Goldfarb launched himself into the darkened warehouse. In the dim emergency lights glowing from the high ceiling, his eyes made out dark shapes, rows of machines, low work tables, storage boxes. The noise from the alarm startled birds that had roosted inside the big building; other staccato movement came from the shadowy rooms.

"Lights!" Goldfarb called into the monotonous din of the alarms.

Jackson slithered farther inward along the wall. "Got 'em."

The bright overhead lights snapped on, banks and banks of blazing fluorescent tubes, and Goldfarb suddenly saw the entire warehouse. Like frozen soldiers, rows of slot machines stood on pallets, some dismantled, some wrapped in sheet plastic. He recognized electronic machines as well as the old mechanical "one-armed bandits." Tools and testing equipment lay strewn across workbenches.

A disembodied voice sounded groggy. "Hey! What the hell is going on?" The alarm bells continued their head-pounding clamor, throwing everything into confusion. "Oh, shit!"

"Hey, you!" Jackson shouted. "Freeze! Over there."

Goldfarb saw a young man staggering away, ducking for shelter between the rows of slot machines. The kid had close-cropped blond hair and wore only a pair of khaki boxer shorts. "Hold it right there! Federal agents!"

Jackson and Rheinski crouched, their handguns drawn, as they went in two different directions to head off the young man. A young woman screamed, then shouted a string of obscenities. Holden ran to investigate as Goldfarb hurried after the kid in the underwear.

"Where do you think you're going?" Goldfarb called impatiently—then the young man lurched up from his hiding place and pointed a handgun at him. Goldfarb scrambled to the side as the kid fired two quick shots. "Aww, not again!"

The two bullets ricocheted off a half-dismantled slot machine. Goldfarb instinctively fired back with his left hand, but his aim was off and the shot went wide.

"Watch it, Ben—don't hit *me*!" Rheinski shouted.

Underwear Boy shoved a big slot machine, crashing it off its pallet as he dashed in another direction, weaving around and trying to get to one of the rear warehouse doors. Jackson stood up, both hands locked around his handgun in a professional firing stance. "Throw down your weapon, sir!"

But the kid shot wildly at him, sending sparks up from another slot machine. Jackson ducked out of the way, a befuddled expression on his face.

The alarm bells continued to rattle with skull-cracking volume.

Goldfarb saw the kid limping severely; one arm and shoulder had been bound and bandaged in a recent injury. Taking cover behind the squat machines, he slid from one row to another, looking for a shot. His broken pinkie throbbed like a jackhammer.

"Johnnie, look out!" a young woman's voice shrilled. Goldfarb turned toward the sound to see a half-naked blond teenage girl struggling against the wall, handcuffed to one of the electrical conduit pipes that ran down a support girder.

The unexpected sight so startled him that he didn't notice Holden until the other Las Vegas agent stepped out from behind Underwear Boy, pressing his handgun right up against the young man's spine.

"I don't think you'll be wanting to resist any more, kid," Holden said. Underwear Boy froze, his face writhing with a storm of desperate emotions—but his eyes seemed unfocused, glazed with some kind of drugs.

Panting, Goldfarb and Jackson converged on him, leveling their weapons as Holden disarmed the captive. He slid the young man's handgun in his own pocket as the warehouse alarm bells rang and rang.

Handcuffed to the wall, the young woman continued to writhe and spit curses at them. Goldfarb ignored her—they would have plenty of time to question the girl later.

Underwear Boy was in his early twenties, his freckled skin pale and bruised. Bandages covered his arm, shoulder, and shin, but other angry red scrapes and contusions showed on his back and chest. Someone had smeared salves on the worst wounds.

"Looks like you're pretty banged up there, kid," Goldfarb said.

"What do you think you're doing?" the young man said slowly. His voice was slurred and his eyes unfocused, as if he had taken massive amounts of painkillers.

Suddenly, merciful silence dropped back upon them. Rheinski came up, patting his hands together. "Couldn't find the trip switch, so I used a wire cutter. Worked like a charm."

"This is private property!" the girl shrieked. "You got no right! Damn Nazis!" She didn't look older than seventeen.

Jackson put his own handgun away, then marched off. "I'll check the rest of the premises. Maybe I can find some clothes for Cinderella," he said.

"Or at least a gag for her foul mouth," Holden muttered.

"Leave her alone—" the young man said, turning to go toward her, but Holden slammed him back. He winced in pain. "Watch the ribs, man! Ah, shit, that hurts!"

"Hey, I recognize you!" Goldfarb suddenly said, staring at the young man's lean figure, short sandy blond hair, freckled cheeks, watery blue eyes. "Back at the bridge in Laughlin. You're our friendly train bomber! Looks like you just barely walked away from an avalanche."

"I'm not saying anything," the young man said. "You can't do this, breaking into a private business. This isn't Russia!"

"No, this is the United States—and here we use search warrants." Goldfarb displayed the paper for only a second, but Underwear Boy didn't seem interested in it anyway. "I'm placing you under arrest for destroying the railroad bridge, conspiracy, attempted murder, reckless endangerment of life, firing upon a Federal agent, resisting arrest, felony destruction of property." He glanced over at the half-naked girl. "And probably statutory rape."

"Yeah, that won't mean much in a little while," the man snorted.

Goldfarb felt cold. "We already know about the nuclear warhead. We've dispatched teams to disarm it."

Shocked, the militiaman took a moment to recover. "They'll never get all the way out there in time. They can't get through the security checkpoints. No way. You've already lost."

Goldfarb frowned. *What security checkpoints?* All the way out *where*?

Jackson came up, holding a military uniform. "Rest of the place is empty. I found his other clothes, all torn and muddy from taking a long tumble into the river."

Goldfarb shook his head in disbelief. "His girlfriend here probably picked him up from the canyon, brought him back here to do a bit of first aid. I bet Dennisons is some kind of a militia safe house."

"You'll never find the bomb," the militiaman said again. From her position on the wall, the girl began to curse again, thrashing against the handcuffs, but Goldfarb ignored her.

"Just read him Miranda," Goldfarb said, leaning against one of the dismantled slot machines. "We sure hit the jackpot here." He fished the man's wallet from the pocket of the uniform slacks and flipped through the papers and ID.

He pulled out a green laminated card and turned it over. The blond man's picture was on the front. "Department of Defense. Staff Sergeant John Marlo, United States Air Force." Goldfarb unfolded a Leave Statement that listed the address of Dennisons Machine Repair as Marlo's place of residence. It specified NELLIS as the sergeant's base.

"I want a lawyer. You can't bust in here and arrest me like this—"

"Oh, shut up," Holden said.

Goldfarb heard the front of the store open, and the SWAT team entered in response to the gunshots fired. He took a moment to calm them, reassuring them that the facility had been secured and the situation was under control. "Get one of the women on the NEST team as a chaperone so we can let the young lady here get her clothes on," he added. "We don't need a sexual harassment suit on top of all this."

Jackson reappeared, carrying a box of ammunition. "We

found what must have been a weapons cache back behind the banks of broken-down slot machines—but it's empty. From the weapon mounts it looks like it held a lot of automatic weapons. This box of ammo was all that was left."

"You don't know anything," Marlo said, his words still slurred, but his eyes had brightened, as if his predicament had penetrated the fog of painkillers. "And you don't have any time left. We're putting a stop to the UN shit, and it's too late to stop us. You hear me? It's already too late!"

"Thanks." Goldfarb tossed Marlo's wallet to one of the other agents. "Let's get on the phone to Craig. Maybe that's all the information he needs to make sense of all this."

CHAPTER THIRTY-EIGHT

Friday, October 24
5:20 A.M.

Dreamland
Groom Lake Air Force
Auxiliary Station

With the land rover parked beyond the razor-wire perimeter fence surrounding the ominous Dreamland facility, Paige remained a captive, helpless.

Waiting.

Mike Waterloo switched off the vehicle and sat patiently in the driver's seat. The clouds remained gray-black even in the dawn, and sprinkles of rain dotted the windshield. He spoke distractedly. "You know, the Trinity Test back in 1945 was postponed for a few hours because of a heavy early morning thunderstorm. The first atomic bomb, with a yield in kilotons . . . not much more than a toy compared to the warheads we make now." He glanced at the back of the rover.

"Megatons," Paige said. "You know that if you detonate that, even way out here, you'll be killing thousands. This storm will spread the radioactive fallout for hundreds of miles, maybe even worse than if you had planted it in an underground parking garage in Las Vegas. Here, there's nothing to stop it—how can that help our country?"

Mike looked over at her, then gestured toward the Area 51

facility. "You're not blind, Paige. You're a smart little girl. What do you think that place is? Do you believe it's a hangar for a crashed UFO and alien cadavers? A chemical weapons plant? A biological warfare research station? No way."

He snorted in disbelief. "Think about it—I'm cleared to handle nuclear warheads. Any day of the week, I can make a few phone calls, get all the approvals, sign a form, and take five megatons from Omega Mountain back to the DAF. I've been in the weapons industry my entire professional career . . . but no one gives me more than a blank stare when I try to find out what's up here."

He narrowed his eyes, squinting through the rover's dusty windshield. "That isn't any weapons manufacturing station. That is no research laboratory. You've been in research laboratories yourself. *Look* at the place!"

"It doesn't look like Livermore," Paige admitted, "but that doesn't mean it's anything more sinister. It could well be a stockpile storage site. Sure, the U.S. might be hiding some of its nuclear weapons, despite what the treaties say. Maybe this is where they keep their ace in the hole. It wouldn't surprise me."

"If that's the case, then *I* would know about it," Mike said, his face flushed. "Believe me, I'm one of the few people they *would* inform if they're going to divert assets out of the stockpile—and they refuse to tell me squat about Area 51!" He shook his head. "This is something beyond the pale of normal defense activities. This is outside the control of our elected government and the rights we as citizens have given to our representatives."

Paige saw his bright eyes, his flushed face. "So what do *you* think it is, then? And why do you need a nuke to get rid of it? Why is it worth contaminating the southwestern United States?"

He answered instantly, as if he'd been desperately waiting for her to ask. "Dreamland is the training ground for a

United Nations Strike Force, whose mission is to absorb the government of the United States into a worldwide political organization. I've seen the planes without markings, the troops. Their efforts are already underway in Third World countries—the UN Peacekeeping Force is just a front." He made a raspberry sound. "Peacekeeping! 'Culture destroying,' more like.

"Other countries can fight their own struggles for freedom. America had to. We have our freedom because we *earned* it. Nobody just handed it to us for free. It was part of our growing pains, but it was also a learning process.

"During the Cold War we achieved a level of maturity to handle the responsibility of nuclear weapons. But do you think other countries, the North Koreas or Bosnias, the Irans or Iraqs, the Indias or Pakistans, are *mature* enough to handle that terrible responsibility? I don't believe it for a minute.

"Despite the flaws and despite all the political arguing between the President and Congress, the Supreme Court, the state legislatures—our government is *ours*! I can't stand by when an insidious UN effort is being put in place with the cooperation of elements of our own society. They mean to swallow up the best parts of what we've achieved and then combine it with other things from other countries, compromises, so that the entire system becomes one giant worldwide average—mediocrity!"

He extended his hand so briskly that he rapped his knuckles against the windshield. "Inside that facility is a UN Command Center, large numbers of troops, weapons, computer systems, plans for a massive takeover of our national infrastructure, our government. We have to eradicate it *all*.

"They've already infiltrated people into high government positions, even the military. They think it'll be a bloodless takeover—but the Eagle's Claw plans to shed plenty of blood. Their blood. Necessary blood for our freedom." The pleading look had returned to his hangdog eyes. "I know this in my heart, Paige, and if you would open your mind, you'd believe it too."

She stared at the vast building, but heard no sound, saw no movement. Isolated for so long in Nevada, working in the nuclear weapons industry, Mike Waterloo had been forced to cooperate with his former enemies to dismantle everything he had built during his career, and it must have driven him over the edge. He'd also had to contend with the shock of his wife's death—not to mention the loss of Paige's own father a year later . . . Paige's father, who would have been a pressure-release valve for him, a sounding board to calm his paranoid delusions.

Mike's expression remained so confident, so frozen in his convictions that Paige knew she had no chance to talk him out of it. He didn't seem to hear her. "So what do we do now?" she said. "Just wait here all day until somebody gives us a parking ticket?"

"Nobody will come out after us," Mike said. "We're camouflaged, and sheltered in this gully. The storm is already covering our tracks. We arrived in darkness, and this vehicle is broadcasting an IFF signal. The sensors automatically ignore us. We've got all the time in the world."

"Why don't you just get it over with, if you want to blow us all to hell?"

"I *don't* want to blow us all to hell," he said. "I didn't want you in this at all. If you'd only stayed away another few hours, you could have been out of this entirely . . . but I don't know how I'm going to set you free now." His sad face looked intensely troubled, but Paige didn't allow her heart to soften.

As they sat in continued silence, Paige heard the faint humming of a vehicle approaching in the dark, audible even over the increasing rumbles of thunder. She turned to look just as Mike noticed it too. Her heart surged with hope—

perhaps an Air Force security squadron would apprehend them.

But when she saw the second camouflaged land rover barely visible against the broken landscape, she realized the vehicle was identical to what Mike had driven, also approaching from the south, as if it had picked its way through the night from the Test Site, through Nellis, here to Area 51.

Mike glanced at his watch. "About time. I'm sure *I* would have been reprimanded if I'd been this late." He climbed out of the rover to stand waiting.

Paige wondered if she should leap out and make a run toward Dreamland. If she climbed the fence, no doubt alarms inside would summon an instant full-force response—but she also knew that Mike or the newcomer could shoot her down easily . . . and if she did manage to reach the fence, it was probably electrified; if not, Groom Lake security teams would probably gun her down before they bothered to check her story.

Out of her own need to know, she turned to see the identity of Mike's other militia accomplice.

His secretary, Sally Montry, stepped out of the second vehicle, dressed in casual clothes and wearing a murderous look on her face.

CHAPTER THIRTY-NINE

Friday, October 24
5:23 A.M.

Rio Hotel and Casino
Las Vegas

Craig used his FBI badge and ID to convince the Rio's night manager to let him into Paige Mitchell's room. But the suite was empty, the bed made, showing no signs of a struggle. She had left no sign of where she had gone or what she meant to do.

Had she for some reason gone out to see her Uncle Mike . . . gotten herself involved in a dangerous situation while Craig was distracted with NEST searching for the warhead in Las Vegas?

In a daze, Craig rushed back through the Rio lobby, not hearing the slot machines or the buzz of gamblers, not seeing the lush jungle decor or the flashing lights and mirrors. He felt grimy, tired, sore, and hungry, and he couldn't see any chance for relief in sight.

Especially not now, not if Paige was in trouble.

He thought again of the paraphernalia Waterloo had left in his house, wishing the DAF Manager had given some inadvertent indication of where the stolen nuclear device was hidden. But he had found no Las Vegas street maps, no diagrams of the downtown area, no target zone in the city. Only those maps of NTS and Nellis and Groom Lake.

Unless the warhead wasn't in Las Vegas at all. Unless it had never been taken from NTS.

What if the bomb still remained on the vast reservation . . . hidden in the test range that covered thousands of acres? Perhaps the militia had simply smuggled the weapon out to an isolated gully, waiting for their chance. Who would think to look for the missing nuke out on the test range itself?

If Paige had figured it out for herself, figured out the connection with Waterloo, he could well believe that she would have made her own way out to the Test Site, snooping around, confronting her Uncle Mike at the DAF and getting herself in trouble. . . .

As he hustled out of the casino, his cellular phone rang. Craig stood at the front doorway, waiting under the bright lights as he flipped open the antenna. Goldfarb's voice came in a rush.

"Craig, we've got the guy who blew up the railroad bridge yesterday! Staff Sergeant John Marlo. Found him in Dennisons, just like your informant said—but there's no nuclear device here. Our guy says it's in a place no one will ever find in time, somewhere isolated, somewhere with lots of security checkpoints. He also seemed baffled when I brought up the President's layover. Chances are he didn't even know about it. His papers say he was stationed at Nellis Air Force Range, north of the Test Site."

Craig suddenly remembered his day up touring the test tunnels, and Waterloo's weird fascination with the secret Groom Lake facility, Area 51—and he connected that with the sketched map he had found in Waterloo's house.

The Eagle's Claw might have wanted to expose the suspicious testing programs, the covert activities at Groom Lake—or destroy them. He felt cold as all of his assumptions fell into place.

"Dreamland," he whispered. If Waterloo could slip past

all the security, it would be the perfect place to hide a nuclear warhead.

"I guess it's good news then," Goldfarb said. "It doesn't look like the bomb is in Las Vegas after all."

"Don't celebrate yet," he said, remembering what Paige had told him. "With the size of that bomb and with this storm blowing, the radioactive cloud is going to kill thousands."

"Go ahead, rain on my parade."

Craig scanned for where he had parked his car in the Registration Only spots. He spoke quickly into the phone. "I'm heading out to the Test Site right now. I just found out that Mike Waterloo is involved in the militia, some kind of big wheel."

"*Waterloo's* in the militia?" Goldfarb squawked. "Holy cow, who's next?"

"I'll explain later—but he's disappeared, and he might even have taken Paige hostage. Meanwhile, have a helicopter meet me at the DAF—there's a pad only a mile away. From there, we'll need to head north into the desert. See if you can convince Major Braden or June Atwood to get me into Nellis Air Force Base. I think Waterloo's got the stolen bomb, and I think he's hauling it to Groom Lake. That's where he'll set it off."

"The militia is going to *Area 51*?" said Goldfarb, sounding incredulous. "What, they want to kidnap the aliens?"

"I'll let you know when I get there." He switched off the phone as he raced for his rental car—and then he felt a strong hand grab him by the forearm. Craig whirled, instantly alert, ready to struggle.

General Ursov stood there in his immaculate brown military uniform, dressed and ready to go. "I have found you, Agent Kreident, and I know something is going on!" the Russian said stonily. He stepped in front of the car door and waited, arms crossed, refusing to move.

His heart sinking as his thoughts whirled, Craig tried to brush past Ursov. "General, you must believe me. There is a national security emergency. I don't have time for this—"

"*Nyet,*" said Ursov, pounding on the hood of the car. Two of the valet parking attendants turned to stare. "*I* do not have time! I will not let you out of my sight until I have answers. Enough of this! Nevsky is dead, information is being buried—you will tell me now."

Craig clenched his fingers around the car door handle, ready to rip it off. It would take him half an hour to get to the Test Site at breakneck speed on rain-slick roads. Goldfarb was already setting things in motion, and he couldn't waste the time appeasing Ursov right now.

On the other hand, he realized, the Russian ambassador had been the first to discover the missing warhead, and he had been murdered for it. In fact, the FBI would never have suspected the nuclear threat or the connection with the Eagle's Claw otherwise.

Besides, he could always leave the general at the DAF once the FBI helicopter showed up.

"All right, General—I guess you're part of this, too." Craig looked forcefully at Ursov. "Get in the car. I've got something to tell you. I'll explain on the way."

CHAPTER FORTY

Friday, October 24
6:03 A.M.

South Gate
Nevada Test Site

Sitting in the front seat of the rental car, General Ursov fumed as Craig raced toward the Nevada Test Site. Daylight tried to seep through the stormclouds, but the rain pattered more heavily on the windshield as he drove. The wipers waved back and forth, keeping his view clear.

"How long have you known Ambassador Nevsky was murdered?" Ursov said, blustering. "You deliberately withheld this information from me and my government!"

"Yes, and I apologize. It was unfair to keep that from you." Craig adjusted his sunglasses, then fumbled in his coat for the cellular phone and laid it on the dash. Goldfarb might be calling him at any minute. "With tomorrow's summit meeting, we were trying to avoid an international incident—but it was just as important to hide that knowledge from the militia members, so as not to tip our hand in the investigation. If you had known the ambassador was murdered, you would have canceled the remaining disarmament activities, thrown the summit into an uproar, embarrassed both of our presidents. . . ."

"True," Ursov said with a dry smile. He spoke in measured tones, as if carefully considering the implications of his own question. "So if Nevsky's killers have stolen a nuclear weapon, why are you taking me back to the Test Site now?"

"Because that's where I think things are going to happen."

"You are aware that you are transporting an official of the Russian government to a destination against his will?"

"Personally, I would rather have left you in the Rio parking lot, General—but you insisted," Craig said without changing his expression and without taking his eyes from the road. He knew Ursov was mostly blowing smoke. The speedometer had passed 95, but he sped onward.

Ursov surprised him by letting his gruff demeanor slip into a smile, then even a little laugh. "It's been worth the trouble, Agent Kreident. You have already told me more in twenty minutes than I've been able to learn in the past three days." He looked at his thick fingers. "I warn you, though—do not try to leave me behind or 'ditch me,' as you say in colloquial English. Even though Nevsky was a drunken ass, I want to help apprehend the criminals responsible."

Craig drew in his breath. *When it rains, it pours.* He would deal with that when the time came. "Just make yourself useful, General."

The cellular phone rang. Ursov looked startled, as if he didn't know what to do. He handed it to Craig, who used one hand to steer while he spoke. "This is Kreident."

"Ben Goldfarb here. I finally got someone at DOE to authorize our FBI chopper to come in for you. The pilot's on his way and should be at the DAF helicopter pad within the next ten minutes. The weather's getting rough to fly in, but he can make it. Do you need any help up there?"

Craig took the Mercury exit from the highway, racing toward the line of guard kiosks. "We could use some backup at Groom Lake once we cross the boundary. We're on our way."

"We? Who's 'we'?"

Craig looked over at the alarmed Russian general. "Let's just say I've got all the help I need."

At the DAF parking lot, Craig managed to identify one of the trucks parked there as Paige's. He had never been so glad, and then so concerned, to see a pine-scented air freshener before. After checking quickly, he discovered she wasn't inside the secure facility—but now at least he knew she had come to the DAF sometime the night before. She had to be with her "Uncle Mike."

Militia member Mike Waterloo.

Craig dreaded Waterloo had taken her as a hostage—if he hadn't already killed her, adding another casualty to the Eagle's Claw bloodbath.

Up in the sky, they heard an approaching helicopter, its chattering engine cutting through the muffled thunder. Craig and Ursov sprinted for the rental car to take them off to the helicopter pad.

CHAPTER FORTY-ONE

Friday, October 24
6:34 A.M.

Dreamland
Groom Lake Air Force
Auxiliary Station

Paige remained seated like a statue in the land rover, feeling each droplet of sweat like a tiny bullet popping out of her skin. So far, the desert had soaked up the sporadic raindrops without a trace.

As Sally Montry came over to speak sharply with Mike, the "secretary's" entire demeanor altered from what she usually showed in the office—now Sally was in control, commanding. The wind caught at her hair, blowing it around in tufts.

The hard-looking woman came to the driver's side door and scowled in at Paige. "I suppose you're here to make coffee for all of us, Sally?" Paige said sarcastically.

Annoyed, Sally whirled to growl at Mike. "Why couldn't you just kill her? You didn't have any compunctions about smashing Nevsky on the skull—and she's just as big a threat to us. Too damned sentimental?"

"Yes, I did have qualms about killing Nevsky," Mike said, clearly trying to stand up to Sally, but weakening. "And I had grave doubts about your wanting to blow up Hoover Dam, and also to kill all those innocent people on the Amtrak train."

"What about all the innocent people who are going to die from the fallout?" Paige asked. Mike glanced at her, then turned back to Sally.

"But I never questioned *today's* action. *This* is what the Eagle's Claw is about. Fighting the enemy." He stabbed a hand toward the Dreamland complex. "Punishing the conspirators—but when Nevsky found out about the mock pit, I did what I had to do . . . much as I hated it."

Sally continued to scowl. "Don't talk to *me* about unpleasant tasks! As far as I'm concerned, I had the worse duty—fucking that slob PK Dirks, just to get him out of the way so we could do our job. You didn't have to feel that man inside you, enduring his sweaty hands, fighting off the urge to wipe away his slobbering kisses. All *you* had to do was crack a thick Russian skull."

Paige's thoughts reeled, but then anger swelled inside her. This woman, a seemingly innocuous "administrative assistant," had been behind the deaths, the terror, the conspiracies. This woman had led Uncle Mike down the dark path to madness, brainwashing him, influencing him. After his wife had died, after his good friend and anchor Gordon Mitchell had succumbed to cancer—Sally had twisted Mike Waterloo during the emptiest time in his life, when he had most needed help.

"In killing Nevsky, you only succeeded in bringing attention to yourselves," Paige said. "Was it so important that you strike a blow against the disarmament team? Sounds like poor planning to me."

Uncle Mike looked at her in surprise. "The fact that Nevsky was on the disarmament team meant nothing at all to us. The inspection was just a show and tell, a political exercise—but the ambassador went through our paperwork more thoroughly than we expected. He was drunk half the time, but somehow he caught our trail of diverted components. We couldn't let him blow the whistle, not so close to what we've planned for years."

Paige clamped her lips together and didn't speak as the puzzle began to fall into place.

Destruction and transportation of nuclear devices out of the stockpile required certain signatures, certain approvals—but the work schedules changed at random, for security reasons. All the militia had to do was wait until the schedules happened to rotate the infiltrators into place, so that Jorgenson could fill out the transportation forms, Mike Waterloo could fill out the DAF receipts, and PK Dirks—the inept but good-natured technician, yet duped in the end—had unknowingly done his part. Sally, being the expert at filing and, if necessary, forging or altering the paperwork, must have succeeded in covering their trail, working until all the right documents were in place. It must have taken nearly two years of maneuvering.

Administratively, the records showed that a specific weapon had been disassembled and sent elsewhere . . . when in reality it had been secreted away until the Eagle's Claw chose to use it. On October 24, the anniversary of the formation of the United Nations.

Out here, at Dreamland.

Sally must have poisoned Jorgenson because too much suspicion would have been directed at him for Nevsky's death; his part in the plot accomplished, the forklift driver had become an expendable fall guy. And since Paige knew the same coronary-inducing drug had been used on the undercover FBI agent, Sally was no doubt responsible for William Maguire's murder as well.

The secretary turned away and snapped her fingers. Uncle Mike jumped to attention like a trained dog. "Stop twiddling your thumbs and go do your work," she said. "Set the timer, take care of the safety interlocks so we can get this show on the road. Our deadline's today."

Crunching around behind the vehicle, Mike popped open the back of the land rover and bent to the stolen nuclear warhead.

Sally laughed, looking at Paige. "When this goes off, the only thing left will be a big crater instead of a clandestine UN base . . . and then the United States can rest easy again. They'll thank us, in the end."

Paige drew a deep breath, sickened at what they were doing. "Don't tell me *you* believe that nonsense too?"

In the back Uncle Mike intently went through the procedures of arming the bomb, preparing it for detonation. He removed a small plastic card and inserted it into an arming mechanism, keyed in a long string of numbers, then withdrew the card, sliding it back into his shirt pocket. Paige watched as he opened the access panel and began to set the rest of the arming mechanisms one by one, confounding the Permissive Action Links. As DAF Manager, Mike Waterloo possessed the security codes, and he had the expertise required. He verified the numbers, then closed the panel and punched the final button.

Mike stood up, then turned away from Paige, as if he couldn't bear to look at her with his sad eyes. His face wore a dead expression as he met Sally's gaze.

"It's armed," he said.

CHAPTER FORTY-TWO

Friday, October 24
6:40 A.M.

Northeastern Boundary
Nevada Test Site

Craig sat in the right-hand seat of the helicopter, next to the pilot. "My life sure got exciting since you came to town, Agent Kreident," the pilot said. "Just don't make me chase any trains today, okay?"

"No, this morning we're going after nuclear bombs."

The pilot shook his head. "And through a thunderstorm yet—sorry I asked."

General Ursov crouched behind him like a powderkeg, his face pushed up against the curved window, peering down at the brown wasteland racing below them. The Russian seemed to be filing away details of everything he saw. Craggy mesas rose in the distance, contrasting with the broad flats used for test aircraft, bombing ranges, and survival exercises.

There was a *lot* of acreage down there to hide a nuclear weapon. If Waterloo had not gone to Groom Lake after all, or if he hadn't yet reached the area, Craig wouldn't know where to begin looking.

He pushed his sunglasses back into place, fidgeting again. He turned to the pilot and raised his voice over the incessant chopping. "Where are we, exactly?"

"Probably nowhere on any Triple-A map." The pilot's

mirrored sunglasses reflected Craig's features. He pointed to the horizon, toward the black thunderheads. "Just crossed the northern boundary of the Test Site into Nellis, I think. The Air Force bombing range starts at the corner of that dry lake bed below us. Let's hope the flyboys got the word, so they don't use us for target practice." The helicopter bumped along on the storm gusts.

"I'll get us the proper approvals," Craig said. "Just keep going straight to Groom Lake. Best possible speed."

Craig sank back in his seat, feeling helpless and desperate to hurry. He tapped his fingers on the console beside him, then glanced at his watch. After his creepy conversation with Waterloo and the other evidence he had found, the connection with Nellis and Groom Lake made so much sense. The militia didn't even have to smuggle the warhead out of the sprawling reservation, only deeper *inside*.

But why? What did they hope to accomplish by blowing up a hidden part of a high-security military base? To destroy evidence of some sort of conspiracy? But the government already denied all activities at the restricted facility. And the aftereffects of the nuclear detonation, even way out here, would be devastating for the country.

The pilot put a finger to his right earphone. "Stand by, one," he said. Reaching down, he pulled out a pair of headphones with an attached microphone and handed them to Craig. "Looks like you're going to have to do some fast talking to convince them we should keep on going into the restricted airspace. They think we're trying to infiltrate under cover of the storm. Do you know how to use these?"

"Yeah," said Craig. He pulled on the snug-fitting headphones, brought the small black microphone to his lips and reached down to push a button on the cord. "Special Agent Kreident."

"Agent Kreident, this is Lieutenant Colonel Terrell, Ops Group Commander in charge of the Auxiliary base security forces. What is the meaning of your intrusion into restricted air space? You are ordered to turn around immediately and wait for the proper authorities."

"Colonel Terrell, I am unable to wait under these circumstances." He glanced at his watch yet again. "You know why we're approaching your base, and what is at stake. I'm sure you must have been informed by Agent Goldfarb and Major Braden, the NEST commander. We require your full and immediate cooperation—this is a matter of national security."

"No," Ursov said from behind him. "It is a matter of *international* security."

"Nobody told me anything about this until just a few minutes ago," Terrell said. "But I assure you our own base security is capable of dealing with the threat. We'll dispatch search teams as soon as possible. I repeat, you are not authorized to enter this area. Please turn around and return to your takeoff point. It is unsafe to fly under these weather conditions."

Letting his annoyance boil just beneath the surface of his words, Craig said, "I'm sorry, sir, but I can't do that. I have been working on circumventing the Eagle's Claw for some time. If you haven't heard anything about the militia until just moments ago, you are not—I repeat not—capable of handling this yourself."

Terrell didn't back down. "Agent Kreident, do not force me to take extreme action. We have been authorized by presidential order to implement deadly measures to prevent compromising the security of Groom Lake."

Craig swallowed hard and interrupted Terrell. "Colonel, this helicopter is also bearing the head of the Russian disarmament delegation, General Ursov, who is himself here by presidential order—the Russian president and our own." Ursov looked over at him, his eyes wide, his lips curving in a grim smile.

"You've got a *Russian* on board?" Terrell growled over the headphones. "What do you think you're—"

"Colonel, may I remind you that your security has *already* been compromised?" Craig snapped. "We have arrested a Staff Sergeant John Marlo from Nellis Air Force Base, who was responsible for the explosion at the Laughlin railroad bridge yesterday. The militia ringleader in possession of a diverted nuclear warhead is from NTS, the Device Assembly Facility Manager, Mike Waterloo."

"Waterloo! I just signed over a shipment of nuclear weapons to him two days ago—"

"He has been planning this operation for some time, sir, and he is on his way to you right now. I think he plans to blow up your Area 51." He drew in a deep breath. "You must let us through so we can stop him."

Finally, Terrell came back on the line. "Tell the pilot to land just north of the bombing range. Do *not* proceed any further. Do you understand?" During a brief pause, only static came over the line. "I'll be joining you personally. In the meantime, my people will check out this Marlo character."

A dark gray military helicopter squatted on the far end of the isolated airstrip. Military personnel wearing sand-colored camouflage battle fatigues swarmed like ants around the craft, bearing Air Force issue M-16 automatic weapons.

Two additional helicopters hovered in the sky, ignoring the storm, waiting for the FBI craft to land. Craig could make out a rack of missiles on the underside of each guardian chopper. "Looks like they're serious," he said.

"Better than Boy Scouts," said the pilot. He reached to his right to adjust the rotors. The staccato thumping sound changed pitch and became a deep roar, which grew louder as the sound reflected off the dry lake bed. Small puddles had already begun to form in low spots. The FBI helicopter flared out as they slowed their forward motion and started to descend. Below, the security men stepped back to clear the landing pad.

"Okay, gentlemen. You're on your own from here." The pilot lowered the helicopter to the pad; it tilted to the right and bumped on one skid before settling down steady. Once they had landed, the pilot reached up and started clicking switches. "Thanks for a wonderful morning."

Craig pushed open the cockpit door, and the wet wind whipped his tie around. As he climbed out, a tall black man in sand-colored camouflage ducked his head and ran toward them. Two military policemen stepped forward from outside the landing circle, keeping their automatic weapons leveled at the intruders. Craig saw three more men run around to the side and signal the rest of the escort detail.

Craig flipped open his FBI badge and held it up as he shouted over the noise. "I'm Special Agent Kreident."

"General Ursov, Russian Strategic Rocket Forces." The squat, broad-shouldered man stood stoically at a half crouch by the cockpit door. He held a hand on his head to keep his wide brown-and-red hat from blowing away.

The black lieutenant colonel warily saluted the Russian officer. "I'm Lieutenant Colonel Terrell, head of base security. It is highly unusual to allow anyone access to Groom Lake without going through the proper security channels—especially a foreign national." Terrell looked upset, yet intimidating. "I hope you appreciate how sensitive an installation this is."

Craig looked the Air Force officer in the eye. "Colonel, if we don't stop the militia, there won't be much of an installation left for you to worry about. You know that Mike Waterloo has the weapon access codes. Your own Staff Sergeant Marlo could have provided the proper base information, IFFs, and the necessary maps."

"Yes," LtCol Terrell breathed. He looked around the secure area, his men standing at alert, weapons ready. "We checked your story about Sergeant Marlo and confirmed he's one of ours. He's a security specialist, and if Waterloo's got an IFF, he can get around all our sensors, the radar—everything."

Craig nodded, glad that he had finally gotten through to the man. "We have to mount a visual search and do it fast, Colonel. Even with your security forces airborne, we're going to have one heck of a time finding them in all this wide-open space . . . unless we start the search at Dreamland."

CHAPTER FORTY-THREE

Friday, October 24
7:12 A.M.

Dreamland

"The point of no return," Mike Waterloo said, his voice hollow and frightened. "Victory for the Eagle's Claw, and a restoration of American ideals." He refused to look at the warhead in the back of the land rover, as if by ignoring it he could forget about his second thoughts.

With the timer on the nuclear warhead ticking down, he clutched his hands in front of him, looked over at Paige, then glanced away.

Paige had watched Mike work as distant helicopters flew high overhead, circling. *They must be hunting for us.* But the search teams didn't know the land rovers had already penetrated Dreamland security and were hidden in the dry gully. The morning rainstorm would already be foiling infrared search equipment, and Mike's stolen IFF had circumvented Groom Lake's other electronic surveillance.

Mike turned uncertainly toward his murderous secretary. Paige thought he was going to change his mind about the warhead, but instead he said, "Let's get out of here, Sally. All three of us can fit in the other rover and head overland. I'm the only one who can stop the detonation now. We have to move if we're going to avoid the worst of the fallout."

The numbers ticked down, like fading heartbeats.

"You're wrong, Mike," Sally said, reaching inside her loose flannel shirt to withdraw a small handgun. "This method is more definite."

With sharp cracks like splintering wood, Sally fired three times into Mike Waterloo's chest, driving him back against the driver's door of the first land rover. His head slammed against the window.

Paige screamed and leaped for him. Sally backed off, watching bemused.

As Paige held him, Uncle Mike's mouth opened and closed in utter astonishment, touching his chest, seeing the blood, watching it run out of him as he slid to the ground. His sad eyes grew round and wide with dismay. Paige grabbed his sleeve, but could do nothing to help.

"Three times should be enough," Sally said, her voice cold as she looked down at the handgun. "Even with a small caliber."

Paige knelt beside Uncle Mike in the wet dirt, grabbing his shoulder. His final breath rattled in his throat, foaming with blood. His eyes glazed over and became vacant. The rain began to fall harder.

She hoped for him to form words, to say his goodbyes, to gasp some sort of farewell with his dying breath . . . but Sally had targeted accurately, twice through the sternum and once through a lung. Mike Waterloo was dead as soon as he slumped to the ground.

In utter shock, with his blood warm and wet on her hands, Paige could not stanch the flow of memories in front of her mind: visions of Uncle Mike teaching her how to hold a fishing rod, showing her how to use a protractor and compass to draw perfect circles and geometric shapes. She recalled Uncle Mike and her father sitting out on the porch in Livermore, chatting about the nuclear test program, about their work at the Lab, discussing politics and the Vietnam war.

It had been no more than conversation then, shooting the breeze. But somewhere along the way it had turned into a deadly paranoia, a warped perception that had finally led to Uncle Mike setting this nuclear warhead . . . and to his death.

Paige stared at the blood on her fingers as the memories continued to sharpen. She wondered if this might be the supposed phenomenon of her life flashing before her eyes. Sally was sure to pull the trigger on her any second now.

But instead, the secretary brought the handgun down, wiping rain away from her face. "Good old Mike. He said he was willing to die for the cause," she said with a glacial smile. "Freedom doesn't come cheap."

"But he promised he wouldn't disarm the bomb," Paige said, wanting to claw the woman's eyes out. "You were supposed to run away together."

"That was the original plan," Sally said, "but the result is the same, and now he can't ever finger me by getting caught. I got rid of Jorgenson for the same reason. Now I leave a clean field behind me. Besides, Mike wouldn't have been worth a damn as a hostage—and you certainly are." She gestured to the second land rover. "If the military or anybody gives us trouble, I can use you as a bargaining chip. Get in, and we'll hightail it out of here. Put enough distance between us and ground zero."

"Why should I bother?" Paige said, crossing her arms over her chest. She had no other way of resisting. "You'll kill me as soon as you get clear."

Sally shrugged. "Depends on how it all turns out. Would you rather die now or in an hour or two? Your choice."

Wiping her hands on her jeans, Paige left Uncle Mike's vehicle and shuffled toward the other land rover. She glanced once more at the gaunt man's body, but saw nothing there. The Mike Waterloo she had known and loved had died long ago.

Surprisingly strong, Sally Montry lifted Mike's body and hoisted him into the front seat of the first land rover, then she closed and locked all the doors as a final precaution to keep the warhead inaccessible before she hurried over to where Paige stood at the passenger side door.

"Don't make me waste time in pointless threats. You know I'll shoot you, and you know I don't have much patience. Get in!"

Behind them, in the back compartment of the other vehicle, the nuclear device continued its countdown.

"Every second brings us closer to the big mushroom cloud," Sally said, "and we're both going to have to haul ass to get beyond the lethal radius in time. As it is, the rain will make overland travel more difficult."

Seething, yet totally helpless, Paige climbed reluctantly inside the land rover. She couldn't think of a way to fight back. Yet.

That was when they heard the helicopter approaching.

CHAPTER FORTY-FOUR

Friday, October 24
7:26 A.M.

En Route to Area 51
Groom Lake Auxiliary Station

In the rear of the military helicopter, Craig sat on a long webbed seat next to LtCol Terrell and General Ursov. The chopper was a no-nonsense craft bigger than the DOE craft they'd flown in earlier, but not as large as the monstrous MH-53 behemoths that had joined the desperate search.

A two-man security detail stood at the open side door, scanning the brown desert with infrared binoculars as the helicopters swept across the sky. The storm blurred all details, erasing the path of ground vehicles, knocking the aircraft about. But they continued at high speed toward their destination.

Toward Dreamland.

Grasping a braided red nylon rope that ran from the front to the back of the cockpit ceiling, Terrell leaned next to Craig. He extended a hand out of the fuselage, shouting over the constant thrumming that washed into the helicopter.

"If Waterloo really has an IFF, he can neutralize our standard electronic detectors, but we've also requested some high-altitude reconnaissance from the Air Force. They're scrambling a TR-1 and an SR-71 sortie, whichever can get here first. They've promised a JSTARS as well."

"How long is that going to take?" Craig asked.

"Could be as much as a few hours."

"That will be too late," Ursov said gruffly.

Terrell snapped a glance over at the Russian defensively. "With the end of the Cold War, we don't keep those aircraft on alert anymore."

"What about the ground search?" asked Craig, putting down his own binoculars. "Have you coordinated with the NEST team?"

"Been there, done that," said Terrell. His dark arm rippled with muscles as he grasped the nylon safety rope. "They're sweeping up from the south with your FBI task force, and we're coming down from the north. We should squeeze the terrorists in the middle."

"Hopefully, we'll have enough time. We might not be able to wait for a full-scale military assault," Craig said. "Luckily, I don't think Waterloo knows we're coming."

"He will as soon as he hears the helicopters," Terrell said. He ducked and stepped across the interior to the cockpit, where he spoke to the helmeted pilot, who pulled a folded map from a leg pocket in his green flight suit. Terrell shook out the map as he made his way back to Craig and Ursov.

Terrell smoothed the plastic map on the webbed seat, then glanced uneasily at the Russian general before he pointed out the Groom Lake base perimeter. Unidentified buildings were marked around the dry lake bed near another airstrip. "We'll concentrate the air search in this area."

Craig studied the brown and green shading that marked the contours of Nellis Air Force Range surrounding the separate, internal area of Groom Lake Auxiliary Station. It reminded him of the crude sketch he had found in Waterloo's home only a few hours before.

Given the size of the desert, he couldn't conceive of searching the whole base visually. No wonder the military relied on technological means to secure so many square miles—but Mike Waterloo had shown how easy it was to circumvent even the best security, given inside assistance, a few gadgets, and reliable information.

"The Eagle's Claw has spent too much time planning this operation to play hide-and-seek in the desert. I'm sure I know where he's going," Craig said. "And I'm half sure he's got a hostage." His chest tightened as he thought of Paige, betrayed by her Uncle Mike, dragged along so she couldn't sound the alarm.

"We cannot allow ourselves to get into a hostage situation," Terrell said, "not with a live warhead at stake. We must take extreme measures, if we feel the situation is warranted. Thousands of lives are at risk."

Craig felt sick in his stomach. "Just make damned sure it doesn't come to that."

He looked out the open helicopter door. Craggy mountains, bare of any trees, contrasted with the dusty arroyos and dry lake beds below. A thousand places to hide.

But Waterloo hadn't come up here to hide—just to destroy. *How much time did they really have left?*

"That's Dreamland down below, gentlemen," Terrell said. A two-mile-long runway had been scribed like a pale line across a white-salt lake bed. Rocks the size of cars punctuated the ground. Immense featureless buildings sat at the edge of the flat playa, surrounded by concentric fences. Two large aircraft sat on a concrete pad at the end of one runway.

Lieutenant Colonel Terrell grasped the red safety line as the helicopter approached the south side of the isolated complex. He leaned forward to study as much of the complex as he could.

"Don't get your hopes up, General," Terrell said dryly. "We keep all the really interesting stuff hidden inside the hangars."

"Yes, I know," Ursov said, straightening. "And you only fly them at night."

"Not necessarily all of them," Terrell said with a faint smile. "Even your spy satellites have certain limitations."

Craig steadied himself as the helicopter descended to begin a sweeping search of the isolated complex, far from the main base headquarters.

In the right-hand seat the copilot twisted around and gestured excitedly. "I think we've spotted something, sir. Camouflaged vehicles in the gully behind Delta Hangar."

"*Delta* Hangar?" Terrell's face drew tight. "Oh, shit." He turned to Ursov. "Sit down, sir. And strap in."

The Russian plopped down in the webbed seat next to Craig. "Nothing interesting there, I am sure—correct, Special Agent Kreident?"

Still fastened in his safety harness, Craig leaned forward to squint down at the fenced-in complex below. A narrow gully ran behind the largest buildings before it widened and opened up into a rocky alluvial fan across the desert floor.

If Waterloo had driven from the south, from NTS, he might have been able to approach the isolated complex by keeping out of sight in the gully, traveling at night, confounding the Groom Lake sensors with his stolen IFF.

The helicopter wheeled around, coming in from behind the forbidding security installation, then rapidly descended toward the ground like an eagle diving for prey. Craig felt his stomach trying to claw its way up his throat.

Maybe Paige was down there. Somewhere.

One of the enlisted security men pointed down at an angle. "There, Colonel Terrell!"

Hidden in the long morning shadows of the broad gully he saw a pair of four-wheel-drive land rovers, camouflaged with mottled brown and gray so that they nearly vanished into the landscape. Craig couldn't see anyone moving around the vehicles. He felt his heart start to hammer. *Was Paige down there?*

Terrell stepped back from the cockpit. "Just where you

said they would be, Mr. Kreident. I think we have it under control at this point."

The helicopter wheeled in the sky, keeping a good thousand feet above the ground. No one stepped from the land rovers.

Terrell leaned toward the copilot. "Get me a radio mike." He pulled on the curled black cord and brought the microphone up to his mouth. "Security detail, this is command post. We'll need a NEST squad and EOD team in the gully about a quarter mile behind Delta Hangar. All units sweep north back to the main complex." He clicked off the mike and said to the copilot, "Put me on Guard frequency. Maybe someone down there is listening. If not, we can always use the loudspeaker."

The copilot punched in the new frequency. The two enlisted men took up positions on either side of the open door. Securing their helmets and strapping into the helicopter's safety lines, they unlatched M-16 rifles from a weapons cache. Craig and General Ursov watched the preparations, feeling extraneous.

The lean black officer brought the mike back up. "Attention, land rovers below. This is Lieutenant Colonel Terrell, Groom Lake Ops Group Commander. You are trespassing on government property in a highly secure area. Throw down any weapons you may have and exit your vehicle immediately. Security teams are approaching. Make no threatening moves."

He waited a moment then spoke again. "Attention, land rover. Make no mistake—we have weapons trained on you and we are authorized to use deadly force. Surrender immediately."

But the two motionless land rovers responded only with silence. Before long, the rain would make the gully unfit for travel even with the rugged vehicles.

"I guess we've got ourselves one of those difficult situations," Craig said. He hoped Paige was safe down there.

General Ursov peered over at Craig. "They know they cannot get away," he murmured.

"That won't stop them from doing anything desperate," Craig said, turning to Terrell. "We can't afford a long standoff here. They might be trying to set off that nuke. Does your security team have anything we can use in a hostage situation?"

Terrell thought for a moment, then said grimly, "Yes, I think we might have a very unusual surprise for them."

CHAPTER FORTY-FIVE

Friday, October 24
7:46 A.M.

Dreamland

The Dreamland facility changed, moved . . . opened.

With a loud shuddering noise in the eerie desert stillness, the great metal doors along the near side of Delta Hangar groaned apart. Generators hummed, and heavy machinery activated with a clamor like an assembly line—but no human figures showed themselves.

But even with its doors yawning wide, Dreamland gave up none of its secrets. The cavernous interior of the building remained dark, like a dragon's lair. The desert seemed to hold its breath, waiting.

Suddenly, banks of interior lights gleamed on, stabbing through the shadows like yellow eyes hidden in the shadows. External spotlights blasted down from automated guard portals around the razor-wire fence, glaring on the sand; the outstretched runway glistened against the white lake bed, blurred by the falling rain.

"Check," LtCol Terrell said into his headset microphone.

In the rear passenger seat of the military helicopter, General Ursov stared with amazement but without comprehension.

Beside him, Craig couldn't grasp the dizzying size of the secret facility either. At the moment, though, his curiosity took a back seat to his concern for Paige Mitchell, who might or might not be held hostage down there behind the massive buildings—and for the stolen nuclear warhead he knew must be in one of the two land rovers below. He wished they would communicate with him, break their silence, negotiate a surrender.

As the helicopter hovered over the two camouflaged vehicles, Terrell handed the microphone to Craig. "Somebody's on the radio for you, Agent Kreident. Hasn't identified herself, but I think it's our friendly terrorist down there—and it's not Mr. Waterloo. She warns that if any aircraft come out of that facility, she'll shoot her hostage. A woman named Paige Mitchell, a DOE protocol officer, if I understand her correctly."

Craig's heart lurched—Paige was a hostage after all, as he had feared. But then the rest of the comment sank in. "*She?* The militia creep is a woman? What happened to Mike Waterloo?"

"Listen for yourself, sir."

Ursov lowered his voice, muttering, as if commiserating with Craig. "We have been giving Miss Mitchell too many difficulties this week."

Craig swallowed hard, squeezing his hand into a fist, wanting to punch someone. He took the microphone and clicked it. "This is Agent Kreident of the FBI, and we demand that you release your hostage immediately. We have full security coverage of the entire area, and you can't get away. Why not just surrender and put an end to this?"

Instead of answering him, one of the two land rovers lurched into gear, spraying sand and gravel as it picked up speed across the desert. It accelerated down the widening gully into the alluvial fan, away from the second vehicle, which remained parked and motionless.

"Where the hell does she think she's going?" Terrell said. "We've got backup zeroing in from all directions!"

Ursov gave a short, loud laugh. "You expect a terrorist just to give up and apologize?"

Then a woman's voice came over the helicopter's radio, iron-hard and suggesting absolutely no compromise. "You need to keep your priorities straight, Agent Kreident." A familiar voice. "You've got some choices to make, here and now."

He sat bolt upright in the passenger seat. *Sally?* Sally Montry? Craig breathed deeply. Mike Waterloo's secretary—a member of the militia? Events clicked in place—PK Dirks's convenient excuse of being absent at Nevsky's death hadn't been his setup, but *hers*. The administrative paperwork for clearing out nuclear weapons, all the dead-end leads . . . Sally would have been in the perfect position to coordinate everything, and to cover their tracks.

And now she had Paige. *But where was the warhead?*

"My priorities are clear enough, Sally," he said. "To stop the Eagle's Claw, to prevent you from further bloodshed."

Sally's short laugh sounded more like a cough. "You listen to me, Agent Kreident. Inside the other land rover you'll find two things. One is Mike Waterloo, a martyr to the cause—make sure he's remembered as a hero, if you all survive yourselves."

Craig gripped the microphone to retort, but Sally continued. "There's also a nuclear device in the back compartment, already armed and counting down. You've got fifteen minutes before the secret United Nations Command Center is obliterated. Make your choice—waste time chasing me and pretty little Paige"—she gave a sarcastic snort—"or try to save the world."

Sally clicked off her transmission. The land rover accelerated across the wasteland.

Taking Paige with it.

Craig and Terrell and Ursov looked at each other in confusion. The military police in the helicopter wore greenish expressions, as if they wanted the pilot to spin about and head straight away from the warhead with all possible speed, as if they had any chance of outrunning a megaton explosion.

Agonized, Craig knew they would have to make the decision Sally wanted. He watched the land rover bounce away with no pretense at caution. Sally Montry knew she had won this round. "How far out is the NEST team?" he asked, desperately hoping. "And your own disarmament teams?"

"Another twenty minutes, minimum." Terrell's face went slack. "We're the only ones available even to try."

"Well, then I'm going down there," Craig shouted over to the pilot. "Come on, let's go—drop this bird!"

As the helicopter descended toward the ground, its rotors roaring, Craig unbuckled and knelt at the edge of the open doorway, holding the support ropes. Before he could convince himself otherwise, he dropped the remaining few feet to the desert, splashing in the rain-wet sand and running toward the motionless land rover.

Every second might count. *Fifteen minutes!* They'd be caught in the blast of a nuclear explosion, if he couldn't somehow disarm the weapon. And he had no idea where to begin.

The military pilot left the rotors turning, just in case they had to flee . . . though it was an open question whether even the high-speed helicopter could actually get far enough away in time.

"I am coming, Agent Kreident," Ursov bellowed, climbing out the back of the helicopter. "Wait for me—I can assist." The MPs shouted after him, but didn't seem too eager to run closer to the ticking warhead.

Craig didn't pause for a minute. Ursov had vowed not to let Craig out of his sight, but neither of them had time for political games. He couldn't waste a second to get rid of Ursov, so he just ignored the squat, muscular man.

Reaching the rover, Craig spotted the scarlet stains splashed on the driver's side door. Before he could blink, he noticed the crumpled, bloody form inside. He stopped short as he recognized the face of Mike Waterloo, his expression slack with death.

Everything Sally had said was true. She had shot Waterloo, and she would not hesitate in carrying out her threat against her hostage. Paige was doomed—and so were they all. He longed to go rescue her, but first, he had to somehow stop the nuclear weapon from going off. He glanced at his watch. Piece of cake. Right.

"How do you expect to disarm the warhead, Agent Kreident?" Ursov said, panting, his face flushed. "Are you an expert in such matters?"

"Maybe it's got an OFF switch," he muttered, shaking his head. He'd had trouble enough with the plastique at Hoover Dam—and now this. "I knew I should have learned how to do this stuff."

His priorities had been clear, as Sally had known, but the procedure was not. Craig had no idea what to do . . . but if he did nothing, the warhead would go off. And if he did the *wrong* thing, the warhead would go off. He just had to hope that somehow, by accident, he would be able to guess the correct method.

The wind picked up, hurling cold raindrops, and the thunder rumbled overhead. Craig peered into the back of the land rover and spotted the nuclear device. He had seen similar warheads in the DAF, and he knew this was not a mockup, not a prop—but a functional nuclear weapon. He understood where it had come from, and he knew that the militia intended to use it.

The LEDs on the warhead's access panel glowed. Numbers on the timer continued to click down steadily one at a time. The bomb was armed, ready to detonate.

Thirteen minutes.

Ursov moved up beside him, puffing, his face flushed with determination. Perhaps he intended to chew up the warhead to dismantle it. He stared through the land rover's window, scowling. "Come, Agent Kreident—we must begin."

Craig grabbed the door handle, ready to jump into the back compartment and get to work . . . whatever it was.

But he found the door locked. He couldn't even get inside.

CHAPTER FORTY-SIX

Friday, October 24
7:53 A.M.

Restricted Area
Groom Lake Air Force
Auxiliary Station

As Sally Montry drove at a reckless speed across the rugged and muddy terrain, fleeing the nuclear demon she herself had set in motion, Paige huddled in the passenger seat. After all she had seen and learned, the death of her Uncle Mike, the insidious plan of the militia and their paranoid fears of a secret UN base deep inside Groom Lake, the ticking timer on the nuclear device, she sat quiet, seemingly cowed, subdued. . . .

Watching for her chance.

Wondering how much time remained on the warhead's countdown clock, and how they would escape the deadly rain of fallout even if they somehow managed to survive the blast itself.

The murderous secretary jammed the land rover into four-wheel drive and tromped down on the accelerator, kicking up chips of alluvial gravel from the boulder-strewn hardpan, splashing brown water from a puddle. The vehicle slewed from side to side, but the speedometer jiggled close to fifty miles an hour. Twelve and a half miles, Paige thought. That's how far they'd make it in fifteen minutes. She didn't know if that distance would put them out of harm's way—how far away were those weathered press bleachers from the detonation zones on Frenchman Flat?

A mile from the fenced-in Dreamland facility, cracks appeared in the ground, wide arroyos carved into the desert where forerunners of a flash flood coursed, eating away the soft dirt. The driving became much rougher.

Slowing as little as she dared, Sally paralleled one of the gullies, frequently glancing into her rear-view mirror, searching for helicopter pursuit or her imagined United Nations security forces that were supposedly headquartered inside the hangar building.

The land rover roared recklessly across the desert, leaving a plain trail. Sally must be counting on the nuclear firestorm to obliterate any tracks. Stern-faced, her eyes flicking from side to side, Sally Montry cruised onward. Paige held onto the vehicle's door to steady herself.

Craig and the others had remained behind at the second land rover, struggling to deactivate the warhead—but she didn't think Craig had any possible way of knowing how to shut down a warhead. Mike Waterloo had asserted that no one could disarm the warhead in time. And Sally had shot him dead.

The bomb would go off, and everyone around it was doomed.

The land rover's left front tire struck a boulder. Sally compensated by jerking the wheel, and the vehicle smashed into a depression, bouncing them savagely.

Paige picked that moment to lash out, reaching over to grab the steering wheel with both hands, jerking it to the right—hard. The rover lurched toward the steep gully churning with runoff water from the rainstorm. If they went over the edge, the tires would jam—the vehicle might even tip on its side, and they would be stranded, mired in the mud. Sally would never get away in time.

She would probably shoot Paige in her helpless rage, but it would do her no good. The vicious woman would still be trapped.

Sally howled and fought, wrestling for control. "Stop it, you bitch!" Freeing her right arm from the steering wheel, she jabbed brutally into Paige's side with her elbow. Paige gasped with a sudden explosion of pain and released her hold.

"If we get stuck, we'll both be fried in the blast!" Sally yelled, jerking the vehicle back under control as she dropped her speed, veering away from the steep arroyo.

"That's the whole idea," Paige growled as she lunged for the steering wheel again.

But Sally clenched her right fist and swung hard backhandedly, striking Paige squarely on the bridge of her nose. The militia woman knew exactly where to hit, as if she had been trained in hand-to-hand combat. The blow caused a silvery explosion of pain behind Paige's eyes. Fresh, warm blood spurted from her nose.

Paige gasped, seeing the scarlet stain spill onto her shirt. She held her head against the pounding pain, wondering if the other woman had broken her nose. "Damn you," Paige said, her voice clogged and gurgling from the flowing blood.

"You don't have a clue what could happen, do you?" Sally snapped. "I should have shot you." She tromped on the accelerator. Loose rocks spewed from under the rear tires, and the land rover leaped forward again, as Sally frantically tried to increase the distance. "Nothing's going to stop me now."

Paige looked up, blinking the red haze from her eyes.

Suddenly something glittered overhead, a silent flash of motion that seemed nothing more than a blur across the sky, lower than the dark clouds. Then the noise came—a muffled passage, a *whoosh* that sounded as if a high-speed invisible truck had just roared past them.

The land rover rattled and jerked from the shockwave.

Through the biting pain in her head, Paige had a fleeting thought that the warhead had exploded after all and the distant shock front had just rocked them—but she knew that couldn't be true. From this distance the flash would have blinded them both, and the blast front would have squashed the land rover like a recycled can.

"What the hell was that?" Sally grabbed the steering wheel, craning her neck to stare up through the windshield, then looking out the side to see what had just soared by, what had attacked them.

The sound came on again, tremors in the sky but not thunder—the rushing, roaring passage of something cruising just above them, close enough to touch.

Paige could see nothing, and neither could Sally. The secretary grew frantic, wrenching the steering wheel with white-knuckled hands, attempting to drive an evasive path—but she didn't know what could be pursuing them.

Paige caught an odd glitter out of the corner of her own eyes: flashing lights moving incredibly fast, then nothing . . . like a mirror in the sky, as if it *almost* wasn't there. . . .

"What is happening here?" Sally demanded, then tugged the land rover to one side to avoid a rugged cluster of boulders. She accelerated all out to get away from the mysterious invisible attacker.

Paige discerned an oval shape beneath the clouds, glowing, indistinct, which emitted a shower of lights that she couldn't quite see. Then the strange craft moved faster than she could follow with her eyes. The image disappeared in the air, swallowed up in an illusion of the sky, once again soaring directly over the land rover.

Sally saw it too and jerked the vehicle to the left as the shock wave hit again—but then, without warning, the dashboard erupted in a shower of sparks. The land rover's engine went dead, as if it had been smothered by a heavy pillow. All the lights and gauges winked out. The ventilator fan stopped. All power systems shorted out.

Sally could no longer steer, but the vehicle's momentum pushed it along a few more feet until it bumped into a boulder and came to an abrupt stop. Dead.

Furious, Sally pounded on the steering wheel, on the horn, but even *that* emitted no peep, no sound at all. She turned the key, trying to start the engine again and again, but the vehicle didn't cough, didn't even try to turn over.

Flinging open the land rover's door, Sally yanked out her handgun, jabbing it toward Paige, who still sat trying to stanch the flow of blood streaming from her nose. She stumbled out of the vehicle into the rain, waving her gun around in search of a target. "What is this? What the hell is going on?" she yelled.

But Paige had no answer for her. She was as mystified as the militia woman. She thought of Doog and his hippie friends, coming up here to search for the hidden flying saucers. . . .

Sally stood, her feet planted on the muddy ground, turning back and forth. The secretary looked behind her toward Dreamland and the armed nuclear warhead, several miles distant. They had not come far enough to escape the atomic blast or the immediate fallout, Paige knew. Not nearly far enough. And their time must be dwindling to zero.

Then Paige heard the invisible enemy again, an approaching whine in the air that developed into a steadily building rumble, the roar of engines so powerful it sounded like an avalanche in the sky.

Enraged, Sally turned to look up, holding her handgun out as if she might fire upon the mysterious craft in a futile gesture—but instead Sally just stared, gaping open-mouthed in astonishment.

"I don't believe it! The nutcases were right all along." She gasped in amazement. "It's a fuckin' UFO!"

Then the blurry mirage thundered past like a self-contained sonic boom, streaking so low and so close that the entire land rover shuddered from side to side. The windows rattled. The open driver's side door was nearly torn from its hinges.

The shock wave hurled Sally to the ground. Seeing her chance again, Paige leaped out, ignoring her bloodied nose and her aching ribs. She tumbled out of the land rover and scrambled to where the secretary lay stunned.

As Sally tried to pick herself up from the dirt, Paige crashed into her, tackling the secretary back down to the mud. She used both of her knees to trap Sally's forearm. Wet dirt and sand splashed both of them. She pounded on the militia woman's hand, trying to get her to release her grip on the gun. When Sally's fingers only clenched tighter, Paige picked up a rock and smashed her knuckles.

With a yelp of pain, the other woman finally released her hold on the weapon, and Paige grabbed it up, standing above the snarling secretary, swaying. Her vision blurred, and the blood flowed down her face again.

But Paige drew herself up tall, her legs spread, both hands tightly wrapped around the handgun. Her finger slipped around the trigger guard. She had watched this woman gun down her Uncle Mike in cold blood. "Just stay right there," she said, pointing the gun.

Sally struggled to her knees, her expression cold and furious. "We've got to run! If we don't get to shelter before that warhead blows, we'll be disintegrated in an instant! We're still too close to ground zero."

"It's too late for that," Paige said, feeling a remarkable clarity coming to her fuzzy thoughts. "But if it happens, you'll have about a microsecond to say 'I told you so' before the flesh gets blasted from your bones."

Paige gave the militia woman a little smile just to show that she really meant it.

CHAPTER FORTY-SEVEN

Friday, October 24
8:02 A.M.

Dreamland

Sweat rolled off Craig's forehead as he struggled with the land rover's locked door. Locked! What a stupid reason for a delay.

In the back cargo compartment, the red LED blinked down seconds on the makeshift timer. A countdown to Armageddon.

He smeared his arm across the back window, wiping away the rain. The warhead itself was a dark, hazy shape half hidden by tinted windows and a sheet of scuffed plastic thrown over the device. Mike Waterloo's limp body lay sprawled in the front seat, stuffed into an awkward position. Blood pooled from wounds in his chest, and his head lolled to one side.

And all the doors were locked.

Behind them, Terrell's Air Force helicopter shot into the air, leaving them. The rotor's noise rolled away as the helicopter thundered straight upward like an elevator being yanked to the top floor, buffeted from side to side in the high winds.

Craig looked up in despair at being abandoned so utterly. Ursov shook his fist. But then he realized with relief that the lieutenant colonel must have directed the helicopter to hover overhead and mark the spot for the approaching NEST and EOD crews as they flew in from the southern part of Nellis. Just in case they could get there in time.

Through the tinted glass, though, he could see that the countdown showed less than ten minutes—not nearly enough time for a team to get here, set up, and accomplish anything. Craig thought that the smarter move might have been just to evacuate everyone out to a safe distance and let the warhead blow.

Now he didn't even have that option.

"Before we can disarm bomb," Ursov said, "we must get inside this truck."

Craig stepped back and kicked at the vehicle's door handle, hoping to smash the locking mechanism with his shoe. Nothing. The side window didn't yield to his kicks either. He needed a crowbar to smash the safety glass. A rock. Anything hard enough to penetrate.

Ursov yanked off his uniform jacket, revealing a white shirt now smeared with dust and dampened with perspiration—and with good reason. The rain poured down, soaking them both.

The general barely glanced at Waterloo's body, but turned back to peer again at the nuclear device through the tinted glass. He looked up at Craig, an intense look of worry on his face. "You must get inside. Now. Time is running out. If this warhead explodes, the fallout will be a thousand times worse than Chernobyl."

"This damned locked door is a simple but effective delaying tactic." Craig kicked at the window again. The heel of his black wing tip merely bounced off the tinted glass.

The military helicopter hovered above them, a thousand feet up, serving as a beacon for the NEST team. But Craig saw no sign of anyone coming to help. Not that it would make much difference. Nine minutes.

Craig pulled the Beretta from his shoulder holster and leveled his weapon at the driver's side window. "Step back."

Raising his forearm to shield his eyes, Craig fired at an angle into the window, which splashed into a spray of cobwebbed cracks. He fired again, and this time the remains of the safety glass shattered. Craig turned to the side and lashed again with his foot, this time kicking in the sheet of glass shards held together with fiber strands.

Panting, Craig said, "Now that we're inside, I don't have the first idea how to disarm that thing. All yours, General."

Ursov crossed his arms over his white shirt. "I have helped to disassemble this model of weapon." He peered inside the land rover. "Perhaps I can figure out something to do."

"You'd better hurry, comrade." Craig reached in and unlocked the doors. "Quick! Open the back!"

Ursov jogged around to the rear of the vehicle. He fumbled with the latch and yanked the back hatch open.

"What can I do to help?" said Craig, feeling terror claw up his throat. *Stay calm,* he thought. The last thing he needed to do was to spook Ursov.

"Nothing—yet," said Ursov, bending over the warhead. He ripped the plastic sheet away and let it drift across the rocky ground. The wind caught it and whipped the plastic away like a lost kite. "Give me room to work."

Craig backed off, feeling awkward and desperate for something to do. "I'll see if they left any clues on how to stop this thing."

Craig stuffed his pistol back in its shoulder holster, then hauled Mike Waterloo's body out of the front seat. No time for ceremony, no time for sadness or anger. He dumped the DAF Manager on the muddy ground, then frantically began to search the vehicle. He sprawled across the front seat and banged on the glovebox. It fell open, and he rummaged through it.

In back Ursov stood over the warhead, studying the device as if he had all the time in the world. But a sheen of sweat sparkled across the blustery Russian's forehead—and that frightened Craig most of all.

From the cluttered glovebox he pulled out AAA maps, a National Park Service map, and a folder of vehicle maintenance records. Nothing about the warhead. Craig tossed the material away. He patted under the front seat, finding only an old wrench and a long screwdriver. He couldn't feel anything else, no *How to Disarm Atomic Bombs in Your Spare Time* manuals.

The warhead would go off in minutes, and he and Ursov didn't have a chance of getting far enough away. Even Paige would be killed along with any other personnel too close to Groom Lake.

Pulling himself back out of the front seat, he turned to Waterloo's corpse lying in the dirt. Sally had shot him three times, well placed and effective. The DAF Manager's gaunt features were pale from death, his body sprawled at an angle.

Craig quickly patted down the man's body. He found only a wallet and a heavy handgun. Then he pulled out a thin RF card from Waterloo's bloody shirt pocket, thicker than a credit card; it reminded Craig of the security access cards he had seen near the DAF. It might have something to do with the warhead, some code for the interlocks.

Protecting it from the rain, Craig jogged around to the back of the land rover. "General, I found an RF card."

Ursov's torso was half inside the back, bent over the warhead. He had opened the casing, but the red LEDs continued to blink, counting down the seconds. Six minutes.

The Russian used his finger to follow wires from the timer to a shoebox-sized package sitting on top of the warhead. He looked up, his eyes red with concentration. "Let me see it."

Craig handed him the card; Ursov flipped it over, scowling. "Do you know the security code for this?"

Craig shook his head. "No."

"It is useless without the code." Ursov tossed the card away and hunched back over the unit. "But it would have helped us a great deal."

Craig stared at the LED readout, still ticking down. "What kind of code would it be?"

"Numbers," said Ursov, his head buried in the workings of the warhead. "A long sequence of numbers. Mr. Waterloo could have set it to be anything he liked. But if you don't have the code, Agent Kreident, then leave me alone so I can work."

"The numerical sequence could be anything." Craig tried to think, watching the Russian work on the warhead's control systems. A matrix of buttons next to the LED took up most of the side of the shoebox, next to the RF card reader. "Can we guess?"

Ursov continued to stare intently, his teeth on edge, as he traced the wires. He didn't look up. "There are too many permutations to try at random. That would be a waste of time. Now stop bothering me."

But it wouldn't be random. *What would Mike Waterloo use—a combination of his dead wife's birthday and Paige's birthday as well?* But even if that were true, Craig didn't have a clue what those dates were. What could be important—

Craig snapped his head up. "Wait, try a date, today's date. October 24." The date the Eagle's Claw had written on the plastic explosives back at the transformer towers at Hoover Dam.

Ursov inserted the card into the unit and punched in the numbers.

Nothing. A loud crack of thunder rolled across the sky.

"Maybe the month and day are reversed—sometimes people do that," said Craig. *Why wasn't this working*?

Ursov withdrew the card, then reinserted it. He tried another sequence. He repeated the procedure—still nothing. "Useless! We are wasting time!" Scowling, he tossed the card to the side, then turned back to the PALs inside the warhead casing.

Craig drew in deep breaths. He felt totally helpless.

The weapon itself looked sleek, highly polished. Seams were barely visible around the steel-colored, conical nose section and toward the flared back. Although not more than two feet in girth at its widest point, the commandeered device took up a good part of the back of the land rover. The nuke looked like an old artillery shell, except smoother and shinier. And much more deadly.

Craig glanced at the countdown clock. They were down to a little over four minutes. Yet Ursov took his time, methodically tracing the wires that led to the rectangular package sitting on top of the warhead.

He heard approaching vehicles, more aircraft, helicopters—but the thought sickened him instead of filled him with elation. They should be evacuating at full speed—but he had no way of getting in touch with them.

Craig leaned over and tried to see what the Russian officer was doing. Here he stood two inches from ground zero with a Russian Strategic Rocket Forces officer—a man who had been trained all his career on how to blow up the entire western hemisphere. Now, Craig's life was in the hands of this ex-communist.

But what could he do—run? The military helicopter overhead couldn't even get far enough away now. They would all be dead in a flash. If the weapon went off, the crater itself would be thousands of yards in diameter, and the fireball would incinerate everything within miles.

All the subsidence craters he had seen out on Yucca Flat had been made by relatively dinky kiloton weapons—this warhead, straight from the nuclear arsenal itself, had a yield of nearly a *mega*ton.

Ursov straightened, then whirled toward Craig, snapping in a hoarse voice. "I need a metal bar."

"A *what*?"

"Something sharp. A crowbar. Quickly. We do not have much time."

"What are you going to do, hit it?"

Ursov looked Craig coldly in the eye. "Agent Kreident, we will both die within three minutes unless you stop asking questions and just assist me." He bent into the back of the land rover and started ripping loose a side panel.

Craig swung open the rover's rear door. He bent to search, scrambling under the back seat. Nothing but a water cooler and thermos jugs, not even a tire jack. It was probably buried somewhere under the heavy warhead.

He thrust his hand under the front seat, patting around. Where were those tools? There, something long, cold, and hard. He yanked out a foot-long screwdriver smudged with oil and grime.

"I've got something."

"Quickly!"

Craig tossed the screwdriver over the back seat. Ursov caught it and immediately began to pry open the shoebox on top of the warhead. Beads of sweat drooled down the general's ruddy face. His close-cropped gray hair was plastered to the side of his head.

The general bent over the device and spoke quietly, almost reverently. "I have learned during these disarmament inspections that you Americans have installed numerous Permissive Action Links so that your warheads cannot be accidentally detonated. Unfortunately, when Mr. Waterloo armed this weapon, he circumvented those protective devices." He grunted as he popped off a cover, then started working with the screwdriver again.

"Therefore, all I must do is to engage the PAL without setting off the explosive lenses surrounding the bomb core—" He slipped and the blade of the screwdriver jammed deep inside the Permissive Action Link. He cursed, flailing his hand and blowing on his skinned knuckles.

Craig felt a chill run through him as he hurried around the vehicle. He desperately wanted to ask what had happened, but he knew he couldn't afford to jar General Ursov out of his concentration.

The helicopter's throbbing rotors broke the desert silence above; Craig heard faint warbling sirens in the distance, coming closer—but the NEST or EOD teams would get here too late. The countdown clock's LED showed only a minute and a half remaining. They would all die together.

Ursov muttered to himself. He swiped sweat from his face with his forearm. Rain blew inside the back compartment. "The timer will not disengage!"

Craig heard a sudden *pop,* then a crackle, as if something had shorted in the warhead. Seconds later Ursov rattled the screwdriver around and pounded on the casing. Craig looked on, his eyes wide. His breath quickened.

Blinking in the sunlight, he shaded his eyes to peer hopelessly up at the hovering helicopter. In the instantaneous nuclear flash, the crew wouldn't feel a thing, wouldn't know what had hit them.

"Stand back," Ursov snapped, not looking at him.

Craig staggered to the front of the vehicle, as if that might protect him. *What else could he do?*

"I said, stand back!" Clenching his hand and hammering with long swipes of the screwdriver, General Ursov chipped away at the breach in the warhead, pounding and twisting in the small hole he had opened in the shoebox.

The Russian looked like a madman, his eyes red, his face full of sweat. He battered at the interior, and tiny beads of a solid material came pattering out. Again and again he struck the delicate systems, digging deep inside.

Suddenly, a burst of metallic shavings and charcoal-gray dust spewed from the hole like a tiny smoke bomb. Craig threw himself backward. Ursov dropped the screwdriver and staggered back out of the cargo compartment. He reeled in the glaring sunlight. The numbers of the LED counted down—less than a minute.

The Russian general stumbled away from the land rover. "Get away!" he cried hoarsely. He waved a hand spattered with gray dust. "Quickly! It is going to explode!"

Going to explode? Craig felt frozen with fear. *Does he expect me to run away from a nuclear fireball?*

But unreasoning instinct kicked in. Feeling as if he were moving in slow motion, Craig sprinted away from the rover, ducking deeper into the washout gully, ignoring the ankle-deep streams of brown water and searching for some kind of shelter. While Ursov ran at an angle from him, Craig bolted for an outcropping of rock, pumping his shoes in the uncertain mud. He tripped over a rock, but he scrambled back to his feet and picked up speed running full bore.

Above him the helicopter tilted its wings and buzzed away, uselessly trying to flee the impending holocaust.

Craig scrambled over a smooth table of rock. Sliding down in a spider-walk, he lunged out to get behind the outcropping. His pants ripped, and he winced as he banged his knee, cutting open a gash. He tumbled into a small depression behind the rocks, drenched with water and painted with mud.

No matter how far he had run, he remained well within the fireball zone. Perhaps it would be better just to stay here.

He thought fleetingly of Trish, but the recent memories of Paige overwhelmed him. Had the vicious Sally Montry managed to drive her hostage beyond the lethal radius of the weapon? Craig sucked in a burning breath as he realized all the opportunities he had missed with Paige.

He couldn't hear General Ursov, and he wasn't about to peek around the natural shelter to find the man, to thank him for trying. But it wouldn't matter anyway since everything around would be instantly incinerated—

He heard the *pop* of an explosion. A laughably small echo and thump.

Startled, Craig waited for something else to happen, but there was nothing. Only the sound of the response team sirens growing louder, and the distant echoes of thunder.

Craig crawled around the rock, wincing as he nursed his battered leg. Some distance away, General Ursov raised his arm, waving for assistance.

Smoke curled up from the land rover, which had rolled onto its side, as if a giant had smacked it aside. The tailgate was bent up and torn away. The small explosion hadn't destroyed the vehicle, but it had been enough to blow away the back end.

Some of the high explosives had detonated, but Ursov had somehow prevented the nuclear core from undergoing a chain reaction. The small explosion had damaged the vehicle, but nothing more. The atomic bomb had been contained.

Dizzily, Craig slumped back against the rock as he heard the sirens grow louder, and the sound of approaching helicopters. Within minutes the place would be swarming with help.

But he still had to make sure Paige was all right.

CHAPTER FORTY-EIGHT

Friday, October 24
8:17 A.M.

Dreamland

One of the Air Force helicopters came low to the ground, kicking up sprays of water and sand; a cloud of mist swirled around the heavily armed behemoth as it bumped to a landing, settling onto the soft ground.

Two armed security policemen jumped down from the passenger compartment and spread out, fanning the area with their automatic weapons—but they didn't leave the immediate vicinity of the craft.

Dressed in white protective gear with hoods, three members of the NEST response scrambled out. One carried a radiation detector and held up a gloved hand, sweeping it from side to side, focusing on the site of the explosion, while the others drew up short. They stood warily back from the remains of the blasted land rover and the ruined warhead.

A hundred yards away, Craig pulled himself up on the slick outcropping of rock and watched the team. *A day late and a dollar short,* he thought. Good thing Ursov had accomplished whatever it was he had done, somehow damaging the stolen warhead enough to prevent it from going critical.

One of the security men spotted the Russian general from his shallow hiding place. Ursov limped toward them, wiping at an ashlike gray substance that clung to his shirt. The stocky man looked dazed, but held himself upright as he painfully made his way across the desert.

The NEST person with the radiation detector motioned toward the main helicopter, while medical teams and decontamination units rushed toward Ursov. Two women hauled out a long hose and started unreeling it, stopping just in front of the Russian. They unfolded a plastic container like a child's swimming pool and instructed the general to step into it. They used their gloved hands to tear off his shirt and pants, stuffing them into plastic contamination bags.

Ursov held up his hands, cooperative, while the NEST volunteers sprayed him with some sort of decon foam. They scrubbed his skin raw with coarse brushes. He winced, but endured all of it.

Craig looked up as another pair of helicopters approached, flying low under the diminishing rain. One was identical to the NEST helicopter; the other looked like LtCol Terrell's escort chopper. The second NEST helicopter landed near the first. Ben Goldfarb jumped out and trotted toward the group, shading his eyes and searching for Craig. Dressed in a dark suit, the curly-haired man spoke into a walkie-talkie, coordinating with the rest of the FBI team. The NEST workers waved him away from the Russian general and possible contamination.

Craig pressed a hand against his throbbing and bleeding knee, then staggered toward the others. Blood oozed from the wound, but he knew it wasn't serious. Yellow sunlight poked through a gap in the clouds, making him squint. He had lost his scratched sunglasses somewhere back at the land rover. Wearily he checked his watch. Not even nine o'clock in the morning, and already the day had been too long.

He saw someone signaling him from inside Terrell's chopper as it bore down, returning from the horizon, the direction in which Sally Montry's land rover had fled. He spotted a flash of blond hair beside the lieutenant colonel in the back. *Paige.* She waved at him.

Two men in white protective gear ran toward Craig, jogging in their full-body suits. One held out a radiation detector and motioned to the other. "He's clean. No radioactive debris made it this far."

"Get him out of here, then. The Russian guy needs to go to the hospital, ASAP. We've got to mitigate this exposure."

Wincing, Craig limped toward the rescue helicopters.

His knee wrapped in a field bandage and his leg elevated on a chair in front of him, Craig sipped a cup of stale office coffee as he eased himself back on the Naugahyde-covered couch. Despite its highly classified location, the Groom Lake Auxiliary Base Headquarters looked like any average military office building.

Air Force memorabilia filled LtCol Terrell's office: photos of Atlas, Delta, and Titan rocket launches; a painting of a mountain range with a plane in the background; two plaques bearing different Air Force seals; a photo of Terrell with two general officers. A portable stereo, complete with CDs and speakers, sat on a black metal credenza.

Through the miniblinds over the window beside Terrell's desk, Craig could see a bustle of activity at the Groom Lake flight line: helicopters took off and trucks crisscrossed the black asphalt surface, bringing in teams, evacuating NEST workers, wrapping up the aftermath of the morning's excitement.

Paige plopped onto the overstuffed couch beside Craig and scooted herself nearer to him. A thick white gauze bandage covered her broken nose, but her smile still showed through when she looked at him. "We make quite a pair," she said. "Like we had a knock-down, drag-out brawl."

"Sometimes I like it when the sparks fly," Craig said with

a smile. He had washed off most of the mud-splatters and dirt, but he still needed a long, hot shower.

Terrell stuck his head into the doorway on his way past. "One more report to Washington. Be right back." He closed the door on them.

Craig smiled. "Your nose is okay?"

"It'll heal—just don't ask me to sing anytime soon." Paige brushed her hair over her shoulder. "How's your knee?"

"Better than it looks," said Craig. "Just don't ask me to dance for a while."

"I didn't think you knew how to dance."

Craig looked at her with mock seriousness. "FBI agents have to undergo rigorous and diverse training, ma'am."

She laughed, then became silent. She folded her hands together, as if in deep thought.

Craig took a sip of the bitter coffee and watched her. Now, after the past four frantic days, it felt good to know the pressure was finally off, both the threat of the militia and Nevsky's murder investigation.

But Paige had been caught in the middle of this, unexpectedly hit by Waterloo's involvement. So much had happened, but Craig could still feel for her. He said, "I'm sorry about your Uncle Mike."

She kept her blue eyes down and nodded. "I don't know what to think. He was so much a part of my life for so long. It's hard to grow up thinking you really know someone, and then they turn out to be a completely different person. Like Jekyll and Hyde. About two years ago Uncle Mike stopped coming to Livermore, quit calling me. I thought he just wanted to start over, that the memories were too much for him."

"He did start over," said Craig. "He just hooked up with the wrong crowd, directed his anger in the wrong direction. Sally Montry played up on that."

Paige grimaced. "God only knows how much power that woman had over him, but an aggressive person can really dominate someone whose defenses are down. Because she worked with him so closely, Sally knew Uncle Mike's weak spots, knew the buttons to push. After Aunt Genny died, and then my father, he was an easy target—lost at sea. She manipulated PK Dirks, too, though she never got him to do anything illegal. He was the perfect scapegoat. Just like Uncle Mike." Paige shook her head. "But that doesn't excuse what he did."

Terrell returned, brisk and businesslike. "Good news about your Russian general. He was exposed to over a rad—serious, but not deadly. He'll live. He was lucky he didn't get more debris blown on him when the casing cracked, and that the decon team arrived within minutes to scrub him down."

"Have they cleaned up the rest of the radioactivity that was released out at your hangar facility?" Paige asked.

"Everything except some trace gases that escaped," Terrell answered. "We're all lucky only one of the high explosive lenses detonated, otherwise the dispersal would have been disastrous. The fail-safes worked.

"We all owe our lives to General Ursov . . . much as it amazes me to say that. He destroyed the weapon's symmetry—everything needs to fit perfectly in these warheads in order to cause a nuclear explosion. Once he damaged the explosives with the screwdriver and cracked the casing, Ursov knew the warhead wouldn't go critical. These things *don't* detonate accidentally."

"But when General Ursov cracked the casing, he got dusted with radioactive material," Craig said. "He couldn't get the PAL to engage, so he tried to bypass it and damage the warhead directly. He knew he might receive an exposure, but he took that chance."

"Good thing you ran, then," Paige said, pursing her lips as

she looked at his injured leg. "Otherwise you might be undergoing the same decontamination procedures. I hear it's about as pleasant as a root canal."

Ironically, Craig thought of his former girlfriend Trish, who continued to study the treatment of radiation exposures at Johns Hopkins. Maybe they would call her in to consult on Ursov's case.

Paige leaned back on the couch and studied LtCol Terrell, narrowing her blue eyes. "There's still something that bothers me, Colonel, and I do hope you'll be forthcoming with an explanation."

"What's that?" Terrell sat up stiffly, guarded.

Paige glanced at Craig, then stared down the black officer. "Something *big* overflew Sally's land rover. I saw all our power systems go out. My watch still isn't working. I know there are rumors about UFOs kept here in hangars up at Groom Lake—"

"That's a familiar story," Terrell said with a forced groan. "We're always having kooks trying to sneak in looking for flying saucers . . . or the secret UN base. Or the Aurora project." He steepled his fingers. "Anytime there's classified work that demands high security, people will speculate about what's behind closed doors." He shrugged. "Can't be helped."

Paige cleared her throat. "Yes, sir, but I *saw* it. It wasn't a NEST helicopter flying in low, and it wasn't a Stealth bomber. It was something shimmering, almost invisible, and extremely fast."

"Maybe you were too excited to know what was going on—"

"Colonel Terrell, don't feed me any lines," Paige said in a no-nonsense voice. "I've got the clearances, and it was nothing I've ever seen or heard before in my life. Now tell me—is there any truth to these UFO stories?"

"Of course not."

"Then what happened out there?"

"I told you," said Terrell. "It must—"

"Colonel Terrell," Craig interrupted softly. He carefully put his coffee cup on the table in front of him and flexed his bandaged leg. "Sir, don't you think you owe us something?"

He nodded to Paige, who drew her mouth tight and sat stiffly on the couch. She watched Terrell as if he might be a snake ready to strike. "Without us, your base would be sitting in the middle of a big crater right now. Come on, tell us what's going on."

Terrell pressed his lips together. "You know, most people don't even know this base exists. Even fewer ever get to see inside. That should be enough for you."

Craig raised an eyebrow. "Sorry, it's not enough for me."

Terrell scowled. He drummed his fingers on his wooden desk, then got up to stride across the room, carefully shutting the door to his office. "It doesn't matter what clearances you have. *No one* has a Need To Know about our Special Access Required programs up here. For example, in the early eighties our Air Force HAVE BLUE project was an SAR program that built the F-117A Stealth fighter."

"You're avoiding the question," Craig said simply.

Terrell stood against the closed door for a moment, then moved to the stereo boom box sitting on the credenza. Putting on a jazz CD, he turned the volume up and stepped over to the couch. Paige and Craig scrunched close to each other.

"You never heard this from me." The lieutenant colonel spoke in a low tone that no one outside could hear over the music. "What you saw was the prototype of a '*visible* stealth' aircraft, code-named HAVE NOT. One of our test pilots overflew you at close range, enough to rattle your vehicle. Then he used HAVE NOT's high-power microwave weapons to knock out every one of your electronic systems."

"Visible stealth?" Craig looked puzzled. "I've heard about microwave pulses to stop a car dead in its tracks—some police forces are starting to use that as a nonlethal countermeasure. But 'visible stealth' seems to be a contradiction in terms."

Terrell folded his hands together. "Just as regular stealth is invisible to radar frequencies in the electromagnetic spectrum, we are developing materials and coatings that are invisible at *optical* wavelengths. The visible light that human eyes can see. It's the same principle." He drew back. "But aliens and UFOs?" He shook his head. "No, I don't think so."

Paige's blue eyes went wide. "An invisible fighter plane using microwave-pulse weapons to knock out electronic systems?" She winced as she bumped the bandage on her nose. "No wonder people think you have UFOs up here."

The jazz music continued to play. "None of that information is scheduled to be released for a few years," Terrell said with a hard edge in his voice. "And since you're both Federal employees, we will file felony charges if either of you allows this to leak to the public." He walked briskly to the stereo, which he clicked off. "And I'll deny everything."

Paige grinned. "Of course you will."

Craig looked innocent. "If *what* gets out, Colonel? That Ms. Mitchell helped stop the militia, single-handedly wrestling Sally Montry out of the land rover and holding her under arrest until help could arrive?"

Terrell shook Craig's hand. "I'm glad we see eye to eye on this, Agent Kreident. Meanwhile, let's get you out to the flight line—we aren't cleared to keep visitors up at Groom Lake this long."

CHAPTER FORTY-NINE

Friday, October 24
10:31 P.M.

Excalibur Hotel and Casino
Round Table Amphitheater

A knight on horseback cradling a twenty-foot lance trotted in front of Craig and Paige, his polished armor clanking. With one gauntleted hand, he raised his visor, saluting the crowd as other riders swirled around him, bearing colorful pennants.

Trumpet blasts announced the knight's entry as his horse whinnied and pawed the dirt in front of the reviewing stands, ready to charge across the arena. In the Excalibur's raised stands, the spectators applauded. Buxom damsels dressed in low-cut flowing dresses threw flowers up at the crowd from the arena.

Craig winced with a twinge of pain as he leaned over to Paige. Although bandaged, cleaned, and shot with antibiotics, he still ached all over. What he wanted most was a long, hot bath and a long, deep sleep.

He studied Paige in the dimness of the stands before speaking. She wore a long black dress, complete with a slit up the side that revealed her shapely legs. Her blond hair lay against the silk fabric, and when she flipped a strand behind her shoulder, she glanced over at him. Only the thick white bandage on her nose spoiled the effect.

"Looking at something?" she said, her voice muffled and nasal.

"Yes indeed." Craig reached for his drink, a bottle of Samuel Adams beer. One of the best beers the Excalibur had to offer, according to Paige.

She sipped her own beer, a thick Guinness, then leaned back against the hard chair with a wistful smile.

The crowd laughed as a court jester was stuck in the rear end by a knight's lance. Regal-looking King Arthur sat on a throne next to his queen, while Merlin performed magic tricks. The soundtrack boomed loudly from the arena speakers.

Paige looked amused at his expression. "Still have your mind on the militia, Craig?" she asked. "Or is it Sally Montry?" She crossed her legs and leaned forward to whisper in a conspiratorial voice. "Or is it those UFOs?"

"Don't get me started," said Craig. "Just don't get me started."

He drained his beer glass and pushed it across the table, then positioned himself to ease the ache in his injured leg. "With the information on the Eagle's Claw we got from Jorgenson's home, and Mike Waterloo's, as well as the people we've arrested—Bryce Connor, Deputy Mahon, and Sergeant Marlo, not to mention Sally—we should be able to unravel the whole militia group. Not only did we save the day, Paige, we also hit the jackpot."

Paige ran a finger around the top of her own beer glass, touching the foam of the thick black stout . . . at which Trish would have turned up her nose. "So what's next for you?"

Craig shrugged. "Oh, I go wherever they send me. I'll head back to the Bay Area, but who knows where the Bureau will want me next? Depends on where a suitable case turns up. I specialize in the high-tech investigations . . . but they could just as well have me investigating parking-meter fraud. What about you?"

Paige remained silent for a moment. Her fingernails ran up and down the smooth side of the glass, and she held his gaze with her striking blue eyes. The longer she looked at him, the stranger Craig felt—out of breath, his cheeks warm.

She glanced down when she finally spoke. "Me? Well, I don't think I'll be able to go back to Livermore, at least not for a while. Too many memories of Uncle Mike there—but it goes deeper than that. Whenever I think of the nuclear community, I remember all the years I had spent trusting him, how he and my father worked on all those tests together."

She hesitated. "It could be a good opportunity, actually. I've never lived outside of California for any length of time, except when I went to college—but now is the best time to go somewhere else. I just need to get away, get my life together."

Anxious to distract himself, Craig took another sip of his beer, saddened that she wouldn't be close anymore, but he also understood why she couldn't stay—not with the memories she had to deal with. It reminded him of Trish's leaving all over again. . . .

But this was different. He could never confuse Paige for Trish, and her reason for leaving wasn't to follow a burning goal that consumed everything else. It was just to find some personal peace. For the time being.

He swallowed. "So where do you think you'll go?"

She took another sip of her dark beer and placed it on the table, running the back of her hand across her lips. In the arena below, the horses thundered around in a circle. "DOE has openings at several of the labs back east—Brookhaven maybe, or Oak Ridge. I've got connections, and good references, and my clearance transfers."

"Brookhaven? Where's that?"

"In New York." She looked out over the court assembling below them, troops of knights in shining armor, flashing their pennants. A princess in a conical hat strutted around the arena, followed by ladies-in-waiting who carried her filmy train. In the front ranks, one muscular knight sat rigidly at attention on his prancing stallion; the knight brought up his sword to salute King Arthur.

Craig felt a sinking feeling come over him. *New York?* The other side of the country. It *was* Trish all over again. In defeat, he gave her a wan smile.

Paige continued. "But I've been looking at going to Argonne instead. Or fermilab, near Chicago. I know some people there, and I'm sure I could get a few good leads just by picking up the phone. I've never really been in the Midwest—it's supposed to be peaceful out there, a lot more laid-back, more neighborly. I don't know. I might stay there for a while, for as long as I can stand the cold winters, then head back to California. The west will always be home for me, but I've got to shake this out of my system."

The waitress brought another beer for both of them. Craig fumbled for his wallet, but Paige beat him to it. "This one's on me." She left a tip sure to bring the waitress back.

Craig clinked his glass against Paige's. "Then here's to all of us good guys."

"Hear, hear." She stared at him with her clear blue eyes as she drank. From her serious expression, she seemed to be reading his own turmoil, his own confused thoughts.

Craig felt his face grow warm. If he let Paige go now without saying something about his feelings for her, he'd end up kicking himself forever. She *wasn't* Trish. And that was all behind him. It was time to move on with his life—and now was the time to start.

He set down his beer and opened his mouth, finally getting up the courage to say—

"Hi, kids!" A slurred voice came from beside him.

Craig turned to look over his shoulder. Maggie the Mind Reader. A bright green parrot sat perched on her shoulder.

Walking with a visible stagger, she stopped in front of their seats. "It's about time you two showed up. I hoped you would make my last show. Too late now."

"We got a little busy." Craig smiled, then looked at Paige. He felt the tension flow from him, leaving a sense of disappointment. *The moment had passed. . . .*

Paige leaned forward, laughing. "When do you go on again? We'd love to see your act."

"Sorry, Sweetie." Maggie placed her hands on the narrow table and leaned toward them. "That was really my last show. I gave my notice. Time to move on, but I'm making one last swing through the pit."

"You're kidding," Craig said. "I thought you told me old showgirls never die."

"They don't."

"Then what are you going to do?" Paige asked.

The parrot squawked and flapped its wings. Maggie turned to give it a *shush*. Turning back, she blinked at them. "I'm going away. Just like you two. But old Maggie's going to get away from all the free booze, then pack it in to San Diego where I'll start over. I've got grandkids there."

Craig blinked. "And do your mind-reading act in San Diego? Do they have enough clubs for that?"

"Clubs? What the hell are you talking about, Sweetie? I'm going to work in a pet store. I love animals."

Craig laughed as Paige patted the chair next to her. "Sit down. How about one more mind-reading before you go?"

Maggie glanced at Paige, then back to Craig. She shook her head. "You kids don't need old Maggie to read your minds—what you need is some time alone." She winked and turned, walking away with a slight stagger.

Paige placed her hand on top of Craig's and squeezed—but she left it there, caressing the tops of his fingers.

Embarrassed and self-conscious, Craig laughed as the old woman left, feeling Paige's touch burning his skin. "Now that's a wild way to end a day. This place is going to miss her. What an act, even if she really can't read minds." He turned to Paige.

She looked at him with her sparkling blue eyes. "Who's to say she can't?"